June Gadsby was born in Felling, Tyne and Wear. She lives in south-west France with her photographer husband, Brian, and her miniature Yorkshire terrier. Her previous novels include *When Tomorrow Comes* and *The Jealous Land*.

TO THE ENDS
OF THE EARTH

Wild and beautiful Gwyneth Johnns is a
Patagonian with a past that shocks the
Victorian ladies of the small pioneering
town in the Valdes Peninsula. She has
sworn never to let any man get close, but a
handsome Spaniard, Miguel, weakens her
resolve. Then, new immigrants arrive from
England. Gentle giant Rob, his brother,
Davy, and the hard-drinking, amoral Matt
with his young wife. Gwyneth is called
upon to teach them how to be *gauchos*.
Reluctantly, she accepts the challenge. But
now she risks losing her life and newfound
love to the cold glaciers of the Andes . . .

Books by June Gadsby
Published by The House of Ulverscroft:

PRECIOUS LOVE
KISS TODAY GOODBYE
SECRET OBSESSIONS
THE ROSE CAROUSEL
THE IRON MASTER
WHEN TOMORROW COMES
THE SAFE HEART
THE MIRACLE OF LOVE
THE JEALOUS LAND

JUNE GADSBY

TO THE ENDS OF THE EARTH

Complete and Unabridged

ULVERSCROFT
Leicester

First published in Great Britain in 2005 by
Robert Hale Limited
London

First Large Print Edition
published 2006
by arrangement with
Robert Hale Limited
London

British Library CIP Data

Gadsby, June
    To the ends of the Earth.—Large print ed.—
Ulverscroft large print series: romance
1. English—Patagonia (Argentina and Chile)—
Fiction 2. Patagonia (Argentina and Chile)—Social
conditions—19th century—Fiction
3. Large type books
I. Title
823.9′2 [F]

ISBN 1–84617–479–1

Published by
F. A. Thorpe (Publishing)
Anstey, Leicestershire

Set by Words & Graphics Ltd.
Anstey, Leicestershire
Printed and bound in Great Britain by
T. J. International Ltd., Padstow, Cornwall

This book is printed on acid-free paper

For my stepchildren:
David, who has also experienced
the magic of Patagonia,
Helen and Caroline

1

First, there was the dust cloud. It appeared small on the Patagonian horizon like tumbleweed; a rolling ball of pampas grasses chased before *El Pampero*. This constant summer wind blew relentlessly across the Andes from the west, until it arrived at the small coastal towns around the Valdes Peninsula.

But this particular cloud of sun-dried, wind-blown dust that day in 1900 was not caused by tumbleweed. As it grew in size, drawing ever nearer to the scattering of log cabins belonging to the tiny Welsh settlement town of Puerto Daffyd, the cloud took form and shape. The hollow thud of hoofs could be heard long before watching eyes made out the shimmering shape of a young woman on the back of a sleek black stallion.

She rode astride, *gaucho* style, long legs clad in guanaco hide trews. Her white shirt in fine cotton, clinging to her breasts left no doubt that she was female — and shocked the group of Chapel ladies watching her arrival from behind prim lace curtains.

'Here she comes,' announced the Widow

1

Evans, whose house it was, as if she was the only one to see.

'Gwyneth Johnns, is it?' One of the other women struggled to see past the heads of the women assembled at the window. 'I never expected to see her again, look you; but she still comes, *brazen hussy* that she is.'

'Aye. How does she have the face to show herself where all is known of her?'

Cups rattled indignantly on saucers, tea was spilled and no attention paid to it.

The Widow Evans, well used to these scathing tongues, ignored them. Her old eyes squinted short-sightedly across the street where Gwyneth Johnns was tying her horse to the hitching rail, and brushing herself down. There were men outside McGinty's Tavern looking for mischief, for wasn't it alcohol they were supping from china cups to fool the Temperance Elders. So transparent were men. All made of glass they were, so you could see right through them.

Blodwen Evans smiled and nodded. Any funny business and Gwyneth would send them off with a flea in the ear. She could handle herself as efficiently as any man, and with less fuss. A flash of those blue-green eyes of hers was usually all it took to make them back off. That and one hand tightening around the rifle she always carried, cocked and at the ready. They knew she would not hesitate to use it. She had proved that twelve years ago when she killed the man who had raped her.

'Look, go you all to your homes until I finish my business with the girl,' Blodwen told the women, her voice as soft as her ancient skin.

'You still do business with her, Widow Evans? Is it wise, look you, after the trouble you had with the Elders?'

'You like your lace and your fancy folderols well enough, do you not?'

'I would prefer to buy lace made by *your* hands, Widow Evans,' one woman, big with her seventh child, complained.

'You all will be back to buy from me the lace that Gwyneth Johnns weaves like an angel,' Blodwen said, holding up her twisted and swollen fingers for them all to gaze upon. 'Look at these deformed old hands. I am hard put to hold a bobbin these days, let alone weave a lace collar. Besides, I taught Brin Johnns's daughter all I know, and good she is, if I say it myself.'

'The girl should not have stayed around after what happened. I have never felt easy with it.'

'At thirteen you would have the child banished? Locked up like a criminal or a crazy person? Her with no family to look out for her?'

'Still, Blodwen, it was too good you were to her then, as now. It brought you trouble from the Elders, going against them like that. You should have done what the rest of us did and — '

'Minded my own business, is it?' Blodwen tucked some straying fronds of silky white hair beneath her starched cap. 'That's as may be, but the Elders know better than to chastise me now. There's not one of them as old as I am.'

She laughed suddenly. It was odd how that laugh of hers could sound so wise, convey so much without her saying a word. She turned back to the window, leaving her visitors to show themselves out. They had drained her teapot three times already and left only crumbs on the cake plates. Enough was enough.

She watched the tall, impressive figure of Gwyneth Johnns striding out, her head held high, broad shoulders pulled back. Blodwen had always admired the pride of the girl. Even more so when she had had the courage to announce that it was her own father who had violated her. When the Elders decreed that it should all be hushed up, thirteen-year-old Gwyneth took her father's rifle and shot him through the heart, and not a person said a thing about it.

Blodwen sighed long and deep. No, they said nothing, did nothing, but their silence and their turning away from the poor child had torn her heart in two. It was as if the whole town had tried and judged Gwyneth Johnns and found her guilty of her father's crime, sentencing her to a life of shameful solitude.

Ah, but she had risen above it. If their treatment of her had made the girl hard, then it was all to the good, for she had to fend for herself in this savage land that broke even the toughest of roughnecks who thought they could make a living off the Argentinean plains.

Blodwen had arrived half a century before with the first Welsh settlers. She had seen the struggles of man and beast against all manner of adversities. They thought they were coming to the *promised land* and for a while it seemed rightly so. But then there were the hostile *Indios*; and the wind that blew horizontally across the plains, bending trees and pampas grass with its fury; the droughts killed the crops, despite the irrigation system put in by far-seeing Welsh engineers; and with typical contrariness, floods came and washed the farms out into the sea.

The old woman from Prestatyn had no more dreams left in her, except the secretly harboured desire to return to the land of her birth. First, however, she had things to do. And this involved the young woman who was now standing on her doorstep, eyes blazing and full breasts heaving, having just brought her hand sharply across the face of a lad foolish enough to approach her.

'Good day to you, Gwyneth,' Blodwen called out from her rocking chair where she could see down to the sea and the boats that came and went. 'Close the door after you. The wind is strong today and I have just cleaned the house.'

She rocked silently while Gwyneth put the door on the sneck and entered the cosy living room with its furniture made from the poplar trees that grew so plentiful in the river valleys.

'You saw that, did you?'

Gwyneth had a strong voice with a hint of Welsh in her accent, along with the Spanish that she spoke like a native, though she preferred to speak in English. Blodwen guessed it might have something to do with the girl's desire to exasperate the folk who adhered to the Old Language, still prevalent in old pioneer towns of the fifties and sixties.

'Take no notice. He is a boy desperate to become a man. You should not look so

6

desirable, Gwyneth. If God had to make you beautiful he should have placed you elsewhere. Not in a land where young women are scarce and men are eaten away with their own hunger.'

'Pah! Will they never learn, Blodwen? I can't help how I look. Would you have me go about with a hessian sack over my head?'

'Dressing like a respectable lady might help, girl.' Blodwen tutted and shook her head at the young woman. 'My, my! I swear you don't wear a corset. Or a chemise. Look at you. You'll not get a decent man like that, miss.'

'I'll stay as I am, thank you very much. I have no need of a husband and well you know it.'

Gwyneth was pacing about the cottage like a caged lioness. Her long black hair had come adrift and as she bent to inspect the lace pattern on Blodwen's old sideboard runner, the sun's rays put a metallic blue gleam into her thick tresses.

There was something different about the girl today, Blodwen decided. A kind of urgent restlessness.

'Come girl, sit you down by me. It's a long time since you have been to visit. Tell me what you've been doing.'

And so they talked. Gwyneth told the old

lady how she had trekked for weeks over the mountains to a valley as green as any in Blodwen's beloved Wales. She had found work at an *estancia* teaching young, inexperienced *gauchos* how to ride and shoot and throw the bolas. She had been sorely tempted to stay, but here she was back again in the town of her birth, where her roots were firmly embedded.

'Why, what is it with you, girl?'

Gwyneth shook her head, hiding her face in a thick curtain of hair, but not before the widow had seen a hot flush surge into her high-boned cheeks. How lucky that the girl favoured her *Indios* mother who died giving her life. She got her height and breadth from her father's genes, but there was little else of Brin Johnns in her, thank the Lord, other than a stubborn streak and a slight shortness of temper when provoked.

'There is a man you like at the *estancia*, eh, girl? Why, the saints be praised. Gwyneth Johnns has finally discovered that she is normal under that cast-iron veneer.'

'It's not like that.' Gwyneth faltered and swept her hair out of the way, retying it with the thong at the nape of her neck. 'I'm not even sure I like him. Oh, Blodwen, I've never felt like this — ever!'

She stopped abruptly, breathing deeply.

Blodwen tapped arthritic fingers on the girl's knee.

'Gwyneth, it won't ever be like it was with your father. Brin Johnns was a wicked man and known as such by all. He took your poor mother from her people and forced her to marry him so he could have female comfort on his treks into the mountains. When she died having you, he went off trapping in the high Andes, leaving you with the Thomas family.'

Blodwen paused, but the girl gave no response, so she went on.

'You were ten when you saw him for the first time and he stole you back and carried you off to his shack. Mr and Mrs Thomas died from the grief of it. He put you in your poor mother's place and abused you the way he abused her. He deserved to die — may God forgive me for saying it.'

'But you would not say that in front of your Chapel friends, would you, Blodwen?' Gwyneth's eyes flashed.

'No. You are right there. I would not say that, but I say it to you, as would many another if they had the courage to go against their pious pride.'

Gwyneth made a small, impatient sound and turned to stare out of the window, her back ramrod straight.

What a fine wife she would make for some good man, Blodwen thought, and not for the first time. The child had become a woman before her time because of the cruelties life had showered upon her. Before long, she would be of an age when childbearing was not advisable unless you were already shedding babies like peas from a pod.

'What age have you now, Gwyneth?' Blodwen asked, her head too befuddled to work it out these days.

'I'm twenty-five,' the girl said, 'and why do you ask?'

Blodwen sucked in air through the gap in her teeth where one of her ancient molars had dropped out last year. Soon, they would all go the same way and she would have to dip her bread in her tea to soften it.

'Oh, no reason,' she said lightly, for it was easy to get a rise out of Gwyneth's temper. 'You're restless, girl. What ails you?'

'Nothing ails me, Blodwen!' It was a sharp response; meaning, of course, that something indeed ailed the child.

'There now.' The old lady chuckled softly, the sound filling the small room with sunshine. 'It seems to me, Gwyneth, that you suffer the same affliction as those young lads out there.' And late it is in coming, she thought to herself.

Gwyneth spun around, stung. 'And what is that, pray?'

Another chuckle from Blodwen, for she knew she was correct in her diagnosis. Hadn't she suffered the very same affliction as a young woman before and after the death of her lovely Huw? It was hard for a warm-blooded female to go without the physical side of love when it raged inside you.

'If you were a horse,' Blodwen said, picking her way carefully, 'it could be said that you are ready to be put to the stallion.'

She saw the dark-haired girl frown, mulling over what she had heard, and choosing to ignore the significance. But she knew her words had hit their mark.

Gwyneth moved restlessly about the room for a moment or two longer, then she threw herself down into an old leather armchair whose horsehair stuffing protruded like chest hair from a fat man's shirt. She indicated the brown paper parcel she had placed on the table. 'There is your lace and I have a list of necessaries . . .'

She pulled out a carefully folded piece of paper and placed it on the table, smoothing out the creases with long, tapering fingers. Since the townsfolk found Gwyneth's presence disturbing, she preferred to acquire her provisions through Blodwen, rather

11

than provoke trouble.

Blodwen got to her feet, grunting with the difficulty of it. She glanced down at the list, tapped it, and smiled.

'Ah! You are not alone at the cabin, is it?'

She heard a quick intake of breath, saw shadows flit across Gwyneth's face, turning the luminous kingfisher eyes a dark emerald green.

'Who would I have staying with me?'

'Your list of supplies is larger than usual. Still, it is none of my business.'

'No, that is true, but I assure you I do *not* have anyone staying at the cabin. I am going back to the *estancia* for the winter. The supplies are for them.'

'Them?'

'They are called Gomez-Pan — Spanish they are. Therese — and Miguel, her brother.'

'The brother is not married?'

Was that another maidenly blush? Blodwen watched the girl surreptitiously. Such a contradiction was Gwyneth Johnns. As fearless as a man in many respects, totally unmindful of feminine things — or so she liked the world to believe — and yet here she was being as coy as a schoolgirl.

'Don't harbour any wrong ideas, Blodwen,' Gwyneth said eventually. 'It is business, that's all.'

'Do they treat you as a daughter or use you as a servant?'

'They don't *use* me, no! They are my friends and I am there of my own free will. It's a good life on the *estancia*. They are self-sufficient. They produce their own meat and vegetables and the corn for their bread. Therese makes good bread.'

'And what does Miguel do?'

Again that rosy hue appeared on the girl's tanned cheeks. She was keeping her face averted for a reason, Blodwen was sure.

'When he is not being a rancher, he dances. Oh, Blodwen, you should see him dance!' She pulled up short and, after a sharp catch of breath, continued in a calmer manner. 'Therese dances the *flamenco* and — and then there's the *tango*. They are teaching me the steps.'

Blodwen was confused and a little surprised. Ranchers that were dancers? And her Gwyneth — *dancing*! She had heard of these dances the hot-blooded Spaniards favoured. They were popular in the cafés and bars of Buenos Aires, and had even found their way to Paris and London by all accounts. They were erotic, so it was said, full of passion; and frowned upon by God-fearing folk who thought that they were the work of the Devil.

'Tell me that you do not dance these

— these gyrations of Satan, Gwyneth!'
Blodwen was a wise, open-minded woman,
but she feared for her protégée. The girl's
reputation was damaged enough. 'If you want
to dance, girl, you can do the traditional
dancing of your own people, the Welsh.'

Gwyneth glanced at her from beneath
black raven's wing eyebrows.

'I don't have any people, as well you know,
Blodwen,' she said. 'Besides, I like the
Spanish music. It awakens something in me,
makes me feel alive.'

Blodwen heaved a long sigh and shook her
head with its wobbling thatch of snowy white
hair. Her dark, blackcurrant eyes fixed
themselves on the beautiful half-breed girl.

'It is to be hoped, Gwyneth, that it is only
your heart that is on fire and not your loins,
look you!'

The tip of the girl's pink tongue showed,
licking her full red lips.

'Don't you worry yourself about me,
Blodwen. I can never love any man. My
father saw to that.'

Blodwen put a hand on the girl's arm. Her
old fingers squeezed the young flesh, seeing
in Gwyneth something of the girl she herself
had once been.

'Go you, girl, and take care. You will always
be my daughter, even though you are not of

my flesh and blood. Remember that, will you?'

Gwyneth's countenance softened. She leant down and kissed the pale, flaccid cheek with its tramlines and pouches and the odd whisker of senility sprouting. She loved the old woman as much as she could love any human being, but their ways were different, their beliefs worlds apart.

'I will be back tomorrow for the supplies, and then again in the spring,' Gwyneth said gently and was gone, swaggering nonchalantly away, her proud head held high, her eyes looking neither to the left nor to the right, even when the drunken sots on the tavern steps hailed her.

'You might be back in the spring, my lovely,' Blodwen muttered as she took faltering steps back to her rocking chair and picked up her Bible, for she got many a comforting word from its pages in the winter of her life. 'But will I still be here to look out for you?'

★ ★ ★

Blodwen was already dozing, head lolling onto her chest, when Mrs Lewis of Lewis the Bread came rushing in, hot in the face, her corset creaking with the exertion. She had run all the way from the harbour where she had been buying fresh fish since it was Friday, and late on in the afternoon it was cheaper.

The two women exchanged stiff greetings once Blodwen had rallied, for she had been deep into a dream of *flamenco* and twanging guitars and the sight of a jet-haired girl twirling, showing legs beneath her skirts up to her thighs and beyond. It had taken the old lady's breath away, for she had never imagined such things before, even when she was in the heat of her youth.

'What is it, Mary? Has Mr Lewis set the bakery on fire?'

And then it all came rushing out, as it always did. A nine-day wonder it was going to be, everybody seeing Gwyneth Johnns in town. And how could the Widow Evans hold her head up high, entertaining such a person in her front room?

Mrs Lewis, like most of the people who knew of Gwyneth's past, preferred not to be reminded of this unwholesome side of life. And that girl was a terrible reminder every time she showed her face in Puerto Daffyd where, if truth be known, other fathers and brothers were committing the same despicable crime within the private confines of their own homes.

'And why do they do it, Mary Lewis?'

Blodwen added, having given the woman the benefit of her opinion. 'Because God hasn't got it right yet, managing this new country of ours. We have too many single men and not enough girls young enough to marry.'

'Well, yes . . . ' Mary Lewis clutched her basket full of fish and the smell of them was starting to fill Blodwen's cottage. 'But what has that to do with Brin Johnns's daughter?'

Another lecture was building up in Blodwen. After all, Brin Johnns might have fathered the child — or, at least, planted the seed — but when did he ever show any fatherly love or concern towards Gwyneth? Or any other human being for that matter? He had merely lusted after the *Indios* girl, a tiny slip of a thing, but beautiful, and it could be argued that her beauty, like that of the daughter she brought into the world, could turn the head of any man.

'Never you mind, look you,' she said with a touch of irritation that was uncharacteristic of her. 'Don't you stand there while your fish cook slowly in my front room. Go and put them in your cold store and leave me to my own business.'

'You'll be up before the Elders again, Blodwen Evans, if they find out that you are still hobnobbing with Gwyneth Johnns. You know how they are governed by their wives. The good women of this town are all Chapel and Temperance and the Johnns girl drinks alcohol and rides astride. Now, is that any way for a young woman to behave? When they banished her to the *Indios* camp they knew what they were doing. She should have stayed there, and not shown her face again in this town.'

'And leave her between two places where she wasn't wanted, eh? The *Indios* were no better than our own good townsfolk. All she had then, and all she has now, is that tumbledown shack of her father's — and don't you lecture me about what's right and what's wrong, Mary Lewis!'

The fish basket was clutched even more tightly to Mrs Lewis's chest as Blodwen showed her to the door, suppressing an amused smile at the sight of a lobster, still with life in it, reaching up and tweaking the woman's earlobe. She screeched and ran across the street, startling a mule train heading for the Andes.

'I don't know why I didn't think of it before,' Blodwen mumbled again to herself as she searched for pen and paper, then sat down at the table to write. 'I have a mission to save this town — and Gwyneth perhaps. Living with a Spaniard who plays the guitar and dances, is it? Whoever heard of any God-fearing Welsh girl doing that? Certainly not in my time.'

She dipped the steel nib of her pen into the bottle of ink and started to write in a firm hand. As far as she knew, her brother was still alive and he had numerous sons and daughters. The last she had heard from him the whole family in Prestatyn were sick of going underground to dig for coal. Perhaps she could finally persuade them to come to Patagonia. It would be a consolation to her in her old age to have relatives close at hand to take her back to Wales. Or to bury her beneath the lilac tree in the cemetery on the hill behind Puerto Daffyd, whichever came first.

One thing she did know and that was she had to do something about Gwyneth soon, for if Blodwen Evans was no longer at hand to see to things there was no-one else the girl could turn to.

'*Dear brother, Colin*,' she wrote, her nib scratching and splotching ink on the thick parchment paper.

'*This will be a surprise to you, no doubt, but I want you and your family to come over here to Patagonia and make your mark for the future. There is work* aplenty for all. They are still building dams after those terrible floods decimated us, so men with muscles trained in digging for coal should find it easy. Boats still come here with immigrants from the Old Country. See that you put yourself and yours on one. I'm sending you the money — all that I have saved these last fifty years since your uncle Huw passed away. Mind the young ones come already married, for there is shortage enough of suitable brides — though a single man or two will also be welcome if they are able and willing . . .

2

Rob Barker usually left his home on Felling Banks at the same time the nightshift pitmen were returning to their beds. He was early this morning, because his boss, Mr Bingley, had asked him to help out with the embalming of a whole family who had died in a fire.

This was the part of his job at the funeral parlour that he found most difficult. Dead people didn't bother him too much on the whole, but seeing people — and in particular little bairns — mutilated beyond recognition was something a person never got used to.

He was halfway down the hill when the sound of tramping feet throbbed all around like a slow heartbeat. Then, the low rumble of conversation reached his ears. There was never much noise. A few words here and there, punctuated by a chesty cough or two.

Rob's younger brother, Davy, was probably among them. The lad hated pit work, like many others, but there wasn't much choice in a town where most of the work was pit-related. Rob had been lucky to get out and find work helping Mr Bingley. At least he

21

got to go home clean every night.

The pitmen gradually appeared, marching towards him, the whites of their eyes startling against the colour of the coal dust.

'How, Rob lad!' came the shout as some recognized him.

'Ye still playin' wi' the deed folk doon at Bingleys, then, eh?'

'Time ye came back doon the pit and did some manly work!'

They were, he knew, only half serious. Not a man among them would turn down the chance to escape working in the mines. The tinge of bitterness in their guttural voices was put there by a jealous resentment.

He got a cheeky grin and a weary salute from his brother, who was bringing up the rear of the group. One day, Rob hoped, there might be a place for the lad next to him at the funeral parlour, if Davy could be persuaded. He had passed some scornful remarks when Rob had announced his change of job a few years ago, though he was not half as contemptuous as Rob's best mate, Matt Riley, who thought that a good career move was to go from nightshift to dayshift in the pit.

'Any sign of Matt?' Rob shouted at the departing back of his brother. Matt had been keeping a low profile lately, which usually meant he was in trouble.

'Aye!' Davy shouted back. 'He was just coming on his shift as we were leaving.'

'Did he say anything?'

'Not to me,' Davy answered, then gave a lop-sided grin and tapped the side of his nose, just the way Matt always did. 'But there's rumours going about.'

'What kind of rumours?'

'What do you think, Rob? Same as usual, ye know.'

Yes, Rob did know. Matt and a woman. Whenever Matt was in trouble, you could bet your best pit boots that there was a lass at the bottom of it. He never learnt, the stupid sod.

'See ye!' Rob gave a parting wave and continued on his way, steeling himself for the work he had waiting for him and hoping that Mr Bingley was going to deal with the bereaved relatives. Emotion wasn't his strongest point.

★ ★ ★

The sheet of paper in George Riley's hands rattled as he struggled to read it, his reading glasses perched on the tip of his nose.

. . . and so I beg of you to come and join me, Colin lad, for I have not many years

ahead of me and it might be that if you do not like this place, then we can return together to the Old Country, to the valley where we were born, and leave the young ones to forge the way to their own next world . . .

George stopped, cleared his throat, sniffed loudly and looked about him. Four coal-blackened faces stared back at him. He had been so excited at receiving a letter he hadn't even let them wash off the dirt of their day's toil before reading it to them.

'Who did ye say it was from, Dad?' Reuben, the eldest of his sons, asked, squatting down on his hunkers with his broad backside to the fire.

'Your aunty Blodwen — great-aunt, that is. I'd forgotten about her. Never even knew she could write in English.'

There was a chorus of sniggers and George was hard put not to join in. His wife had talked about Blodwen Evans with little affection. The family had never forgiven her for up and going to that foreign land halfway around the world with a fella she hardly knew.

'Ye'll not get me on the high seas in no boat!'

'Me neither!'

'I'll take me chances doon the pit, me!'

George looked from one to the other of his sons. He had four and only three had spoken.

'Well, Matt. Ye've not put your three ha'pence in yet. What do ye think?'

Matt Riley shrugged, continuing to dig the coal dust out from beneath his nails. He was the second-born son and even though he was a grown man and brawny with it, he was more trouble than the rest of them put together.

'We don't live in Wales,' he said through a dark frown. 'In fact, we've never lived in Wales — have we?'

'No, but your mam did,' George said, grinning because his sons had no inkling that their roots were indeed well planted in green Welsh valleys. 'I went there looking for work. That's where I met yer mam. We moved back to the North-East after we got married. There was too much prejudice down there, ye see, me being Irish and all.'

'And you never went back?'

'There wasn't anything to go back for, son. The old'uns had passed away, as did yer ma. We never had a home there. Just this one, such as it is. Aunty Blodwen, begad! Who'd ha' thought we'd ever hear from her?'

'But she's not writing to us, Dad,' Luke reminded his father. 'Doesn't she know that her brother's dead, eh?'

'Obviously not, son. Nor does she know that the only survivors of her family are the Rileys of Gateshead. Now, should I write back and tell her about these brave Geordie lads o' mine that daren't put a foot on board ship for fear of droonin' in the ocean?'

The voices faded in Matt's head as he read and reread for himself Blodwen Evans's letter, penned in an elegant script with only the slightest tremor betraying the age of the sender. He had heard about Patagonia, and the people who went there as pioneers. He had always envied them. However, once he grew up, his fascination with adventure soon faded when he discovered women.

Women! His dad always said that his favourite pastime would earn him a one-way ticket to Hell. Well, he might be right at that, for he was in dire trouble right now and it needed to be settled pretty damned quick, though for the life of him he didn't know how. Marrying either of the girls involved would only tie him down and he wasn't a man born to wear a collar and chain.

On the other hand, if he stayed around here much longer, chances were that he would be frogmarched to the altar, or end up dead down some back alley, for the girls had fathers and brothers and they were up in arms already. As for Matt, it wasn't in his nature to 'do the right thing'. In any case, he could hardly appease both families.

'Why can't we go?' Matt's eyes looked big, showing too much white, as he stared around the room. 'A new life, Dad! Isn't that what we all dream of? Eh? Luke? Colin? Reuben? Dad, yer not too old, either.'

'No, I'm not too old, son, but . . . ' George Riley screwed up his face, hawked, spat out some sooty phlegm into the roaring flames of the kitchen fire and listened to it crackle. 'Nah, it's not for me. Besides, look at yer aunty's letter. Look what she says. They want young married men mainly.'

'That's our Matt out then, eh?' Reuben said and they all laughed because Matt was something of a family joke the way he avoided wedding bells as if the Devil himself were tolling them.

'Well, it just happens that I'm going to get married soon,' he told them to gasps of disbelief.

His father looked at him suspiciously. 'Well, son, much as I would like to see all my sons marry and settle down, you are the last one I expected to actually do it.'

'I've got hidden depths, me.' Matt smiled broadly, showing strong white teeth.

'When did this happen, then?' George

wanted to know. 'And who's the lucky lass?'

'I'll tell ye's all later, when I've had a chance to speak to her.'

'Gan on wi' ye!' Reuben said, giving his brother a punch that raised a cloud of coal dust. 'I'd like to see the lass who'd consent to marry thee, lad!'

'Aye, wouldn't we all!' laughed Luke and the others agreed.

* * *

A few days later, full of new resolve, Matt took himself off to see his best mate. It was late on a Saturday night, but Rob Barker would undoubtedly still be working down at the funeral parlour. He was a glutton for punishment, was Rob, but a better mate no man could have.

They had gone through school together and it was Rob who constantly got Matt out of trouble. Although Matt was big, Rob was bigger and stronger, a veritable gentle giant and much respected. Like Matt, he had started life in the pit at thirteen, but by the time he was fifteen, he was already seeing a better future for himself than his father and grandfather before him. Rob liked working with his hands and was particularly good with wood, so he got a job making coffins for the local undertaker. He was soon taking orders for things other than coffins, which he made in his spare time.

Matt felt a stab of guilt as he wended his way through the dark back lanes. He had been a fool to play Romeo with those two daft females. How was he to know they would try to trick him into marriage by getting pregnant — and at the same time?

He shuddered as he turned the corner into the cul-de-sac where the Bingley Funeral Parlour was situated. Through a pane of frosted amber glass Matt saw a faint glimmer of yellow light and a moving shadow, which meant that his pal was still there.

Rob showed surprise when he opened the door to Matt's knocking.

'Matt! What are you doing here at this time of night? There hasn't been a death in the family has there?'

'Hey, divvint say that, man!' Matt was superstitious; he didn't like talking about death; he didn't like being here, but needs must when the Devil drives. 'Can I come in, then?'

Rob pulled the door wide and stood back so that Matt could enter the wide passageway. When the door closed behind him a darkness descended, bringing with it a chill that had nothing to do with the time of year.

'Howay, man, where's the light?' Matt stood stock-still, unable to put a foot forward in case he stumbled over a coffin, his imagination fired with the thought of dead bodies lying cold and putrefying.

'Hang on,' Rob told him, striking a match and lighting the gas mantel fixed to the wall a few inches away from Matt's dark head. 'I never thought. I know my way around this place like the back of my hand. Just go straight through to the back, will you. I'm finishing something off for a client and he wants it by the morrow.'

Matt made the mistake of looking to the left where there was an open door leading into the funeral parlour itself. He could make out the silhouette of a draped coffin, and gulped audibly, his eyes snapping shut.

'Tell me there's nobody in that casket,' he said, his voice wobbling nervously in his throat.

'Aye, there is. Funeral's on Monday.'

'Aw, flamin' Norah!'

'Don't be daft, Matt. There's nowt to be afraid of.'

'I suppose ye're gannin to tell us now that the dead canna walk,' Matt forced his quaking legs to work sufficiently to carry him to Rob's workshop.

He heard his friend's laugh behind him and

felt his flesh crawl.

'Well, not walk exactly,' Rob said, enjoying the moment. 'But I did have one fella sit up and belch right in me face.'

'Aw, God, Rob!'

'It was nothing. Just the gasses in the body. They keep escaping even after they're cold on the slab.'

'Well, I can tell ye, if I was dead on your slab right now I'd be fartin' mesel' silly. Every time I'm nervous it's blow-off time. Plays havoc wi' me love life.' Matt jumped as something moved across the beam of light coming from the workshop. 'What was that?'

Rob looked over his shoulder and Matt could smell sawdust mingled with the odour of linseed oil and fresh varnish. And above all, the sickly sweet smell of embalming fluid.

'Probably just a mouse. Mr Bingley's talking about getting a cat to save on the cheese he puts in the breakneck traps.'

'Mean old sod, is he?'

'Not so you'd notice,' Rob defended his employer. 'He taught me his trade, pays me well enough and gives me space to do my own bits on the side. I'd call that pretty generous, wouldn't you?'

'You could do a site better. That's what I'm here about.'

Rob turned up the wick in his oil lamp and

settled himself at a work table where he was putting the finishing touches to a child's writing desk.

'Birthday present for a five-year-old,' he explained, smoothing his hand over his work with pride.

'Bliddy lucky she is too. I used to get a book.'

'I know,' Rob said fondly. 'You used to give them to me. I enjoyed them and have them still to pass on to my own bairns, if and when I have any.'

'Well, now . . . ' Matt cleared his throat noisily. 'It's that very subject that brings me here th' night. I'm gettin' married.'

Rob's mouth dropped open in surprise. 'I don't believe my ears! Who is it?'

'Ach, yell find oot in good time, man.' Matt looked about him shiftily, pulling on the lobe of his ear. 'By the way, how would ye like to emigrate to Patagonia with us?'

They stared at one another like ghosts at a funeral. The silence was palpable. Somewhere in the recesses of the old building a clock ticked solemnly.

It was an age before Rob could speak and, as he said later, it was a good job he was already sitting down, or he might have toppled over with the shock of Matt's double news.

'You can't be serious,' he said.

'Oh, I'm serious all right. Me great-Aunty Blodwen has sent the money all the way from Patagonia — a place called Puerto Daffyd. She wanted all of us to go, but the others aren't interested. Anyways, that's when I thought of you. They're mad keen on attracting fellas like yersel'. Me, I'm just a labourer, if ye like. But you — well, ye're a specialist, aren't ye? There's plenty of work and more land than anybody knows what to do wi'.'

Rob rubbed his chin, which had grown bristles since his morning shave, but they glistened like golden needles in the lamplight. His grey eyes looked thoughtful.

'I don't know, Matt.'

'Aw, come on. We're mates, aren't we?'

'But why would you want me to string along if you're going to be taking a bride with you? And you still haven't told me who she is.'

'Well, it's all hush-hush, ye see. No need to spread the word, eh?'

'Matt? What are you up to?'

'Are you comin' or what? Only we've got to get oorsel's to Wales and join the next boatload for Patagonia. I've got enough money for the tickets.'

'I'd have to work me notice with Mr Bingley. He won't be well pleased, but . . . '

'Ye're gannin'?'

'And I'll have to take me tools with me.'

'Wouldn't gan without them, man!'

'But Matt, we're not Welsh. Will they still take us?'

'Well, ye might not believe this, cos I didn't knaa mesel', like, but though me father's Irish, me mother was Welsh. Anyway, I hears there are other nationalities over there. Not just the Welsh. Happen there'll be a Geordie or two an' all, eh?'

They looked at each other and laughed and Rob brought out his secret bottle of whisky he kept stashed away for moments when his spirit needed lifting. He wasn't a drinking man like Matt, but there were times when it was right. This was one of them.

'I'll think about it, Matt,' he said, pouring out two tots. 'But no promises, eh?'

Long after Matt left, Rob sat mulling over his friend's incredible proposition. A little trickle of excitement ran through his veins like an electrical charge. It was some time before he thought of Margaret and how she would react to the idea. His fiancée of three years did not strike him as being the adventurous sort.

As he put the light out and locked up the parlour, Rob felt a damp, heavy blanket descend, extinguishing the excitement. Maybe Patagonia wasn't such a good idea after all.

3

Rob knew he had been a bit rash finally saying he would go with Matt to Patagonia. Now that he'd had a chance to think about it, he wasn't so sure. Tynesiders didn't move about much. They stuck to home and hearth where their roots were strong.

His mother would throw a fit. As for his father, things had been bad enough when Rob left the pit. They'd not been on good terms ever since. Rob's family had been miners for generations in and around the Durham area and Edward Barker was a supervisor. He wanted his sons to follow in his footsteps.

Rob's younger brother, Davy, would likely see Patagonia as an exciting challenge, but he would be hard put to believe that either Rob or Matt were serious about going. After all, Rob was engaged to be married, not footloose and fancy-free like Matt, despite the claim that he was getting himself hitched. If it were, indeed, true. Rob grinned and shook his head, then thought again of Margaret. Of course, if he could persuade her . . . *Nah! No way!*

Now why did his stomach lurch like that? Anyway, he couldn't drag the poor girl to the back of beyond, and expect her to be happy. Margaret was the quiet, homely type. She would want her family around her and know where she was at.

There was nothing wrong with that. For most men, that's all they ever wanted in a wife. It was too damned bad that he, Rob, seemed to want so much more. Always reaching for the moon, his mam was fond of saying about him. Well, if the moon were his for the taking, he'd be a fool not to have a go. And he'd have himself a pocket full of stars too, if they were up for grabs.

Only they weren't, were they? What chance did he have, stuck here in this pit village? He might as well admit it. All he was good for was embalming dead folk and making coffins. The smell of the embalming fluid lingered about his person and he hated that. But he did at least make the best burial boxes in the whole of Tyneside and that was something to be proud of.

Rob swore softly to himself as he looked out at the wet Saturday evening. From his room at the back of the miner's cottage he could see, in the glow of the gaslights, nothing but stone walls and cobbles and the backs of the houses in the street opposite. It wasn't a very exciting place to spend a whole lifetime. Everything revolved around Washday Monday, Fish Day Friday and any titbits of gossip that could be sifted from the days in between. The men slogged their guts out down the pits, struggled to pay the rent and feed their families. The wives scrubbed floors, raised children and, a lot of the time, fought to keep them alive.

He wasn't a miner, thank God, but he didn't have much to offer Margaret, or any other lass. They had already been to see a house that was for rent further down the street. It was a hovel — two rooms, a scullery and a lavatory at the bottom of the yard — but it was all Rob could afford unless his cabinet making took off. Then he would need proper premises and that took money. Margaret said she didn't mind waiting. Rob suspected that she would be happy to wait forever, while he got hot under the collar, and other places, and had to fight off the temptation to sort himself out with the kind of women Matt frequented.

'I'm off out, Mam!' he called as he passed the kitchen where his mother was meticulously scrubbing the whitewood benches with soda water.

'I hope ye're not goin' to the public house, our Rob,' she shouted after him, and he looked at her, his face creasing into a deep frown.

'I might call in at The Swan on the way back, Mam, but I have to go and see Margaret first.'

'See Margaret? But the lassie's coming to tea tomorrow afternoon, Rob. What on earth do you have to go and see her about that's so urgent?'

'There's something I have to discuss with her — personal, like.'

'Oh, aye? Eeh, our Rob, you haven't got the girl in trouble or anything, have you?' It was Annie's absolute fear that either of her sons planted their seed before they were respectably married.

He almost told her that chance would be a fine thing. Margaret was as pure as the driven snow and not about to rectify that in the near future. He hoped to God she would see things differently once they were married, but there were times when he had grave doubts. There was something about her attitude that he couldn't quite figure out.

'Stop worrying, Mam.' He darted into the kitchen and gave her a peck on her warm cheek. 'I'll be back for me supper.'

'And don't you go drinking with that Matt Riley. You know what he's like. Always in and out of trouble. You've had more than your share of pulling him out of it by the scruff of his neck.'

'Aye, Mam.' He smiled and patted the cheek he had just kissed; she was lovely, but she definitely did not understand men or their ways.

'One of these days he'll drag you down with him,' she went on. 'Your dad and I couldn't bear it if you got a reputation the likes as he has.'

'Yes, Mam.'

'When he was a bairn, he was a canny enough lad, but he's changed. You mark my words, our Rob, he'll come to a sticky end and I don't want you around him when he does.'

'Yes'm,' Rob grinned and pulled his forelock, trying to ignore the fact that she was usually right in her predictions, even if he did act the big sceptic in front of her.

'Oh, go on with ye!' She gave him a playful slap and laughed as he sidestepped deftly away from her and hurried out into the street.

★   ★   ★

It was strange the way life could change in the space of a few hours. Rob had thought his future was all cut and dried. He'd continue working at the funeral parlour, marry

Margaret, have a bairn or two, save up for his own workshop; and take young Davy on as an apprentice to save him from the pit that he hated. It was all so settled in his mind. Then Matt had to come along and upset the apple cart.

Rob twisted his face and stuck his hands deep in his trouser pockets, hunching his shoulders against the rain that was beating down on him in slanting torrents.

'If the truth be known,' he thought, 'I was already unsettled. I just didn't want to admit it. I was going along with the flow, because that's what people do, generally.'

He had called in on Margaret, who showed no particular pleasure at his visit, being in one of her quiet moods. She had been sitting in the front room, reading her Bible. It was the only book she read and Rob couldn't help thinking that this, in itself, was a mite worrying. All that religion, to the exclusion of all else, was enough to turn a person's mind.

Margaret's parents were down at the Evangelist Hall, where her father was a lay preacher and her mother played the piano. They were preparing for the Sunday service. There was no rousing organ in the hall, which was cold and void of any ornamentation, religious or otherwise. Rob found them a dreary lot and he had not looked forward to his wedding being held there.

But that secret dread was now lifted. There wasn't going to be a wedding after all. He lowered his head even further and his feet splashed through the puddles where the pavement was uneven. The cold, muddy water seeped through his trouser bottoms and ran down into his socks and best boots, which he had taken care to shine with copious amounts of black Cherry Blossom polish that morning.

The squishing of water between his toes was uncomfortable, but he paid it no mind. Every few yards, he did a little hop, skip and a jump as relief sank in and an incomprehensible sense of excitement took over. He kept it contained. After all, his fiancée had just given him the push. It was hardly an occasion for celebrating.

The Swan Inn was full to the gunnels when he got there. It looked like every miner in Gateshead was exercising his elbow after breaking his back down the pit. Rob pushed his way through, nodding to all and sundry and ignoring the jibes about his sodden state. He could see Matt propping up the bar, surrounded by a bunch of fellows who looked far from jovial. In fact, as he approached, one thickset young man grabbed Matt by his lapels and looked as if he was going to land him one with a big, clenched fist.

'Hey, what's this?' Rob latched on to the man's wrist and held it. He was the only person in the place taller than Matt and his broad, muscular build tended to make people back off.

'Am I glad to see you, mate!' Matt's eyes signalled for Rob to get him out of there.

Rob released the man and saw that hostility was simmering and might come to the boil any minute.

'What's going on, then?' he asked, keeping it light and signalling to the barman for two pints of pale ale.

There was an explosion of voices all around him, until he held up his hands and called for the eldest among them to speak out.

'He's had his hands on me daughter and now he's desertin' her. And her with a bairn in her belly,' said the man, his face red and his eyes glassy.

'Aye, and he's done the same to *wor* lass an' all.' Another man joined in, his anger so great that he spat the words out through clenched teeth.

Both speakers were short, brawny miners in their forties. Not real fighting men like the fellows who did knuckle boxing in the pub's back room on Saturday nights, but angry enough to make each blow count. Still, Rob held off, thinking it was high time his pal was taught a lesson. He was too free by half, putting it about among the canny lasses of Gateshead.

'I thought you said you were getting married, Matt,' Rob said to disbelieving murmurs and raised eyebrows.

'Aye, I was — I mean, I am — but not to *their* two lasses . . . '

Matt looked more than a little uneasy as there was a surge forward, bodies pressing in on all sides. Rob picked up the two pint tankards and passed one to Matt.

'You've really burned your bridges this time, mate,' he said, watching as Matt swigged back his ale in swift, thirsty swallows.

'Oh, hey, come on,' Matt said, banging his empty glass on the bar counter and wiping his mouth with the back of his hand. 'It's the lassies' word against mine. Nobody can prove anything.'

'Why, ye bugger, ye . . . '

The two fathers of the disgraced girls grabbed Matt while Rob held back the restless onlookers. He saw Matt's plaintive expression, then his friend was being dragged off and Rob was strategically calling for beers all round, throwing money at the barman and placing himself with his back to the door, preventing anyone from leaving.

The men were disgruntled, but they didn't take much persuading once they saw he meant business. Tyneside didn't grow many young men in Rob's mould. He was over six feet tall, broad-shouldered, with muscles of steel. And he knew how to use them, too, when provoked.

The offer of free beer worked a treat and the men were nicely distracted. A few minutes later, the door nudged his back and he moved to let in the two aggrieved fathers. They had bloodied knuckles and were panting fit to burst, but they had had their moment and their anger had abated.

'Ye can go scoop up yer mate, lad,' one of them said. 'But you tell him that we're not finished with him. Not by a long chalk. Tell him, will ye, that today was just a warnin', like.'

'Aye,' Rob said, stepping out onto the street. 'I'll tell him.'

He found Matt struggling to get up from the gutter where the rainwater was running black and gurgling down a sewer grill. His long legs had a rubbery look about them. He was bruised and bleeding, but there was nothing too serious to be concerned about that Rob could see.

'Why the hell didn't ye give us a hand, Rob?' he said, spitting out bloody saliva and a piece of broken tooth.

Rob hauled his friend to an upright position and marched him up the road, like two lads running a three-legged race.

'I figured you deserved all you got,' he said lightly. 'Besides, I was in no mood for a scrap.'

Matt stared at him, squinting through swollen eyes that would shine black and blue by morning.

'Wot's up wi' thee, then?' he said.

'Me and Margaret. The engagement's off.' Rob looked away, overcome with self-consciousness.

'Oh, aye?'

'Aye, but I'm not too fussed about it. I figure I wasn't really looking forward to getting married after all.'

Rob shrugged his shoulders at Matt's curious stare.

'Come on, Matt. I'll take you home. I suggest you keep your head down for a bit if you don't want to lose the rest of your teeth.'

★ ★ ★

There were stony faces around the supper table. Rob's mother nearly fainted at the state of him when he got back. He had stayed an hour with Matt and they had downed half a

45

bottle of whisky between them. By the time he got home, he was more than a little tipsy and it showed.

He had a quick wash at the kitchen sink and changed into dry clothes, then the family sat down to a delayed meal. Young Davy had his wide blue eyes fixed on his big brother. Rob was something of a hero to him, and he had never seen him drunk before. Rob's father concentrated on his meat and three veg, looking up occasionally from beneath bushy grey eyebrows, speaking only to ask for the gravy.

'Well, that is bad news, son,' Annie said at last, when he thought the silence was going to continue right through to the pudding. 'Did Margaret give you any reason for this sudden change of heart?'

Rob swallowed a piece of rabbit pie, licked his lips and knew that if he didn't say something now he never would and the whole idea would be lost for all time.

'She doesn't want to go to Patagonia with me,' he said and three sets of eyes popped out of three raised heads.

'Where's that when it's at home?' Annie asked, her fork half way to her mouth, dripping brown gravy down her clean floral pinafore.

'And why would you be going there in any

case?' Ted Barker banged his cutlery down, rattling everything on the table.

'Patagonia!' Davy breathed. 'Why, that's . . . '

'South America,' Rob told them and felt some of the pressure ease now that the subject was out in the open. 'I'm going to emigrate there with Matt.'

'*You're going to do what, our Rob?*' His mother's face was parchment pale and her chin was already beginning to quiver.

And so Rob told them his plans, which he did not know were his plans until that moment. The thought of having to marry Margaret had held him back. He had no fancy, somehow, to start a new life with someone who was so lacking in vitality that he was very often bored in her company.

When he told her that he was thinking of going to Patagonia Margaret's reaction of horror came as no surprise. '*I really don't think we were made for each other, do you?*' Those were her very words. And now that he'd had time to think about it, full of truth.

'When are you leaving, Rob? Can I come with you?' Davy was so excited he was spitting out globules of mashed potato all over the table.

'He's not going anywhere!' stated Annie Barker flatly and her elbow gave her husband a meaningful nudge. 'Ted, speak to your son,

47

for goodness sake. I suppose that Matt Riley is at the bottom of this? It's the kind of brainless thing he would get up to.'

Rob fixed his mother with a determined eye.

'It was Matt's idea, Mam, but don't think for one minute that he's influenced me. I've been restless for a long time. What is there here for the likes of me, eh?'

'You've got a respectable job, son,' Annie Barker said. 'Mr Bingley thinks highly of ye.'

'Aye, it's better than being down the pit, anyway. And, I'll never be short of work, will I, making coffins. But I want more out of life. I'm tired of smelling like a corpse meself. I want to see something of the world beyond Gateshead. I want to get away from the rain and the cold of the North-east. And the rows and rows of pit houses and little else. I want to live where the air is soft and the sun shines every day and there are trees and — '

'Ye can get that by goin' to the Lakes in Cumberland,' his father reminded him, though they all knew that it rained harder over there than it did in Durham county.

His mother was on her feet now, leaning her red, work-roughened hands on the table, directing all her force his way. Rob was looking at his father, surprised to find him so quiet and not laying down the law as he

48

was known to do.

'Annie,' Ted said softly, touching his wife's arm. 'Sit down, lass, will ye. Our Rob's right. He was born with itchy feet and he'll not settle until he's had his fill of what he thinks is right for him.'

'Oh, Ted!' Annie sat down heavily, her expression more shocked than ever. 'I never thought I'd hear you say anything like that.'

'Now, Rob, lad,' his father was regarding him levelly. 'How much do you need to take you to this 'promised land' of yours? And how are ye proposin' to live once ye get there?'

'Twenty pounds all told if we share a cabin, but I'm going on Matt's ticket,' Rob told him, slowly stirring the vegetables in the gravy swimming on his plate. 'His great-aunt sent enough money for the whole family, but most of them are dead and Matt's brothers aren't interested.'

'He has people over there! Where did you say it was?' Annie was recovering slowly, but her chin still quivered uncontrollably.

'Patagonia, Mam,' he replied. 'It's Argentina actually, but — '

'Oh, don't confuse me with the geography of the place, son.'

'It's in South America, Mam,' Davy piped up, shoving the old family atlas at her, jabbing the page with a thick finger. 'Look!'

'Is it civilized, that's what I'd like to know?'

'It's full of Welsh people, Mam.' Rob gave a lopsided grin and helped himself to another piece of pie. 'Is that civilized enough for you?'

'I'm not sure that's a good sign or a bad one,' Annie said, her forehead creasing like a concertina. 'Anyway, what's he doing, going to join the Welsh?'

'Aye,' her husband nodded. 'Funny lot, the Welsh. Never know how ye have 'em. Not much sense of humour, by all accounts.'

'Well, I wouldn't know about that,' Rob said. 'Anyway, Matt's only Irish on his dad's side, but Welsh on his mother's, apparently.'

'It's no wonder the lad has problems,' Annie said and then they all began to laugh; first Davy, then Rob, then his parents. And what a blessed release it was.

* * *

It was a few weeks later when Matt arrived at the Barker house driving a rickety old horse and cart packed with his belongings.

He had set the date with Rob, having made contact with Mr Dai Griffiths, the one uncle he had still living in Prestatyn, and the one who had sent them Blodwen's letter. Mr Griffiths had instructed them to come first to him. He would, he said, have the necessary

50

papers ready, for there was a boat leaving Liverpool within the month headed for Rawson in Patagonia. A group of Welsh were already formed and their passages booked. It would be a tight squeeze, but Matt's uncle had strings to pull, him being related to Blodwen Evans. The woman was something of a living legend, apparently, and many a person looked upon her as a heroine.

At the moment of departure, Rob embraced his family with a mixture of emotions tightening his throat. They told him to be good and to write often and to come home soon, as if he was thirteen and off on holiday to Whitley Bay. Davy, he noticed, darted back into the house before the goodbyes were over, no doubt to nurse his disappointment in not going with them.

Rob hadn't seen much of Matt since their decision to emigrate. His friend seemed a touch on the cagey side and Rob couldn't help wondering if there was something more than the unfortunate business of two pregnant lasses bothering him.

As they approached the cart with its knobbly boned horse snorting and pawing impatiently at the cobbles underfoot, Rob noticed someone sitting on the seat in front.

'Who's that?' He glanced at Matt and saw a

shadow of guilt sweep over the other man's face.

'Erm . . . ' Matt took out a pocket watch and studied it. 'It's me wife.'

'Your *what?*' Although Matt had spoken of his intention to get married, he had never actually produced his 'intended'. 'Matt? What kind of wool are you trying to pull over my eyes now, eh?'

'Who? Me? Never!' There was the famous incorrigible grin that had fooled many a person before now, but Rob was wise to Matt's tricks.

'Come on, Matt. Be honest, for once in your life.'

He heard a deep intake of breath. 'I kid you not. She is truly my wife and I have the certificate to prove it.'

'You actually . . . ' Rob gulped at the ridiculousness of it. 'You *married* one of them?'

'One of . . . ? Oh — er — no, mate. Not either of those two lasses, but we'll not say nowt to Dora about that little shenanigans.'

'Dora?'

'Aye. Dora Milligan.' Matt looked decidedly pleased with himself. 'Now Mrs Matthew Riley, as of this afternoon.'

Rob's steps faltered and he nearly dropped his end of the tool chest. Of all the young women in the world, Dora was the last he could imagine as Matt's wife. Dear, sweet little Dora, who didn't appear to have much between her ears, but was liked by everyone for her gentle ways.

'I don't believe it!' Rob said, his voice thick with incredulity.

Matt's face twisted and he pulled on the lobe of his ear.

'Sorry, mate, I know you was going to be me best man, but it happened quick, like, if ye know what I mean.'

They had reached the cart and Dora was anxiously looking down at them, her dinner-plate eyes bigger than ever, her tiny, rosebud mouth tightly pursed. She looked like a child afraid of the dark. Rob felt anger rise in him as he thought of the way Matt treated his women, and guessed that Dora had a shock in store for her. She was the kind of girl that people wanted to protect, because she certainly didn't know how to protect herself.

'Dora.' Rob nodded and she gave him a tremulous smile.

'Hello, Mr Barker,' she said in a tiny whisper of a voice with the slightest hint of a lisp, her china doll face flushing with embarrassment.

Dora had been a foundling. Nobody knew

her history. Once she left the orphanage at fifteen, she had been looked after by the kindly old soul who ran the local sweetshop. The woman had died recently and the girl was again on her own, though people looked out for her as much as possible. Where were they, Rob wondered, when Matt went sniffing around?

As much as he liked Matt — they had grown up together — he was not blind to his faults. For a start, he could not be trusted around women. Some women, of course, knew what they were letting themselves in for. But not Dora. She was too naïve by far.

'Congratulations,' Rob said and forced a smile, trying not to show the concern that was twisting inside him. 'I hear you've married my best mate here.'

She nodded shyly and her fair, unruly curls bobbed like corks on springs. Dora was not beautiful by any stretch of the imagination, but she had a natural inner glow.

Rob frowned deeply, wondering if the girl knew what she had let herself in for. Had Matt told her anything at all of what lay ahead? The poor bairn probably couldn't believe her luck. How would she feel once she discovered that luck or, God bless her, *love*, didn't come into it?

He caught her looking at him with some

trepidation and hurriedly gave her a reassuring smile.

'Let's be off, then.'

Matt sounded impatient as he pushed Rob from behind until he climbed up and sat on the seat beside Dora and they set off, the girl sandwiched tightly between them.

They reached the station in good time. Rob stood with Dora on the platform, surrounded by their luggage, while Matt disposed of the horse and cart on a grassy patch of spare ground. The poor animal would at least have something to eat until its owner came along to reclaim him.

With a toot and a puff of steam, and sulphur fouling the air, their train arrived at last. They tumbled into the first carriage that presented itself, storing their bags, parcels and boxes as best they could. Matt was asleep and snoring almost before they chugged out of the station, so it was left to Rob to tuck a travelling blanket around Dora. The poor girl was shivering convulsively from the chill in the air, her delicate face pinched with cold and fatigue.

'For a new husband, Matt is not very attentive, Dora,' he said kindly and saw her clamp her lips together and swallow with difficulty.

'He must be tired, Mr Barker,' she said.

'Call me Rob, pet. I hope we're going to be good friends from now on.' He saw her shy nod and felt his heart clench, for if he was not mistaken, this tiny waif of a girl was going to need a friend if she was to cope with Matt's unruly ways.

It was a long journey to Liverpool, with station changes all along the route. There was rain the whole way and it was cold and windy. When they finally alighted and stood looking around them, they already felt as if they were in a foreign land. It sounded like it too. The local accent was barely understandable to the three young Geordies who, until now, had never travelled beyond their county border, other than to Newcastle.

'My uncle said there would be transport running to Prestatyn,' Matt said, looking around him and spotting the exit. 'Come on, this way.'

He picked up his own valise and left Rob and Dora with the heavy toolbox. Rob was about to call him back when a voice hailed him from behind.

'Need some help, mate?'

Rob's head snapped around on hearing the familiar tones, and he stood gawping at what he saw.

'Davy! What the hell . . . ?'

His brother tossed him a cheeky, blue-eyed

56

grin, then he looked beyond Rob to the fragile-looking girl.

'I didn't know there were four of us going to Patagonia,' he said. It's going to be a right laugh, isn't it, eh?'

Rob opened his mouth, then shut it again with a snap.

'Davy,' he said, his teeth gritting, 'you get yourself on the next train back home or I'll have your guts for garters.'

'No way, man! I'm coming with you.'

And he did.

4

Gwyneth turned from grooming the stallion, Diablo, and leaned on the hitching rail in front of the stables. The sweet smell of horse was still warm in her nostrils. She was glad to be back at the *estancia*. Here, on the Andean plains, she could be anything she wanted, rather than a woman with a dark past.

The atmosphere was heavy, the sky thick with purplish grey storm clouds. In the distance, thunder rumbled. As she gazed out at the flat green expanses around the ranch, great splotches of rain kicked up the dust, scarring it with minute craters.

Diablo whinnied and stamped his feet. Gwyneth did not change her position, but spoke to him softly, her voice a caress, as she continued to stare into the distance. She was trying to empty her mind, but finding it impossible. This feeling of urgency that gripped her body refused to let her go.

She took off her neckerchief and wiped around her perspiring neck and between her breasts, willing the cooling rain to come quick and heavy. Rain always brought relief after a period of great heat. The long summer had at last run its course.

On the roofed terrace of the *hacienda*, Therese was preparing the table for the evening meal. With the graceful movements of a seductress, she floated a checked poplin cloth down the length of the long, communal table. Then, broad Spanish hips undulating, she laid out cutlery, humming to herself, swaying all the while, her movements graceful, yet with an underlying vivacity. Although past forty, Therese never stopped dancing, even when there was no music.

This evening, however, there was music aplenty. It floated from somewhere at the back of the house, accompanied by the familiar *clack-clackety-clack-clack-clack* — the tapping of Miguel's high-heeled dancing boots, and the sharp clicking of his fingers to the hot tempo that grew in speed and intensity, blotting out the chorus of cicadas from the surrounding pampas.

Therese looked up and saw Gwyneth hovering by the stables. She waved, the broad smile on her face welcoming.

'Hurry, Gwyneth! Supper is almost ready!'

Gwyneth responded with a wave of her own. It never failed to amaze her that in so short a time they had become friends. Therese never sat in judgement. They were almost like a family, Gwyneth thought.

However, Miguel still kept his distance.

'I must wash,' she shouted, indicating with a jerk of her thumb the wash house where she had her own private corner, separated from the men's.

Therese nodded, then disappeared into the *hacienda*, no doubt to stir the inevitable meat stew and slice up the bread she baked freshly each morning.

Gwyneth's feet faltered on the way to the wash house and turned her in the direction of the small arena behind the *hacienda*. She knew Miguel preferred to rehearse without being observed, except for Antonio who played guitar for him. However, if she were very careful, she could creep up on him.

Pressing herself against the end wall of the *hacienda*, Gwyneth slowly inched forward until she could see Miguel. His slim, graceful figure seemed to glide as he went through his steps, then his body snapped to attention as he affected the stance of a bullfighter. Although he had no tools other than his expressive face and hands, there was no doubt that he was mimicking the swirling of the cape and the plunging of the sword into the imaginary bull on its knees before him.

Miguel had been a matador in Spain before travelling to Argentina to become a dancer. His sister, Therese, on the other hand, had always been a *flamenco* dancer. She was good, but she was no longer young. Fights often broke out between brother and sister as he put her through endless practice sessions, introducing new and more complicated routines. Gwyneth had seen Therese practise until her feet bled, but even then Miguel would not let up on her.

Gwyneth peered around the building until she had a good view of Miguel. It was not the first time she had secretly watched him, and not only while he was dancing. Miguel fascinated her with his taut, handsome face that tended to look sad and angry at the same time. He had wonderful, gleaming black eyes, but they never flashed in her direction.

She shivered suddenly, though the temperature was still high, despite the drizzling rain and the stiff breeze that was moving dust and tumbleweed about the arena. Miguel's feet stamped out a fast and sensuous rhythm, legs and body working in such perfect harmony to the throbbing strings of the *flamenco* guitar.

'Hola, Señorita Gwyneth!'

Gwyneth jumped guiltily as Juanita Rodriguez, the long-time family retainer, grabbed her arm and pulled her back into the shadows, her wise old eyes squinting in the lowering sun, her thin slit of a mouth puckering about the edges.

'Juanita! I wish you wouldn't sneak up on me like that.'

Juanita's eyes narrowed critically as she directed them to Gwyneth's rain-spattered shirt clinging almost transparently to her breasts.

'Is not good, señorita, watching Señor Miguel in secret. Is not respectable, this dance that he does.'

'Oh, Juanita, it's so beautiful, don't you think?' Gwyneth tried to look at Miguel again over her shoulder, but the old Spanish woman tugged at her until she had to give in and head reluctantly for the wash house.

'Huh! All that passion. Is not good, I tell you.'

'You don't object to Therese dancing like that,' Gwyneth said, but Juanita wasn't in a good mood today.

'That Therese!' She threw up her hands. 'She was born with *El Diablo* in her soul. How could I, Juanita Cecilia Maria Rodriguez, simple peasant that I am, stop her dancing? *Dios mio!*' Juanita crossed herself twice, closed her eyes tightly and shook her head. 'It cuts my heart like a knife to see her — and you too, senorita, but with the father you have in you . . . '

Gwyneth blinked down at the little Spanish

woman and slowly licked her dry, dusty lips.

'What do you know about my father, Juanita?' she asked, her hands balling into tight fists, for she had believed she was far removed from her past.

The Spanish woman's chin dropped onto her chest.

'I should not have spoken, but . . . ' The beady eyes flashed knowledgeably. 'All the world and his brother know about that father of yours, señorita. He was bad, all the way through. I see that passion in you and I tell you, you should be afraid.'

Gwyneth's spine stiffened and she pulled herself up to her full height, squaring her shoulders. Not even the Widow Evans spoke to her like that. It wasn't true, it wasn't! She had spent years trying not to be like her father, trying to forget him and what had passed between them.

'I am *not* like my father,' she said.

'I have seen how men look at you,' Juanita said. 'And I have seen how you look at Señor Miguel. The bad seed will find a way out!'

Anger boiled up in Gwyneth. She wanted to deny vehemently what the woman said about her inheriting her father's bad seed, but a part of her held back. Perhaps it was true after all. Every time she looked at Miguel, something inside her stirred. It exhilarated her to such an extent that she could hardly control her body. The fact that Miguel was barely aware of her existence disappointed her sorely.

Gwyneth avoided the woman's discerning eyes and spun on her heel, entering the wash house and peeling off her damp clothes. Inside the dark, timber building, it was cool, but she burned even more and stayed longer than usual underneath the cold, healing water of the shower, using more than one bucket, almost pulling them down on top of her when she yanked furiously on the rope attached to them.

'Damn, damn, damn!' she cursed under her breath as the cold water hit her head and shoulders and flowed over her heated body.

She was not cursing the coldness of the water or the fact that she had been a little too vigorous in pulling on the rope. What bothered her was the way Miguel made her feel. She hated men and all they stood for, yet here she was panting after a man who appeared oblivious of her presence. As old Blodwen Evans had so rightly indicated, she was exactly like a filly on first heat. An old filly, at that, having a quarter of a century behind her.

★ ★ ★

'You are late, Gwyneth.' Therese frowned at her as she slid into her place and passed a plate of stew down the table.

'I was hot and dirty, Therese,' Gwyneth said apologetically. 'I must have taken longer at my ablutions than I thought.'

'It is to be hoped the water was good and cold for you,' Juanita whispered in her ear as she passed the bread.

The young ranch hands nearby grinned and nudged one another, used to the housekeeper's taunting criticisms. It no doubt made an amusing change to have Gwyneth targeted. They respected her expertise with horses, but resented her aloofness.

There was some talk and ribald laughter at the head of the table where Miguel was sitting, though Miguel himself did not join in. Instead, he shot her a sly look, catching her off guard. His black eyes flared just once, then he dropped his gaze and muttered something into his plate that she could not make out.

'Si, si, si!' Therese reached over and patted Miguel's hand, then she fixed Gwyneth with a flashing smile. 'After supper we are going to dance. Gwyneth, you are to be Miguel's partner. I have told him that you are ready, but my brother, being the stupid, pig-headed person he is, does not believe me.'

A small hiss of air escaped Gwyneth's slightly parted lips. She felt a warm sensation creep up her throat and into her cheeks as heads turned expectantly her way. Antonio kept shaking his head, but Miguel simply nodded in reply to his sister's proposal.

'It is settled, then,' Therese announced in an even louder voice. 'The rain has stopped. Tonight we will dance and drink and be merry. Juan! José! Set up the benches around the arena. Juanita, fetch more wine. I want to have fun tonight. What do you say, Gwyneth?'

Gwyneth smiled weakly. Usually, she only watched these social functions from a distance, never eager to join in. Therese had been giving her private dancing lessons after she had spied Gwyneth's tapping foot. She had been unwilling, at first, to admit that she enjoyed the music and the dancing. She had never danced with Miguel, but she imagined what it must be like, especially when she watched Therese dancing with him, winding herself around him, clinging to him with all the passion in the world written on her face. In the heat of the *tango* it was hard to remember that they were brother and sister.

'You must make the audience believe that you are passionately in love with your partner,' she told Gwyneth.

'But he's your brother,' Gwyneth said.

'How can you make it look so real?' Therese shrugged and gave a small, amused smile.

'I am an actress. I make a living at fooling people. Or, I did, until I became too old and too fat.'

'My sister seems to think you might be an excellent new partner for me.'

Gwyneth jumped at the sound of Miguel's thickly accented voice. He did not usually speak to her in English, so it came as a surprise. She had been so deep in her thoughts that she hadn't seen him approach. Tongue-tied, she pushed back her chair, rose and started walking away from him, but he followed, lightly touching her elbow with cool fingertips.

'Well?' he demanded. 'Is she right? Are you that good?'

Something riled inside her, hating his arrogance, but at the same time she was unable to suppress an excitement that rose from the soles of her feet and spread through her like a licking flame.

'I doubt it,' she said flatly, subduing her enthusiasm. 'However, we shall see, won't we?'

Then Therese was there, fussing about her, dragging her back to the house so that she could put on a suitable dress.

'You cannot dance with Miguel looking like

a *gaucho*,' Therese said with a grimace. 'I have a dress that should fit, though it will be a little short on you.' She gave a quick gurgle of laughter. 'That will prove that you really are feminine beneath that armour of yours. The men are beginning to doubt it.'

'Therese, I can't do this . . . '

'You can and you must. You are a natural and Miguel needs a partner. I no longer excite audiences. Whereas you . . . *come*. We will dress you so that even Miguel will fall in love with you.'

Therese walked away, laughing. Something alien stirred in Gwyneth's stomach and her heart missed a beat, then tripped along at a faster than normal rate as she followed Therese into the house. She did not understand what was happening to her. She did not *love* Miguel. She could never love any man, of that she was certain. Yet her body betrayed her with an emotion she had no control over.

★ ★ ★

'Howay, man! Get a move on or we'll still be trying to find me uncle's house this time th'morrow.'

Matt was striding out ahead, valise in one hand, makeshift map in the other. From time to time, he stopped and peered at the street names and the numbers and compared them with the address he had been given.

It had been a long, harrowing journey, but they had finally put down at Prestatyn in North Wales. Rob exchanged glances with Davy, who smothered a yawn.

'Hey, I thought they were speakin' a foreign language at Liverpool,' he said, 'but this here Welsh is ten times worse. I canna understand them.'

'Me neither.' Rob shook his head and glanced over his shoulder to where Dora was trailing behind, almost asleep on her feet. He called out to Matt. 'Matt, hold up a minute, will you.'

Matt took no notice. He was crossing the road and showing his bit of paper to a passer-by. The woman eyed all four of them with suspicion and hurried on without a word.

'Matt!' Rob was running short on patience, for he had been required to bite his tongue the whole length of the journey, so appalled was he at Matt's careless treatment of Dora.

'What, man?' Matt was peering through the steamed-up windows of a public house, from which came the sound of male voices singing in surprisingly good harmony.

'Have a thought for your wife, man. The

poor lass is exhausted. We all are.'

'Aw, she's all reet, man,' Matt said without even looking at the young woman he had married. 'Howay, the lot o' ye. Let's get some liquid refreshment.'

Without waiting for a reply, he opened the door, letting out clouds of tobacco smoke into the inky blue night. Rubbing his hands together gleefully, he disappeared inside.

'It's a grand pity his uncle wasn't there to meet us,' Davy said, pulling his coat collar up and his cap down as the rain fell more solidly on their heads and the wind keened about them like a lamenting banshee.

'Aye,' Rob nodded and indicated to Davy to put down the box of tools they were carrying. 'But the train was late, as you know, and if Matt's uncle is anything like Matt, he wouldn't be wanting to hang about twiddling his thumbs.'

Matt was not exactly over-endowed with patience, as they well knew. It was in his character to want things passionately, and when that happened there was no stopping him, though he often came off second best, thanks to his irrational nature.

'Are we goin' in there for a drink, then, our Rob?' Davy looked as tired as Rob felt, but had perked up at the idea of putting himself around a pint of beer.

'I doubt we'll find Newcastle best brown in these parts, lad,' Rob told him, though he thought they might just have some of that Irish Guinness stout. It looked like treacle in the glass, but it was fair drinkable and some folk gave it to sickly babies to enrich their blood.

'Let's try, anyway. I'm parched.'

'Haven't you forgotten something, lad?' Rob inclined his head towards Dora, who was swaying perilously and looking near to collapse. 'Ladies aren't welcome in public houses.'

'Oh, aye. I nivvor thought . . . ' Davy frowned apologetically.

'Nor did Matt, it would seem,' Rob rubbed his aching arms, then went to Dora and pulled her gently but firmly onto the pavement, thrusting her at Davy. 'You look after Dora. She can sit on me toolbox until we get back.'

'Aye, but — aw, Rob!'

'Don't argue, Davy, or I'll send you back to Gateshead with your tail between your legs. You shouldn't be here and you know it.'

Davy dropped his gaze to his feet. His best shoes had lost their shine. They were his pride and joy, having been the only bit of footwear he owned that weren't pit boots or clogs. Now, they were scuffed and muddied and they didn't keep his feet warm anyway.

Rob gave Dora a little shake and her eyes flickered as though he had disturbed her most private thoughts, though in reality she had probably been asleep with her eyes open.

'Go on, Dora, pet. Sit down for a few minutes while I go and fetch your ruddy husband.'

'Where's he gone?' she asked, her wide eyes glazed with fatigue.

'He's just gone into the pub to ask for directions,' Rob lied. 'You stay here with Davy. I'll be back in a couple of minutes.'

He waited long enough to see her sink down thankfully onto his toolbox, then he pushed his way through the ranks of men standing shoulder to shoulder in the pub, some talking, some singing, all of them lifting their elbows to their own rhythms.

Matt was leaning on the high bar, surrounded by a group of miners still covered in coal dust. They were pouring over the makeshift map. The miners spoke in the Welsh language, but the landlord, it seemed, had a good grasp of English. He was studying the map intently, stroking his black, handle-bar moustache, and stabbing a finger at the centre of the paper.

'If your uncle is Dai Griffiths, nephew of Colin Griffiths the blacksmith who should have sailed to Patagonia, but didn't, like his uncle before him, then this here is where he lives.' He sucked in air through his misshapen teeth and shook his head. 'Only he's not there, for he's gone to Prestatyn Station to meet family? He told me so this morning.'

'Well, that would be me — *us*, I mean,' Matt said, brightening. 'Only he wasn't there to meet us, so we had to find our own way.'

'I hope you've not come to find work in the mines, because there's little enough for our own men.'

'Oh, no, no, sir,' Matt said, whipping off his cap and puffing out his chest with pride and satisfaction. 'We're here to catch the boat to Patagonia.'

At his words, heads shot up, expressions became interested, ears stretched from all corners of the pub and Rob felt a surge of uneasiness spreading up from the pit of his stomach.

'Patagonia, is it? You'll be lucky, my lad. The boat's been full these last three weeks. There are lads in this town who have been turned down, look you. What makes you think that there'll be a place for you, English, eh?'

Before Matt could start something he couldn't stop, Rob grabbed his arm and put a meaningful pressure on it. The Welshmen were a hefty bunch and looked mean.

'If you've found out where your uncle lives, Matt, let's be on our way.'

Matt was obviously feeling belligerent and Rob groaned inwardly as his friend pulled away from him and leaned more heavily on the bar, eyeballing the landlord.

'And what makes you think I'm not Welsh, just because I don't have that silly accent of yours, eh? Eh?'

'Matt!' Rob hissed in Matt's ear. 'Let's just go, eh? Come on. Dora and Davy are waiting outside. We're all on our last legs.'

'Just a minute, Rob.' Matt was fumbling in his clothing, searching all his pockets until he finally produced the crumpled and well-read letter that had been forwarded on to his father. 'There you are, see?'

The barman took the letter, his mouth moving with every word as he read. No-one was singing now. Every capped and mufflered miner pressed forward around the two Geordie lads, eager to hear what the letter said.

'Well, now, this is a letter written by Mistress Blodwen Evans . . . ' He looked around the bar as a buzz of interest passed from man to man. 'It certainly looks authentic, so I suppose I must accept that you are a relation of hers.'

'That's very big of you, mate,' Matt said, pulling the letter back into his possession and folding it tightly before tucking it back into his inside pocket as if it were a passport to Paradise. 'Now, I think perhaps you owe me and me pal here a drop of something liquid, eh?'

'A drink, is it? Oh, aye, indeed to goodness. Where are my manners? Nothing but the best for a member of Mistress Evans's family, and on the house, eh?'

Rob received a roguish grin and a wink from Matt.

'Ye see? Remind me to give me aunty Blodwen a big kiss when I get to meet her, will ye?' He then addressed the barman's back, speaking over the clink of glass upon glass. 'Make mine a double, if ye don't mind.'

There was a hiss of liquid hitting the glasses and the barman turned, two frothy drinks in his hands, which he placed on the bar counter. Matt's astonished nose twitched as he sniffed the air curiously.

'Two large ones,' the barman said and smiled magnanimously. 'On the house.'

'Hey, what's this?' Matt picked up his glass, eyeing it suspiciously; he tasted the contents and spat the liquid out in a great fountain. 'What the hell!'

'That's our best sarsaparilla, young fellow,

75

and I'll thank you kindly not to waste it.'

'Sars . . . ? What did ye say?'

'Of course, if you don't like it there's always our best lemonade. Perhaps you'd like to try that?'

There was a growing titter of muffled laughter. Rob grabbed a handful of Matt's jacket, ready to hold him firm if his fists started flailing; and prepared to drag him back out to the street if necessary.

'Ye've got to be jokin', man!' Matt's eyebrows were meeting his hairline. He wiped his mouth with the back of his hand and shuddered. 'What kind of bar is this, when it's at home, eh?'

'It's a Temperance bar, my English friend.'

'A what?'

'There's a movement afoot to put an end to the demon drink,' the man explained carefully. 'It's a strong movement, so a lot of the public houses in Wales can no longer obtain a licence to sell liquor. Maybe you would like a cup of hot chocolate instead?'

Rob heaved on Matt's coat and propelled him in the direction of the door. The Welsh miners, now laughing openly, opened up like the Red Sea for Moses. At the door, however, he stopped, turned and faced them all.

'We have a young woman waiting for us outside,' he said, still hanging on to Matt.

'She's exhausted and frozen to the bone. Would you object if I brought her in for a minute and gave her a hot drink?'

'Well, that would depend on what type of young woman she is.'

Rob looked the man straight in the eye.

'A decent, respectable, married lady,' he said, nudging Matt who stood briskly to attention because it was difficult not to with his friend's big iron fingers digging into his back.

'Aye.' Matt nodded. 'She's me wife an' all.'

'Then she'll be welcome. Bring her in and take her into the snug where my wife will serve you all with hot chocolate.'

'I'm not drinkin' no hot bloody chocolate!' Matt said through gritted teeth once they were back out on the pavement.

'In that case,' Rob told him, 'you stay out here and mind our belongings while Davy, Dora and I join the Temperance men. And don't wander off or we'll have nothing to take with us to Patagonia — that is, if we ever get there.'

Rob was surprised to find that Matt had not budged by the time they rejoined him ten minutes later, much revived by the hot chocolate. Even Dora had perked up, though she didn't object when Davy put his hand under her skinny elbow and took her weight as they continued on their way.

They arrived at Matt's uncle's address at the same time as the man himself. He drove up in a pony and trap, looking for all the world like a fire and brimstone preacher in search of a misguided congregation.

'I am not at all happy about this whole situation,' he informed them as Matt introduced himself and the others. 'The least you could have done was wait for me at the station.'

'The train was late,' Matt explained. 'We thought we had missed you.'

'Yes, well, you had better come in before we all get washed away and frozen solid.' Matt's uncle looked from one to the other of them, puzzled. 'I did not expect four of you, nor did I know about the young woman. Lodging you will be difficult since we only have one spare bedroom with a double bed in it.'

Matt laughed and slapped the man's shoulder, a *bonhomie* the Welshman did not appear to appreciate.

'Well, it's going to get cosy for a night or two, isn't it, eh?'

'A night or two? The boat for Patagonia is already full. I could not get passages for you, not even for Blodwen Evans's relations.'

Matt looked stunned. Rob and Davy

exchanged worried frowns. As for Dora, she gave a little sigh and would have sunk to her knees had they not supported her.

'So,' Matt said, speaking with difficulty, for he was still trying to assimilate the news. 'What does this mean? When's the next boat, then, Uncle Dai?'

His uncle shook his head. There was not going to be another boat, he informed them as he ushered them into the narrow, dark hallway and they dripped on the shabby linoleum. Not for some time, maybe months.

'Not another boat!' Matt couldn't believe his ears. 'But that's daft, man. We've come all this way because me aunty Blodwen sent for us and you stand there and tell us — '

His uncle held up his hands.

'Please,' he said. 'You will wake my wife and daughter. Come in, come in, and take off your wet things. There's a fire in the kitchen. When you're warmed and fed on Mrs Griffiths' broth and dumplings, we'll see what can be done about sleeping arrangements until you can go back to England.'

'Go back to England!' Matt shouted in disbelief. 'Not bleedin' likely. I've not come all this way, me, just to stay the night and gan back to bliddy England. I'm gannin' to Patagonia by hook or by crook and nobody's ganna stop us.'

'Yes, well . . . ' Dai Griffiths looked uncomfortable. 'Perhaps there will be cancellations. If you had come last year the boat sailed half empty.'

Later, much later, while Dora shared a bed with Uncle Dai's young daughter and Davy slept on an old horsehair sofa in the front room, Matt and Rob talked in low voices as they clung to their respective sides of the small and lumpy double bed.

'Aa divvint care wot me uncle says,' Matt was saying fiercely. 'Somehow, I'm goin' to get meself aboard that boat.'

'What about the rest of us?' Rob asked, shivering and pulling the quilt up to his chin, thus exposing his bare feet sticking out the end of the bed. 'What about Dora? You can't leave her here.'

'Oh, aye, I can, mate, if that's what it takes.'

Matt had ignored Dora from the moment they left the Northeast. It had shocked and puzzled Rob that his friend could be so callous and inattentive. Dora was a sweet little thing, full of innocence and trust. What she must be feeling right now gave Rob a wrench to his heart.

'Why did you marry her, Matt?' he asked, seeing Matt's chest heave in the twilight of the room. 'We both know it was nothing to do with affection.'

'Well, ye know . . . ' Matt bounced about in the bed until he had turned his back on Rob. 'I thought she would come in handy, in case I couldn't get any out there in Patagonia. It seemed like a good idea at the time, like.'

A good idea? Rob thought. Matt had brought himself some feminine comfort rather than go without, but what comfort would poor Dora get? Matt would find women more experienced and less fragile than Dora, wherever he went. As for love? That was a different matter altogether. Rob wasn't at all sure that any of them would find *that* in Patagonia any more than in Tyneside.

5

It had taken a few minutes for Gwyneth to lose her self-consciousness after Miguel led her into the arena to a scattered assortment of handclapping and some lewd jeering from the ranch hands. What she had learnt with Therese had seemed easy, but there had been no-one watching.

She did the opening steps without fault, despite the uncomfortable beat of her heart. She approached Miguel, who was not even looking at her, but staring out across the waving sea of pampas grasses, as if his mind were a million miles away, though his dancer's body was tensed and ready. Like a serpent about to strike, she thought. At that very moment, the music changed. Miguel turned and faced her, one hand outstretched, his face a mask, but his eyes on fire.

Gwyneth stepped forward, extending her hand in his direction. As his fingers closed on hers, she stumbled slightly, her feet becoming suddenly clumsy. She swallowed hard and held her breath, expecting him to dismiss her with an arrogant toss of his fine head. Instead, he turned her around and pulled her to him, pressing her back hard against his chest.

'Stay with me, Welsh girl,' he murmured in her ear.

Gwyneth took a deep breath and felt him move, taking her with him. They swayed, they stepped out slowly, then danced with increasing pace and rhythm. Antonio's throbbing guitar was joined by the plaintive notes of Fernando Garcia's gypsy violin, while Therese took up the castanets, playing them high above her head as she circled the couple on the floor.

As the final notes of the *flamenco* died and Miguel threw Gwyneth to the floor, spinning her around so that her skirts splayed out like a matador's cape, the whole place erupted. Gwyneth had not been prepared for such an ovation. It was, after all, a dance that Miguel and Therese had performed many times over.

'Well, well!' Miguel said, inclining his head and smiling a rare smile as he helped her to her feet. 'Therese was correct. You do dance as though you have fire in your blood. Come, we will do the *tango* now. For this, you must have real passion in your heart, little one.'

She smiled at his use of the familiar 'little one', for she was as tall as he was. Moving to the side with him, Gwyneth was aware of his hand placed lightly in the small of her back. It sent a shiver up her spine that produced an embarrassed flush to her already hot cheeks. In the ring of spectators, she spied Juanita scowling and shaking her head.

'Antonio! Fernando! The *tango*, if you please!' Miguel signalled to the two men with a snap of his fingers.

'Oh, I don't know if . . . ' Gwyneth began to draw back, but he had her wrist fast in his grip. 'Perhaps you should dance with Therese now.'

She looked over her shoulder to where Miguel's sister was standing, but saw that Therese was clapping her hands and nodding her head encouragingly and the others in the crowd followed suit until it became a demanding applause, everybody chanting: 'Tango, *tango*!'

Miguel turned to her, his eyes half closed against the setting sun.

'You are not afraid. This much I know of you. You dance better even than my sister.'

'Oh, I don't think . . . ' Gwyneth was still breathless from the last dance, and now her heart was beating strangely because of Miguel's closeness and the thought that the *tango* would bring him even closer, for it was a dance of love. They would have to move as if their bodies were fused.

'Si, si!' Miguel raised her hand to his

mouth and pressed his lips briefly to her fingers, sending tingles through her. Then he looked into her face and gave a short laugh. 'You have nothing to fear from me, *cara*. Come! Dance!'

★ ★ ★

Behind the rain-washed windows of the little terraced house in Prestatyn, Rob and Matt paced the worn carpet, their faces as gloomy as the weather. Every few minutes, one of them went to the window and looked at the grey street outside, then turned away with a disgruntled sigh.

'Hey, man, I canna stand this,' Matt growled, running fingers through his shock of dark, unruly hair.

Rob stopped his pacing and dropped into a sagging old armchair by the window. He adjusted the curtain in an attempt to cut off the keen draught that blew and whistled through a gap in the window frame, then tapped his fingers idly on the chair arm.

'Aye, it's bad luck to get this far and be forced to go back home and face all those who thought we were headed for fame and fortune.'

'Bad luck, nowt! I don't believe in it, Rob, lad.'

Matt banged his fist on the high mantel-shelf and sent an ornament flying. It landed on the hearth, shattering. He paid it no more attention than an impatient click of the tongue before kicking the pieces to one side.

Rob started to speak, but changed his mind. Matt was in no mood to reason with. It was therefore best to keep quiet. Outside, people were hurrying by, crouching beneath great black umbrellas, battling against the wind that blew the rain in horizontal sheets. Even the horses pulling carts and carriages had to lean into it with all their might.

'Look at them, will ye,' Matt rubbed a clear patch in the misty condensation on the window. 'They've all got some place to go and we're bloody stuck here in this flamin' hole. Well, I'm not gannin' back, I tell ye. Somehow, I'm ganna land me a passage on that there boat.'

'How are you going to do that? People are leaving already and heading for Liverpool in groups. I saw some of them yesterday. It seemed like half the town was emigrating.'

'I'll find a way.'

It was when Matt spoke so low like that, almost in a whisper, that Rob knew trouble was in store. They were in a foreign land, here in Wales. Trouble was the last thing

86

he needed right now.

They both looked up at the sound of the front door opening and Davy's chirpy voice could be heard, together with Dora's light laughter. Rob grimaced. It must have been the first time that poor lass had laughed since they left Gateshead. They had been here in Prestatyn four days now and he hadn't even seen her smile. Except when Davy suggested a walk.

'Where the bleedin' hell have yous two been?' Matt's voice cut through the patter of rain and the amiable chatter of the two young people entering the room.

'Matt . . . ' Rob sent his friend a gentle warning, which was ignored.

Dora froze as she saw her husband's angry expression. She backed away from him as he came towards her with a face like thunder. Matt looked at the toffee apple she was clutching, and at the sticky traces of it around her mouth. His hand came back, then swiped the apple to the other side of the room.

Dora gasped and her eyes, like shiny glass orbs, stood out from her head.

'I'm sorry,' she whispered, wincing as his fingers bit into her shoulder through her worn-out woollen cardigan.

'Sorry? I'll make ye sorry all right.' He

pushed her roughly out of the room. 'Gan on wi' ye. Ye seem to have forgotten ye're me wife, ye silly bitch.'

As he followed her out into the hall, Matt turned to Rob with a sneer.

'I take it ye'll not mind sleepin' in a chair th' night, Rob?' he said.

Rob swallowed hard, wanting to sink a fist into Matt's face. Davy, too, had his fists clenched into tight balls and his mouth was set into a grim line.

'Leave her alone, Matt,' Davy said through gritted teeth. 'It wasn't her fault we were so late back. If you're wantin' to hit anybody, hit me.'

'Who said anything about hitting?' Matt said, a smirk on his face.

When the couple had closed the bedroom door tightly behind them, Davy looked at Rob, who shook his head in response to his brother's unvoiced question.

'She's his wife, Davy,' he said and went, once more, to look at the rain-washed street outside the window.

He was pretty certain that the marriage had not yet been consummated. The girl was an innocent. Heaven help her, he thought, for he couldn't imagine that Matt would take her sensitivities into consideration.

'Can't we do something?' Davy wanted to

know, pacing the floor behind his brother like a young lion.

'They're married, lad,' Rob told him, and left it at that.

★   ★   ★

The rowdy applause took a long time to die down, even when Miguel held up his arms and showed them his palms. They demanded more.

'They love you!' Therese cooed in Gwyneth's ear. 'Did I not tell you that you were made for dancing? Hey, brother. Was I not right?'

Miguel regarded her with a vague smile, then his gaze slid to Gwyneth.

'Si,' he said. 'It is true. I will consider you for my partner.'

Without another word, he turned on his heel and walked away. Gwyneth saw him snap his fingers in the direction of Antonio, who jumped to his feet and hurried after him, watched by several pairs of curious eyes.

Therese's forehead creased as she watched them go. Something was bothering her. Gwyneth was about to ask her what the problem was, but her attention was caught by a hand on her shoulder and she found Fernando Garcia standing beside her, his

89

fiddle tucked under one arm.

'Do not take any notice of Miguel, señorita,' he said, smiling benignly. 'It is just his way. Your dancing impressed him. He has been looking for a new partner for some time. Is that not so, Señorita Therese?'

'Si, Fernando. It is time for me to tend my garden and sit by the fire in the long winter evenings. I am happy that my brother has found a new partner.' She gave Gwyneth a sisterly hug. 'And more than happy that it is you, *cara*.'

'Oh, but . . . ' Gwyneth was lost for words. Of course she loved dancing, loved it even more now that she had danced with Miguel. But professionally? No, she thought not.

'Tomorrow, I will ask Miguel to speak to you. But for now, it is time to say goodnight. Come, Gwyneth, I will walk back to the *hacienda* with you.'

They returned to the ranch house arm in arm, and although Therese chattered on, Gwyneth remained silent throughout. Things were happening too fast for her. It troubled her the way she felt about Miguel, but it bothered her even more that he had danced so passionately with her, and then simply walked away. She would never understand these hot-blooded Spaniards who were so cold on the surface.

'Well, goodnight, *cara*,' Therese kissed her on both cheeks. 'Who knows? You may soon be dancing in Buenos Aires.'

Gwyneth closed her door behind her, leaning heavily against it. Buenos Aires! She dreamed of visiting this city she heard so much about from the *gauchos* who came to work at the ranch. And from Therese herself who had spoken of renting a small house there so she could give dancing lessons in between growing roses.

With a heavy sigh, Gwyneth threw herself down on her bed and stared blankly up at the ceiling. One day, she thought, I will have a nice house with roses around the door, and horses, and dogs that will not chase the guanacos. I will have . . . I will have . . .

Had she been about to say 'children'? She swallowed hard as a lump rose in her throat. She would never realize such a dream. What was the use of thinking about children when you didn't like men? No man was going to get the better of her again the way Brin Johnns had done.

As for being a dancer of the *flamenco* and the *tango*. Why, that had never entered into her plan of things. Not even Miguel Gomez-Pan could persuade her to change her life so drastically.

Rob and Davy were playing dominoes in the kitchen when Matt returned from his night-prowl. He was a regular Tomcat. Somehow, he always came back with a self-satisfied grin and a skinful of alcohol, despite the strict Temperance laws. That night was no exception.

'Where's Uncle Death, then?' he asked with a lopsided smile.

'You'd better not let your uncle hear you call him that or he'll chuck us out,' Rob said.

'Aw, howay, man. I canna get me head around callin' him 'Uncle Dai'. What kind of daft name is that, I ask ye?'

'It's a Welsh name, Matt,' Davy said, hiding a grin behind his hand.

'Divvint ye start, young-un,' Matt pointed an accusing finger at the lad. 'Ye're as bad as yor brother, ye are.'

Rob and Davy ignored him and turned their attention back to their game.

'Where is she?' Matt asked, looking around the room as if Dora might be hiding in a corner somewhere.

'If you mean your wife, the lass has a name, Matt,' Rob said, anger prickling under his skin.

He didn't look at his friend, but studied the

black and white domino chips in his hand. They had been at Matt's uncle's house for three weeks now and his patience was wearing thin. Dora never complained, but he could see the hurt in her eyes, a mingling of physical pain and confusion.

'Aye, well, whatever,' Matt threw himself onto the horsehair sofa and put his feet up, boots and all.

'She's gone to bed,' Rob told him, still not meeting his eyes.

'She went early,' Davy supplied and banged his hand of dominoes face down on the table. 'Her cold's worse and she was all done in.'

'Bloody women! Who'd have them, eh?' Matt made himself more comfortable among the cushions and spent a few minutes silently and diligently picking his nose. After a while, he sat up and threw a cushion in Rob's direction. 'Well, aren't ye goin' to ask us where I've been th' night?'

Normally, Matt didn't welcome questions on his whereabouts, so Rob and Davy had learnt to keep their mouths buttoned. When his temper flared he took it out on Dora and neither of them wanted to be responsible for igniting his short fuse.

'So, where've you been, Matt?' Rob said guardedly, noticing that Matt wasn't as drunk as usual. In fact, he seemed perfectly sober, though it was sometimes hard to tell these days.

'I've been down town to see the fella what organizes the immigration groups.'

'Oh, aye?'

'Aye. Just had a little word in his ear and that, ye know.'

Rob and Davy said nothing. They watched him as he got to his feet, took something out of his inside pocket and slapped it down on the table. It was an official, buff-coloured envelope.

'What's that, then?' Davy said, poking the envelope as if there might be something dangerous inside it.

'Tickets,' Matt announced proudly, and just for an instant he looked like the old Matt of their childhood when he and Rob had been inseparable.

Rob picked up the envelope and peered inside, fingering the contents and frowning at them curiously.

'Go on, man,' Matt shouted, banging his fist on the table in excitement. 'Look at them. Four passages on the *Patagonian Princess* — and not *steerage* mind. A cabin with four bunks and all the comforts of home. Well, what do ye's say to that, eh?'

'I'm speechless!' Davy said, his eyes round like marbles.

Rob riffled through the papers, checking the names, checking the wording and the signatures and the official government stamps. It looked genuine enough, but he was worried.

'How did you come by them, Matt?' he asked. 'How could you persuade the authorities, when your uncle couldn't?'

'Aw, divvint worry, Rob. It's all above board. There was a family that pulled out at the last minute, that's all. I just happened to be in the right place at the right time. Aren't ye proud of yer old mate, eh?'

Davy grinned broadly, but Rob's smile was forced. Something niggled at his conscience, but he preferred to give Matt the benefit of the doubt, for now.

'Aye, Matt. It's a relief to know we can go to Patagonia after all. I was beginning to give up hope.'

Matt took a bottle out of his pocket. It was a single malt whisky and it hadn't even been opened.

'Right, set up the glasses lads. This calls for a celebration.'

'What about Dora?' Davy wanted to know, heading for the door. 'She should be in on this too. Should I go and fetch her?'

'Nah,' Matt shook his head. 'Ye know what women are like. They don't appreciate the way we fellas celebrate with a drop of the good stuff. Leave her where she is. I'll have me own private celebration with her later.'

He pulled on his earlobe and tapped the side of his nose, leaving the other two men in no doubt as to what he had in mind for Dora. Rob could only hope that when he did go to his wife, he would be gentle with her. Dora had done her best to hide the bruises, but Rob had seen some of the discoloration on her pale, translucent skin and it made his blood boil.

★ ★ ★

Rob stood in brooding silence, his hands deep in his trouser pockets, his eyes staring straight ahead, but seeing nothing. They were due to leave in an hour with the Welsh party heading for Liverpool and the *Patagonian Princess*, but he had a bad feeling gripping his gut.

It was early morning and the little terrace house was creaking with suppressed life and movement. The door behind Rob opened and closed softly. He didn't turn, for he knew it was his brother. Davy was a big lad, but he was quiet and gentle, even if he did have a raucous sense of humour at times.

'Rob?'

'Aye?'

There was a short silence. Outside, the dawn was far from breaking, yet people were already abroad, hurrying past, huddling together beneath a heavy sky. The rain had been incessant since they arrived in Wales. And now it had sleet in it.

'Dora's crying. She's not makin' a fuss or nowt, but she's crying all right.'

Rob sighed and threw a glance over his shoulder, enough to see Davy's look of concern. Over the last three weeks he had seen the lad mature into a surprisingly sensitive young man. It had warmed Rob's heart to see how Davy could always make Dora smile. His brother would make some girl a good and loving husband one day.

'What's that bugger done to her this time?' he asked, his jaw set.

'Nowt, for once,' Davy shook his head. 'Dora's upset because Mrs Griffiths gave her some hand-me-down clothes and the little lass has given her a rag doll. I've just left the three of them upstairs on the landing all cuddling and crying together. It kind of tugs at your heart, ye know.'

'Aye.'

Rob sighed deeply. He could imagine how Dora was feeling. Despite everything that went on with her and Matt, these last few weeks had seen her as part of a real family for the first time and now she was going to leave it all behind. No doubt she was dreading the sea voyage, not knowing what she would find at the end of it. Aye, and dreading married life with Matt. Well, she had made her bed and now she must lie in it, God love her.

'Davy . . . ' Rob started to speak, then hesitated, turned and looked his brother full in the face the way brothers should when there was a serious matter to be discussed. 'Davy, lad, I've decided not to go.'

'Ye've what? Aw, come on, man, ye don't mean it. What's up with ye? Ye're no coward, our Rob, so what is it?'

'It's Matt,' Rob said, after a moment's pause. 'He's changed so much I hardly recognize him any more. Do you know what I'm trying to say, Davy?'

'Aye, yes, I see what you mean, but he's been like that for a long time, only you refused to see it because he's your pal.'

Rob gave a short laugh. His little brother had an old and wise head on young shoulders. He was right in what he said, too. Matt had been sliding downhill for years and Rob was always too ready and willing to drag him back, by the scruff of his neck if necessary, rather than lose their long friendship. But this stay-over in Wales had opened his eyes to the truth. Matt was no good. He didn't know when it had started or why, but the friendship they had once enjoyed had gone.

'I've been a fool, Davy.'

'Aye, mebbe you have, but that shouldn't stop you going to Patagonia, eh?'

'Davy, there's something deep down inside me that tells me . . . '

'Aye?'

'I'm afraid that if I do go, there'll come a day when I'll regret it.'

'Aw, divvint talk daft, our Rob!' Davy said hastily.

Rob's fists clenched and unclenched as he weighed up his innermost feelings.

'Come on, Davy,' he said. 'Let's just forget about Patagonia, eh? Let's go home.'

It was a long moment before Davy answered. For a while, he stood there, facing Rob, his mouth hanging open, his eyes sending out messages of incredulity. Rob saw him swallow and take a long, deep breath.

'No, Rob,' Davy said. 'I'm going with them on that boat, come hell or high water. If you don't want to come, that's too bad. But one of us has to go and make sure that Dora's all right.'

So that was it. The lad was in love. If Rob was honest, he had seen it coming, but had pushed it to the back of his mind. Davy was young, barely a man. He had a lot to learn about life, and everything to learn about love.

'She's married to Matt, lad,' he said softly and saw his brother flinch uncomfortably.

'Aye, I know, but . . . ' Davy shrugged and stared down at the Griffiths' family Bible lying on the big Welsh dresser amidst a collection of blue and white pottery. His fingers reached out and touched it briefly. 'The marriage is wrong, Rob, honest to God. He should never have married her.'

'We both know that, Davy, but it's none of our business. Now, are you coming back to Gateshead with me or not?'

Davy shook his head, his expression firmly fixed. 'No, Rob.'

Rob sucked in air and let it out again slowly. He rubbed a hand over his face, glanced at the clock, then back at Davy.

'In that case I'd better come with you, for somebody's got to look out for you while you're looking after Dora. Is that not so, lad?'

'Aye, Rob,' Davy said, his face breaking into a happy smile. 'Howay, I'll give ye a hand loading that old toolbox of yours, and then we'll be off.'

It wasn't long before they bundled themselves aboard a packed omnibus. Everyone had got good and wet waiting for it to arrive. They were all steaming, the air between them rank with the smell of damp wool and leather.

They didn't know the people they were travelling with, so it was a long, unsociable ride, the Welsh not being very forthcoming with foreigners. They chattered among themselves in their strange mother tongue, but now and then a name cropped up repeatedly.

Rob turned to the man next to him. He wore a priest's collar and Rob had heard him speaking English, so knew he understood well enough when he asked who this Lewis Llewellyn was that their travelling companions kept on about.

' 'Tis a sad case,' the rector said in a morose, sing-song voice. 'All ready to come with us, they were. A married couple and two children. Poor man met with an accident and his young widow had to sell their tickets, for she couldn't face the journey without her husband, you see.'

Rob was beginning to see all too clearly.

'When was this?' he asked. 'The accident. When did it happen?'

'That would be Saturday morning early, I'll be thinking, as Lewis came home from the candle factory where he was a night watchman. Some brigand set about him and left him for dead.'

Rob felt Matt shift uneasily beside him. Something cold seemed to slither around in his innards and his mouth went dry and numb.

'Oh, aye?' Matt was saying, fidgeting with the fastening on his travelling bag. 'So did he say anything afore he died, like?'

There was a long, stony silence, then the rector shook his head.

'No. He was too far gone by the time he was found, God rest his soul. He was a good man. The Llewellyns would have been more than welcome in the new country.'

'Aye, I bet they would an' all. Bad luck that, eh, Rob?' Matt was doing that all too familiar pull on his earlobe.

Rob nodded, but he couldn't trust himself to speak. The tickets that Matt held so preciously in his breast pocket had originally been made out to Lewis Llewellyn, his wife Mary and his children Morgan and Glenys. And on Friday, Matt had stayed out all night and come home with blood on his clothes and his knuckles grazed almost to the bone. A barroom brawl, he had told them. Just a bit of fun with the lads.

Rob exchanged glances with Davy, who licked his lips and lowered his eyes to the floor where too many pairs of feet were jostling for a comfortable amount of space.

'It's to be hoped they catch the one who attacked the poor man,' Rob said, aware that his words were coming out in a shaky, staccato beat, for his heart was vibrating in his chest.

'Let's hope they do, an' all,' Matt said, not to the people inside the coach, but to the passing landscape through the open window, where the winter wind caught his words and carried them away.

'A sad business,' the minister said, closing his eyes and preparing to sleep for the rest of the journey.

'Aye,' said Matt, rubbing the side of his long nose. 'Sad for some.'

Then he started to whistle a gay little tune that no-one felt like joining in.

6

'*Dance! Dance, girl, dance!*'

Miguel was angry. He was shouting at Gwyneth. She gave him one last dirty look and sank down exhausted on the floor of the arena. How could he expect her to dance like this, so coldly, without joy? Antonio played the guitar reluctantly, all the time following Miguel with dark, brooding eyes. He said nothing, but Gwyneth felt his resentment. Only Fernando Garcia smiled his sympathy as he took time out to tune his old fiddle.

'I am not a dancer, Miguel,' she cried at last when she could catch her breath. 'I do not even *want* to be a dancer.'

'Si, you are a dancer.' He ground out his words. 'And you will do as I say!'

'No!' Gwyneth's fiery temper was taking over. 'You cannot make me. My feet hurt. The dancing is over for today.'

She looked down at her thin canvas slippers and saw the same red stain, just as she had seen on Therese's feet. It was seeping through where a sliver of wood had pierced the thin material. Therese would have got up and gone through the steps again, ignoring the pain. For Gwyneth, dancing was something to enjoy, not to endure like torture at the hands of an unfeeling man.

Miguel swore at her in Spanish and walked away. After a moment, Antonio, silently and sullenly, followed him, like an obedient dog.

'What is wrong with that man?' Gwyneth muttered, picking up a fistful of grit and throwing it down again.

'He is not like other men, *cara*.'

Her head swivelled round and she saw Therese standing a few feet away, the Spanish woman's eyes glistening with suppressed tears.

Gwyneth struggled to her feet and limped over to her friend. Therese's face sagged beneath the wretchedness so evident in her voice.

'Therese? What's wrong? Why does he treat me so — so badly, as if he doesn't care?'

Therese looked at her for an instant, then tossed her head and started back towards the *hacienda*.

'Therese, please — you must tell me. What have I done wrong? I've done everything in my power to please him, but he is so cold . . . '

Therese had reached the wide terrace with its hanging drifts of wild honeysuckle sweetening the air with heady perfume. She

105

sat down on a cushioned swing seat and motioned for Gwyneth to join her.

'Gwyneth, I must ask you . . . ' she took Gwyneth's hand, speaking to her as she would to a young child. 'Are you in love with my brother? Please be honest with me.'

Gwyneth bit down hard on her lower lip and shook her head. She pondered the Spanish woman's question, struggling to understand what it was exactly that she did feel for this complex man.

'I'm not sure,' she said after a long pause. 'Oh, Therese, I made a pledge never to love any man. What happened to me as a child spoiled everything.'

'But you are in love with Miguel.' It was a statement rather than a question, which made Gwyneth frown even more deeply.

'I can't tell you how I feel, Therese. I don't even understand it myself. I tell myself that I should hate him. He is a man and it was a man who took my childhood from me. However, Miguel stirs something deep inside me. And yet, I feel it is not my heart that speaks — nor my head.'

'Ah.' There was a world of wisdom in that one syllable. 'I think I understand. He has this effect on most women, Gwyneth. He is beautiful, is he not? He has mysticism rather than charm. It is not difficult to fall in love with a man who is so good-looking, so full of talent — and passion. His every movement, when he dances, is filled with such ardour, si?'

'I suppose so, Therese, but you haven't told me what the problem is with me. Why does he hate me, so? Is it because I am not pure?'

Therese's laugh was low and husky. Her dark, gypsy eyes rested a moment on Gwyneth's face.

'My dear, dear, friend. You really do not know the problem that afflicts my brother? *Cara*, you are more naïve than I imagined.'

'What do you mean?'

'Miguel is not like other men, as Fernando has already told you.'

'I still don't . . . '

'In Buenos Aires, the men in the bars dance with other men. It is not considered respectable for a woman to dance so intimately with a man. This suits Miguel. I began to dance with him to save him from ending up in prison, but Miguel's fire does not burn for any woman. Now do you understand?'

Gwyneth squared her broad shoulders and blinked furiously, not daring to voice the thoughts that entered into her befuddled head.

'I . . . ' Her words stuck in her throat as

realization dawned. 'He — he prefers . . . other men?'

'Si, *cara*. He has affairs with other men. Men like Antonio. They have been partners for many years. They are, if you like, *lovers*.'

'Oh! Oh, I see, but — but that's . . . '

'It is *prohibido* — forbidden. You must tell no-one of this.'

'No. No, of course not.'

Something in the pit of Gwyneth's stomach churned, curdled and rose into her throat like bile. She had heard of such men. It was considered a grave crime against normal society and when they were found out the authorities locked them up like hardened criminals. In her mind she had pictured these misfits as abnormal, perhaps misshapen creatures, ugly and without intelligence. Not men like Miguel.

'Now do you see why he treats you so harshly?'

Gwyneth inclined her head. 'Yes, you have made it very clear.'

'I have known many women who have tried to — shall we say 'heal' him. It does not work. Please believe me.'

Gwyneth got up and paced the terrace. The cicadas were starting up their evening song. In the kitchen Juanita was singing softly to herself as she clattered dishes in the old pot sink. Fernando, down by the *gauchos'* campfire, was playing a mournful tune on his fiddle. Everything seemed so normal, yet she felt drained and let down. Not by any one person in particular, but by life itself.

'What I felt for Miguel was not love,' she said calmly. 'I do not think I could ever feel love for any man. What I had inside me was something far more — *physical*. Now, even that is dead.'

'There will be other men, *cara*,' Therese picked up the patchwork quilt she was working on to warm her bed in the cold winter nights. 'You will find one who is — shall we say — more suited to your needs.'

'Never!' Gwyneth looked off into the middle distance, her gaze automatically seeking out the solid, unchanging beauty of the Andean plains. 'I don't want to feel like that, ever again.'

Therese's needle flashed in and out as she attached a new piece to her quilt. The steel point embedded itself in her finger. She swore softly and sucked at the wound.

'Never is a stupid word, *cara*. Do not believe it.'

'Oh, I believe it, Therese.'

Therese smiled sadly. 'Ah. We shall see, eh? We shall see.'

★ ★ ★

The Widow Evans was sitting on her veranda, rocking gently in the old chair she had brought with her from Wales when she was still young. The wood was broken here and there and had been roughly mended; the worn cushions had been re-upholstered in cotton and lace and these covers were now showing signs of dilapidation. The chair was not as comfortable as she seemed to remember during those first hard years when it was all she had to remind her of home. But then, her old body was hardly the same as it had been then, crippled as it was with rheumatism, bent and twisted with advancing old age.

Down at the bottom of the street, the jangle of the Telegraph Office doorbell made her look up from her morning gourd of *maté*, the invigorating local drink made from the leaves of the yerba plant. Blodwen's eyes brightened considerably at the sight of Willard the Telegraph galloping down the street towards her, a piece of paper fluttering in his hand.

'Good morning, Widow Evans,' he greeted her importantly. 'I hope you are well — there's news for you.'

Blodwen let her face relax into a curious

smile, then she drew deeply on the bombilla pipe, sucking up the bitter, greenish liquid of the *maté* with relish. She swallowed, smacked her lips and put her head to one side, regarding the tall, lanky figure of Thomas Willard.

'Well, now, Thomas,' she said. 'I am as fine as can be expected for one of my age, but tell me, how is that wife of yours — and the new baby she has presented you with.'

'They are well, Widow Evans.' The piece of paper rattled in the breeze and he kept glancing at it, anxious to impart the message it conveyed. Blodwen was convinced that the poor man got all his enjoyment out of other people's news, good and bad alike. She was in no hurry to read the telegraph. If it were good news, it would be all the more pleasing for being delayed. If it were bad — it could wait as long as it liked.

'And what are you going to call this daughter of yours, eh?'

'We will name her Meredith after her grandmother . . . ' Then to forestall any further time-wasting questions, he continued rapidly. 'She weighs nine pounds, has a head full of auburn-coloured hair, hazel eyes and two teeth already. Looks like my grandfather, she does. Here's a message for you, Widow Evans — very important it is and all.'

'Two teeth, is it?'

'The telegraph . . . ' He pushed the paper under her nose and she fumbled for her eye-glasses, taking more time than was necessary, but at bottom she was dreading reading what was written there, for not a word had she received from her family since sending her letter at the beginning of summer. Now it was coming up to autumn, though the temperature, even for an old lady with thinned blood, was still balmy.

'Will you let me see it, then, Thomas?' she said, suddenly impatient and holding out her hand to him. 'Is it from my brother, perhaps?'

'No — erm — no, it's not from your brother, but from the boat itself that's bringing a new lot of immigrants.' Thomas Willard handed her the paper, but still held on to one corner, a long finger pointing at the pencilled message as if she were senile and couldn't read at all.

'The *Patagonian Princess*,' she read aloud, her face stretching into an impressed smile. 'Well, doesn't that sound grand, eh?'

Her head went from side to side as she read the message written in Thomas's spidery hand, her mouth moving with every syllable.

'Well,' she said eventually, sinking back among her cushions with a tight little sigh. 'It is very nice of this person, who claims to be my relative, to let me know he is coming. Not that I have heard of him, but then I have heard so little in the last fifty years. Tell me, Thomas . . . ' She passed the telegraph back to him and closed her eyes. 'My eyesight is not so good these days and neither is your handwriting. What does that last bit say, eh?'

Thomas gulped audibly, then he read out what he had written. Half the town would likely know all about it by now. He had not been alone when he had taken it down, mouthing every word as he wrote.

'It is signed,' he said carefully, 'by one Matthew Riley, nephew twice removed of Dai Evans and great-nephew of your brother, the late Colin Griffiths.'

Blodwen kept her eyes closed. A dull pain settled in the centre of her forehead. She ought to have known that her brother would have departed this life before her. He never did have any staying power. And now she was to expect a family member she had no knowledge of and, if she had read the telegraph correctly, he was bringing three others with him. And a name as Irish as the Emerald Isle itself. *What, in all Heaven, was her world coming to?*

'And the boat, Thomas,' she queried, trying to ignore the emotion that rose suddenly to her throat. 'When does it arrive?'

'In a few days, Widow Evans, if the weather doesn't change for the worse. I took the news to the Committee of Elders early this morning, for they will have to be prepared for the new intake.'

'It is a good thing for us.' Blodwen was almost talking to herself now. 'This land needs more good people, new blood. It is to be hoped that there are plenty of strong young men on board the *Patagonian Princess*; and not too many women past childbearing age.'

Within half an hour Puerto Daffyd was buzzing with the news of the forthcoming arrival of the immigrant boat. Women flocked to the town hall and the chapel with their spare bedding, and everywhere else that had space to put up the newcomers, for it would take a while to sort them out and find work for the men, and accommodation for their families.

Mary Lewis, as usual, was the first to show her face on Blodwen's doorstep, a loaf of still-warm bread in her hands for the widow, so as not to be thought nosy. Close on her heels, Winifred Jenkins came snooping more openly. Winifred was a widow of long standing, desperate to find herself another man. With those crossed eyes of hers and a temper to match, Blodwen held out little

114

hope for the poor woman.

'So, you've heard the news, have you?' Blodwen intercepted them on the veranda, her arms tightly folded over her flaccid breasts. She wasn't about to let them over the threshold, not with all the work she had waiting ahead of her preparing for the arrival of her 'family'.

'What news is that, then, Widow Evans?' Mary Lewis looked all innocence.

'Of course we've heard the news, Blodwen,' Winifred said with a lift of her angular shoulders and a loud 'tut' in Mary Lewis's face. 'Why, it's all over Puerto Daffyd that there's a boat due any day and that you have relations on board.'

'Not all of us listen at keyholes, Winifred Jenkins,' complained Mary, looking suitably put out at not being the first to speak of the event.

'There's no need of that. The very air we breathe is alive with it.'

'Well,' Blodwen said, a benign smile masking her impatience, 'if you know what's going on, why are you here on my doorstep? If you think I have more to tell you, I do not. Now, Mary Lewis, is that bread for me or are you going to stand there hugging it until it's not fit even for the birds?'

'Oh dear!' Mary breathed out and her

cheeks flushed crimson. 'Oh, do take it, Widow Evans. It's good and fresh and newly out of the oven.'

Blodwen took the loaf and cast a sideways glance at Winifred, her smile turning into something more mischievous.

'I don't suppose you've brought me a pat of butter, Winifred, to go with this delicious bread? Or a jar of your famous strawberry conserve? No? A pity, it is, but never mind. Thank you both for calling. I'm sure you have things to do, so don't let me keep you. Good day to you, ladies.'

And with that, Blodwen stepped back into her tiny vestibule and closed the door in their astonished faces. She lifted the bread to her nose and inhaled the fresh, yeasty odour of it, her taste buds oozing. Any other day she would have cut herself off a thick wedge and enjoyed it at leisure, with her own butter and jam, which were a sight better than anything Winifred Jenkins made. Today, however, she had too much on her mind. Her head felt light and her heart was fluttering with excitement. Had she been twenty years younger she might have lifted her heavy skirts and done a jig. Instead, she bustled about her little house, light of tread and singing her favourite hymn, 'Guide Me O Thou Great Redeemer'. It never failed to remind her of the little chapel on the hill just outside Prestatyn where she attended Sunday service when she was a bit of a girl. She sang the words in the Old Language, even though it brought a tear to her eye.

'Arglwydd, arwain trwy''r anialwch, Fi bererin gwael ei wedd . . . ' Blodwen trilled, putting as much vigour into it as the hymn demanded.

She stopped at the Welsh dresser in her living room and picked up a much-faded sepia photograph of herself with Huw, taken on their wedding day. She sighed wistfully and kissed his kindly face, though she could no longer make out his features.

'Ah, Huw,' she whispered to the photograph. 'We're going to have visitors from the old country. Family, look you. Strangers to me, they are, but never mind. Family is family and they might not want to stay. If they decide to go back, I'll be ready to go with them and that's a fact.'

She picked up a corner of her black shawl and gave the glass and the silver frame a bit of a polish, then set it down, her heart full of nostalgia and dreams of a tomorrow soon to come.

★ ★ ★

'Ach, gawd, I thought I'd never see land again,' groaned Matt as he joined the other passengers hanging over the boat's rail, everybody pointing and chattering together with mutual excitement. The shout of 'land ahoy' had gone up a few minutes ago, after interminable weeks afloat on a turbulent sea.

'It'll be a long time before I'll want to set foot on another boat,' Rob said with a heartfelt shake of his head.

'Me too,' Davy agreed.

'Aye!' nodded Matt, his steely eyes seeking out the contours of the land they were approaching. 'Especially one with cows and pigs pukin' and shittin' all ower the place.'

With difficulty they had endured the long and arduous voyage. The seas had been merciless and hardly a person on board had escaped bouts of seasickness, including the animals they had brought with them. Matt had been one of the lucky ones, though he hated the sea and spent most of his time hiding himself away somewhere, sinking pints of ill-gotten rum.

Rob and Davy suffered little more than a passing queasiness on days when the waves were twenty feet high and the boat rode up and down like the shuggyboats at a fair. It was Dora who came off worst and had to be looked after around the clock for the first three weeks before the waters had calmed themselves to a tolerable swell.

Davy was her self-appointed nurse in between the kindly ministrations of the women on board, who were unimpressed by Matt's lack of sensitivity towards his young wife.

Rob, too, did his bit, because he felt part-way responsible for landing little Dora in this predicament. He doubted Matt would have come on the venture without him. As for Matt, he simply shrugged his shoulders at the disparaging remarks thrown his way, and steered well clear of his sickly spouse.

'Come on,' Rob said, as the boat sailed on calmer waters past islands teaming with sea lions and tiny waddling penguins, and the startling white buildings on the quay came into view. 'Let's go get Dora. She didn't ought to miss this moment.'

'I'll fetch her,' Davy said and was off like an arrow.

Two minutes later, he reappeared with Dora in tow. The girl was staggering on weak legs, but looking considerably better, despite having lost weight that she couldn't afford to lose. When she saw what everyone was looking at she bit her lip and cried blessed tears of joy and relief.

'Oh, it's lovely! Is that really Patagonia?'

'Aye, Dora,' Davy told her. 'That's our new home coming up. What do you think of it, eh?'

'All that space!' she breathed. 'I'm scared I'll get lost.'

'But doesn't it look good, eh? Better than Gateshead any day.'

Dora's eyes grew large and Rob laughed. He reached over and tousled Davy's curly head.

'Don't be daft, lad,' he told his brother. 'She hasn't had time to see anything yet. Who knows? They could have places like Gateshead over here too.'

'Nah, nivvor! Not on yer life, our Rob!'

Rob dragged his attention back to the skyline, watching the land closing in. Everything seemed so flat and clean and bright. It was February and yet the sun was shining fit to burst. And there was heat in it too, enough to make his skin prickle. Back in England it would still be raining and windy and cold enough to freeze the nose off your face.

'Is the weather always like this here?' he said to a passing crew member, who laughed raucously.

'Hey, mate, what do you expect? It's summer here. You wait till the winter hits you. It'll freeze your . . . ' He glanced around him at the women within earshot and lowered his voice. 'It gets bliddy cold, so I hope you've brought your long winter drawers with you.'

'I don't care how cold it gets,' Dora said, hanging on to Davy's arm for support as the boat rose and fell with the undulating waves racing for the shore. Her pale cheeks were tinged with rosy patches of pleasure. 'It looks lovely! It really does.'

The boat changed direction and manoeuvred itself into the port where people were cheering and waving all along the dock. There was a sign strung across a large white building that said: 'PUERTO MADRYN WELCOMES YOU.' And it said it in Welsh and in Spanish too.

So, this is Patagonia, Rob thought, noticing that there wasn't a dark, gloomy street in sight, and no mine heads showing on the skyline, and the only hills were green ones, not pit heaps where colliery bairns played and often died. He couldn't see any mountains, either, but apparently they were something like three hundred miles away.

Davy let go of Dora when Matt joined them, with black brows beetling as he drew deeply on a long, slim cigar that he must have filched from somewhere or other.

'What now, Matt?'

'How should I know?' Matt shrugged and

cast a sharp glance around the scenes that were playing out on the quayside. 'I asked the captain to telegraph me aunty Blodwen, so I suppose she'll be comin' to meet us.'

'She's eighty years old, Matt,' Rob reminded him. 'I doubt she goes far from her door these days. Anyway, once we register with the authorities, Davy and me — well, we'll just go off and do our own thing.'

Davy looked at him, stunned, and Dora gave a small cry of alarm.

'Oh, no, Rob!' she said, her eyes swallowing him. 'Please don't leave us.'

'Dora's right,' Matt said, for once in accord with his wife. 'We came together and together we'll stay.'

'If it's the money you're thinking about, Matt,' Rob said quickly, 'I'll pay back every penny, just as soon as I get set up in business.'

'I wasn't thinking about the money, mate, but since you mention it, I did pay for the pair of yous to come here. Ye do owe us summat, I'm thinking.'

'As I said, Matt, I'll pay you back as soon as I can, but I don't think Davy and I . . . '

Davy was tugging at his arm.

'Rob, what the hell are ye on about, man? If it hadn't been for Matt — well, his aunty — we wouldn't be in Patagonia th' day.'

'Davy's right,' Dora nodded vigorously,

obviously more than a little reluctant to be left alone with her husband, and Rob couldn't blame her.

'Think of Dora, man,' Davy whispered behind his hand while pretending to cough.

It took Davy's reminder to prick Rob's conscience. Like his brother, he had become fond of the little lass with the whispy, cotton-wool curls and the big dinner-plate eyes. But he had no wish to stay anywhere near Matt. Especially now. He more than suspected that his one-time best mate had had a hand in the death of the man whose tickets they had come with.

He was about to speak when a haughty voice with a strong Welsh accent addressed them from across the quay.

'Matthew Riley, is it?'

They turned and saw a small, round figure, dressed from top to tail in black, sitting erect on the seat of an open buggy pulled by two impatient mules that looked almost as old as she was.

'*Jesus wept!*' Matt exclaimed. 'It's bliddy Queen Victoria!'

Davy sniggered, then both he and Rob gave Matt a dig in the ribs to remind him of his manners.

Blodwen Evans's snowy white hair was escaping from her lace cap in floating tendrils. Ignoring it she stared with interest at the little group.

'Well? Which one of you is my far removed nephew?'

'Are you Mrs Blodwen Evans, then?' Matt called out, squinting into the morning sun and whispering out of the corner of his mouth, 'My God but she's more ancient than I expected.'

'Well come along with you,' Blodwen said, her bright eyes flashing with the vitality of one half her age. 'Jump up behind. I don't have all day. Come along, girl. Get up here beside me. Look sharp, will you.'

Rob saw how twisted her hands were and wondered how on earth she had the strength to take up the reins.

'Would you like me to drive?' he asked hesitantly. 'I'm used to it.'

She looked at him and the hint of a smile graced her mouth.

'Are you, now?'

'Aye, he used to drive a hearse back home,' Matt informed her and her fine, almost non-existent eyebrows shot up.

'A hearse, is it? And what are you by trade, young man? An undertaker?'

Rob shook his head. She kept on staring at him with those piercing eyes of hers, and he found it more than a little disconcerting.

'I used to help on the undertaking side of things,' he said, 'embalming and such. Me job was making coffins. Sometimes, I try my hand at cabinet making and carving — that sort of thing.'

He swallowed hard. It wasn't an out and out lie. He'd done his fair share of making coffins, from plain pine to ornately carved oak. It was the latter he enjoyed, but there hadn't been much call for posh coffins in Gateshead. Miners and dockers weren't exactly known for their wealth.

'Ah! Just like your uncle Huw. He could turn his hand to anything.'

'Oh, but . . . '

'*He's* not your nephew, Aunty Blodwen,' Matt sounded put out. 'I'm Matthew Riley and this, here, is me wife, Dora. Rob's me best mate. We've been together since we were little lads in short pants wi' snotty noses.'

'How interesting!'

'Aye, and the young lad's Rob's little brother.'

'Well, there's a thing for you.' Blodwen heaved a sigh and continued to stare hard at Rob. 'For all that, you have a look of my Huw in you — Robert, is it?'

'I prefer Rob, Mrs Evans, if you don't mind, though it's Robert Barker on me papers — and me brother here is David

Barker, but we call him Davy.'

Blodwen looked from one to the other, her expression hardening slightly when her gaze lingered on Matt.

'Rob and Davy it is, then.' Blodwen took up the reins and clicked her tongue at the mules. The animals threw up their heads at the sound and jerked into motion, glad to be under way. 'Don't you worry about me, Rob Barker. These mules of mine could find their way to my house in Puerto Daffyd blindfolded and with their legs tied together.'

'Hey, ye bugger!' Matt exclaimed as the buggy swerved to avoid a head to head clash with an oncoming mule train heading in the opposite direction. 'Be careful, Aunty Blodwen. Divvint get us killed afore we get there.'

The Widow Evans looked straight ahead, saying nothing, though she did reach out to pat Dora's hands that were clasped tightly in the girl's lap. Rob decided immediately that he liked this tough old Patagonian. She might be ancient, as Matt had said, but he would bet the price of a new pine coffin that she still had all her mental faculties, if not her physical ones.

'What d'ye think of her then?' Matt said eventually in Rob's ear as they jogged along the uneven track towards Puerto Daffyd.

'I'd say you'd be hard put to pull any wool

over *her* eyes,' Rob said, hanging on grimly to his side of the rocking and rolling buggy and wondering how long it would be before he and Davy could get the hell away from Matt. Patagonia was a big country. Many times bigger than the whole of Great Britain. They need never see one another again, ever. It was a thought that was beginning to nag at him and the more he pondered on it, the more attractive it seemed.

'Hey, come on, man, what's with all this aggressive talk ye're givin' us? I thought we was pals to the death.'

'Aye, Matt.' Rob stared at the coastline sliding past with its miniscule boats, and fishing fleets, getting smaller and smaller as they sailed out to the horizon. 'Aye, I thought so, too, but maybe we've both changed and neither of us noticed.'

'What the hell are ye gannin' on about now? Ye've been actin' kind of funny for a while. Don't think I haven't noticed, cos I have.'

'Look, Matt, let's just try to make the best of it for now, eh?' Rob indicated the old woman's stiff back with a jerk of his head in her direction. 'Later on . . . well, we'll see.'

The widow had brought with her a small hamper and they stopped en route for a picnic of cold lamb, freshly baked bread, sheep's cheese and fruit. They all enjoyed it, not realizing how hungry they had become now that they didn't have the rolling sea beneath them. Even Dora ate a little and kept it down with a jubilant smile.

'You're too thin, girl,' Blodwen said to her. 'But I think you'll fatten up nicely.

'Yes, thank you, Mrs Evans.'

'Around here I'm known as the Widow Evans. It's almost a badge of office, look you. But since you are family, you can call me Aunty Blodwen or just plain Blodwen — and that goes for you too, young man — Rob Barker, is it? And your little brother, who is far from being little, though he has a way to go before he reaches your dimensions.'

She gave one of her quick, secret smiles and Rob couldn't help but return it. From the way she looked him up and down like a prize bull, he half expected her to give his muscles a squeeze and ask to see his teeth.

It was the middle of the afternoon when they reached the first straggling, white-walled houses of Puerto Daffyd with their red-painted corrugated roofs. It was hardly a town with only two rows of spaced-out buildings on either side of a wide dirt track. To the east side there were glimpses of the sea with breakers crashing on the rocks in a curving crescent moon of a bay. To the west, miles of verdant plains ran to the foothills of the distant Andes.

'I've not seen anything like it!' Davy was in awe.

'Why, man, it's as good as this at South Shields,' Matt said, then hawked and spat into the road.

They all laughed, but then Rob realized that Matt was serious. The landscape of any country would fail to impress him. He was more interested in what he could get out of the people who lived there.

As they off-loaded their baggage from the buggy, Matt was already surveying the local feminine scenery, making eyes and grinning cheekily at two young women walking past. The women flushed scarlet, pushed out their bosoms in indignation and hid their faces in their bonnets as they hurried away. Fortunately, the Widow Evans was too busy opening up her tiny house to notice.

'Welcome to my home, such as it is,' she told them, holding the door open and beckoning them to enter. 'Matt and Dora will occupy the room at the back, which was the bedroom I shared with my Huw the short time he was alive. I've never slept in it since. I prefer the pull-down bed here in the living room. It's quite convenient and cosy in the winter when the stove is kept going. You, Rob, and your brother, must make do with the small attic room above, until we can have a bit more house added on.'

'And when do we have to register, Aunty Blodwen?' Matt said, anxious to get his new life started.

'That will be taken care of in due course.' She spoke almost sharply, then turned to Rob and Davy. 'The two of you will also go down in the register as 'family of the Widow Evans'. I don't suppose that will inconvenience you? It will help when you want to find work, for we have quite a tight little community here in Puerto Daffyd. Very strict Welsh, you understand. I hope you all are good Chapel people. It will be frowned upon otherwise by the Committee. And I have enough trouble to put up with in that direction. I do not want more.'

Rob felt a secret nudge from Davy. He looked up to see a dark, brooding expression clouding Matt's face. Further down the street, next to the chapel, was the Temperance Hotel. It wasn't unlike the one in Prestatyn and, like that place, the only bottles being advertised in the windows did not purport to contain alcohol.

They were, Rob felt, in for a rough ride with Matt. If he was forced to stay sober they would all suffer. Most of all his quiet, fragile

130

wife. Dora, right now, in the company of the brusque but kindly Blodwen, was looking happier than she had been for a long time. How long, Rob wondered, would that pretty, innocent smile last? His heart bled for the lass.

7

'Dora, my lovely, would you go down to the Co-op store and get me a few items?'

Blodwen had been sitting for half an hour composing a list of groceries, though most of the time had been spent in deep thought and in licking the end of her pencil stub without a word being written.

'Yes, Aunty Blodwen,' Dora said, jumping to her feet, so eager to please the old lady that she upset the skeins of wool she had been sorting.

Davy was quick to help her pick them up and as they did so they bumped heads and shoulders and indulged in a great deal of touching of hands that did not go unnoticed. The Widow Evans sucked in air through her teeth and her tongue made a clicking sound. She didn't quite know what to think about those two, and what she did think didn't bear thinking about.

'No need for all that rush!' she told them and saw their faces light up crimson. 'The wool was a long time on the sheep, look you. And it will be lying in my cupboard a long time before I can persuade these old hands of mine to take up the knitting needles again.'

'Oh, Aunty Blodwen,' Dora said, her arms full of tangled woollen loops that were in danger of getting more ravelled. 'Will you teach me how to knit?'

'You want to knit, is it? And why did your mother not teach you, girl? Most girls are knitting before they're eight years old. Have things changed so much in the old country?'

'No, I don't think so, only . . . ' A quick glance at Davy, who cleared his throat noisily and took the wool from her with gentleness unusual in one so young.

'What is it, girl? Have I said something to upset you?' Blodwen was painfully aware that in the space of a second, her nephew's little wife had lost her look of joy and found one of sadness.

'I'll just go and wash my face before I go to the Co-op,' Dora said with a little catch in her throat and hurried out of the room.

'So, Davy Barker,' Blodwen gave the boy a sharp look. 'Are you going to stand there like you were turned to stone, or are you going to tell me what the problem is with that girl? Apart from that husband of hers, that is — though I say it as shouldn't since he's my own kith and kin.'

'Maybe I shouldn't say anything, either,' Davy said, shifting uncomfortably from one foot to the other. 'He's me brother's best mate and if it weren't for Matt, Rob and I wouldn't be here.'

Blodwen pursed her lips and stared at him in the way that she did when she meant business.

'That's as may be, lad, but you and your brother owe me a little something, for wasn't I the one who found you work and gave you a roof over your head? I was good and criticized for that, you being English, but I stood up to the Elders on your behalf, isn't it?'

Davy smiled through his frown, for no amount of scolding from Blodwen Evans ever made him feel hateful towards her. She was hard, but she was fair and he always admired that in a person.

'Dora never knew her mother,' he said in a low voice, glancing at the door to make sure that Dora wasn't on her way back already. 'Nor her father. She was found wrapped in newspaper, so the story goes, lying on a grave in the cemetery on a Sunday morning.'

'A foundling, was she? Poor little soul. No wonder she looks so melancholy and undernourished.'

'The village sort of adopted her,' Davy said and his face twisted. 'She lived with the woman who had the sweet shop, but then old Mrs Hardy died and . . . well, things have

134

never been easy for Dora.'

'And to crown it all, she married Matthew Riley. So all ended happily, is it?' Blodwen's head was on the side and she was regarding Davy with profound curiosity. 'Well? Is that how it is, boy?'

Davy slowly licked his lips, stuck his hands in his pockets and shuffled his feet some more. He looked at her with furrowed brows.

'I don't know how it is, really,' he said, but Blodwen figured that he knew a lot more than he was prepared to let on. 'It's not my business.'

'No, you are right there. And nor is it the business of your brother, but the pair of you look after that girl as if she was a newborn lamb and you not wanting her to be taken to the slaughter.'

'Aye, well . . . '

'Aye, well, as you say, Davy. I'm not one for meddling in affairs that don't concern me — and don't you look at me like you don't believe me, for it's true. There's a difference between meddling and protecting and I'd say the girl needs all the protecting we can give her. Is that understood, my lovely?'

Davy chewed on his mouth for a second or two, then gave a short, sharp nod as Dora returned, her face newly washed and carefully composed.

'Well, here's the list, Dora,' Blodwen said, passing over the scrap of paper. 'And don't you be letting those Co-op people fob you off with anything less than the best butter. And tell Mr Humphries in the butchery department that I don't want his bacon if it's full of fat like the last time.'

'Yes, Aunty Blodwen.'

'Here's my purse, now. Nothing on account, do you hear? I cannot keep track of things at my age and they have a tendency to make illicit adjustments to the bill as it adds up.'

'Yes, Aunty Blodwen.'

'And see if they have a bit of nice chocolate to keep me sweet — and a cake for you and the boys.'

'Yes, Aunty Blodwen, but isn't it all on the list?'

'No, it isn't. It's just escaped out of the top of my head. I never could think clearly with a pencil in my hand. Now look sharp, girl — oh, and ask for some nice ham for Sunday tea.'

Dora was looking worried. She was glancing at the list and also at the ceiling, reciting under her breath the extras that Blodwen was giving her from the 'top of her head' in order to memorize them.

'I'll go with you, Dora,' Davy said, already

preceding her to the door. 'Two heads are better than one.'

Blodwen caught the girl's expression, which was a mixture of pleasure and doubt.

'Go on, girl,' she told her. 'Make the most of Davy today, for on Monday he starts work up at the Dutch farm.'

Davy's jaw dropped a mile, then he grinned.

'You got me some work, Aunty Blodwen!'

She smiled and flapped a hand at him.

'Go on with you. Go and help Dora with my purchases — and make sure she doesn't get cheated on the change. We'll talk about your work when you get back.'

* * *

Rob paused to wipe the sweat from his brow. The days were cooler now that autumn had set in, but work on the new dam called for all the strength and muscle he had. For weeks he had worked on it, side by side with Matt, their backs breaking, their veins popping with the strain of it. His dream of setting up in business as a carpenter had not come to fruition. There were already too many carpenters these days, and not enough demand, especially for a foreigner of little experience.

He was a patient man and hid his disappointment well. He would have to bide his time, or move out to further fields. He had heard that there was a good living to be had from the pastureland at the foot of the Andes. Maybe he would need to change tack completely and become a farmer. With that in mind, he was willing to take on any job that paid enough to have something left over for savings after he had given rent to Blodwen.

'Hey, you! Geordie lad! Stop leaning on that sledgehammer and put some muscle behind it, will you.'

Rob shook himself out of his daydreaming and saw Matt, further down the line, grinning at him. Matt skived more than any man there, but he always managed to get away with it. With an almighty sweep of the sledgehammer, Rob severed a rock in half just as the shift whistle blew and all the men downed tools with a loud chorus of groans and sighs.

'Got yer fingers slapped there, didn't ye?' Matt, covered in dust and sweat, swaggered over to him. 'They're buggers, these Welsh types.'

'They're not so bad,' Rob said, dusting himself down and slinging his canvas bait bag over his shoulder. 'At least they pull their weight. Not a slacker among them, I'd say.'

'Gan on, man,' Matt sneered, looking

138

around him as the gang of workers straggled away, heading for the wagons that were waiting to transport them back to the towns along the coast. 'They're miserable sods, every last one of them.'

He spoke in a loud voice and it was obvious from the glances he got that his words had not gone unheeded. It wasn't the first time he had caused a rumble of discontent among the workforce.

Rob shook his head in despair. It seemed like Matt was forever looking for a fight. It was almost as if he needed to draw blood, even his own, to get anything out of life. Rob thought, with a sense of sadness, that it was Matt himself who was the miserable sod. Aye, and he was making everybody else miserable with him.

Every night, Rob dreaded going back to Blodwen Evans's little house where Dora would be waiting, trying to look keen, but only managing to look nervous and twitchy. And the widow herself took on a grim expression every time she looked upon her great-nephew. Not even when Matt was being his old humorous, likeable self, did the tight expression soften on her face.

Soon after their arrival, Blodwen got Rob to build on an extension to her house and moved Matt and Dora in there so that they could have their own private quarters. Rob now occupied their old room in the main house, and comfortable it was too. Davy still slept in the loft without complaint. The lad slept so soundly nothing short of an earthquake would disturb him.

The wagon, full of workers, jolted along on the rough track and never seemed to travel faster than walking pace. However, the men were too exhausted to complain. They sank gratefully into the wooden slatted seats, eyes closed, heads lolling. It had been a long day and the night would seem too short before they had to start work again tomorrow.

Matt was more than usually on edge, Rob thought, as he caught sight of his friend during waking moments when the jolting was too much of a shock to the system to sleep through. Matt's restlessness seemed to worsen, his eyes darting this way and that, as they negotiated a particularly rough stretch, with mules and wagons crossing a fast-flowing stream.

'What's up with you, then?' Rob said, though he wasn't particularly interested. They had little to say to one another these days.

'Nowt!' Matt slid his eyes slyly over Rob's face, then his attention was immediately captured by their rugged surroundings.

Rob scanned the bright emerald green of

the pasturelands that poured down from the foothills, spreading out like a luxurious carpet. The landscape was wild here with jagged rocks reaching skyward like horny fingers. On the high pastures there were sheep, like tiny blobs of white on the green of an immense canvas, but there was no farm on this side of the ridge.

It was said that land was so plentiful a sheep could have a whole acre of it all to itself and could roam all day without meeting another animal from its flock. Maybe that was true, maybe it wasn't, but he never failed to be impressed by the vastness of the land in this wild country and the isolation that existed between the homesteads.

Further down the hillside, Rob spotted a few moving light brown shapes nervously darting away from the rattle of the wagons. The gentle-faced guanacos trotted out of reach, stopped, looked over their shoulders, then continued to graze. These attractive llama-type animals were to be found everywhere. And they were good for everything, it seemed. The locals wore clothes made from their skins, used their faeces as manure and ate their flesh.

He saw the log cabin and the figure moving in front of it just as Matt stiffened and let out a gasp and an expletive that awoke the man slumped next to him.

'I knew I was right!' Matt said, his jaw set and his fists tightly clenched as if ready to go into battle. 'Look at that, will ye . . . '

Rob was looking, but he wasn't too sure he believed his eyes. The fellow next to Matt was giving a wry smile and shaking his head. Matt thumped him on the shoulder.

'It *is* a lass, isn't it? I'm right, aren't I?'

The man, who's name was Ivor Jackson, straightened his shoulders, but he didn't turn and stare like the two Geordie lads. He gazed down at his hands, clasped together and hanging low between his knees.

'Who is she?' Rob found himself asking, his eyes narrowing as he tried to get a better view without looking too obvious, for that was no ordinary woman striding across the valley wearing trousers, yet looking more fervently seductive than any woman he had ever seen.

'You don't want to know that one,' Ivor Jackson told them, the smile turning into a mean grimace. 'She's got bad blood, that one.'

Rob could see the heat build up in Matt, could see his chest rise and fall. Matt had his sights set on a new prize. Rob recognized the symptoms well, though he had to admit to himself that this *prize* was totally different to any other Matt had gone after.

They drew closer to the moving figure, who now acknowledged their presence with a long, hard stare before she tossed her head and strolled proudly in the opposite direction. The time it took her to turn from them had been long enough for Rob to see her face. Even at that distance, he knew she was the most beautiful girl he had ever seen. No, not a girl. A young woman of about his own age, tall and imposing. One of the *Indios*, perhaps, with that long black plait of hair down her back.

As he looked, the woman stopped in her tracks and waited. She was facing away from them now and it wasn't clear what she was doing, though it looked like she was speaking to someone, beckoning slowly with her hand.

'What the hell's she at?' Matt said, then gave a low whistle as a family of guanacos approached her and one of them nuzzled against her thigh while the youngest, a baby, took food from her fingers.

'She has a way with animals,' Ivor said, finally casting a wistful glance over his shoulder, but returning it quickly to his clasped hands and the floor of the wagon. 'In fact, it's said she has a way with many things. Some of the old'uns say she's a witch — aye — or bewitched by the Devil.'

'I'd like to have *my* way with *her*,' Matt

said, his eyes glued to the woman and the guanacos. 'Devil or no Devil.'

'It's been tried by better men than you,' Ivor said grittily. 'No man in his right mind would touch that cursed female.'

Matt was riled. He didn't like anyone telling him what not to do. Especially a Welshman. Rob braced himself, expecting to have to step in between them. However, for once, Matt did not respond. The wagon had turned, following the contours of the hillside. He sank back in his seat and closed his eyes.

'I thought your friend was married,' Ivor said a few minutes later when Matt's open mouth and loud snoring competed with the noise of the wagon wheels moving over the stone-filled ruts.

'He is,' Rob said with a brief nod.

'Well, then, don't let him get mixed up with that Gwyneth Johnns. She's trouble and, as you can see, she is no lady.'

Rob's mouth twitched as he forced a smile.

'I thought she must be an Indian,' he said, 'but with a name like that, she's surely Welsh — one of yours.'

'Not one of mine, look you! No! By God, no decent family — Welsh or *Indios* — would want to claim a bloodline there. She's of mixed blood, you see, boy-oh. And it's a dirty history. My advice is to stay well clear of it.

You ask the Widow Evans where you are staying. She will tell you the truth, if you really must know.'

Rob shrugged his shoulders, imparting an expression of careless disinterest. If she was as bad as all that, beauty or not, he wanted no part of her. As for asking Blodwen about her, there was no point in lifting stones in order to see what worms would crawl out from under them. His father had taught him that.

Hold on to your discretion, lad. Asking questions can lead to dangerous answers you might wish you'd never heard.

An hour later, the wagon train stopped in the main street of Puerto Daffyd and the men stretched, yawned loudly and tumbled down onto the dried mud road.

'Right, Rob, lad,' Matt said, scratching his chest with one hand and pulling at his earlobe with the other. 'Off ye go and tell them back home that I'm doing a double shift th' night.'

'What?'

'Just do as I tell ye, Rob. It's no big deal, but I've got something to do that's a whole lot more fun than eating Aunty Blodwen's cooking and sampling the skinny desserts offered me by Dora.'

'Matt . . . ?'

But with a slap on Rob's shoulder, Matt was swaggering away down the street and heading for the part of town that everybody knew about, but nobody talked about for fear that God would tear out their tongues.

★ ★ ★

Blodwen was slumped in her chair dozing spasmodically. She preferred to call it resting with her eyes closed and claimed that although she appeared to be sleeping, she missed nothing. This was most likely to be true, for she had an uncanny knack of knowing things without being told.

She heard Rob come in, smelled the dust and the sweat on him and dreamed fleetingly of a long-lost husband returning home to hearth and wife after hours of pounding an anvil. Her dear, sweet Huw might have been with her still today, had it not been for his weak heart that nobody knew about.

The rattle of a poker against the grate brought her out of her reverie. Opening an eye, Blodwen saw Rob's backside as he bent to tend the fire. She let out a soft sigh, thinking how easily this could have been Huw's grandson and, therefore, hers, had they been blessed with children. He was a world removed from the true relation she had inherited. No matter how hard she tried, she could not bring herself to like Matt. It was said that blood was thicker than water, but she would take the water of this grand young fellow here before her any day and be proud to call him her own.

'I could have done that for myself,' Blodwen said, her eyes remaining half-closed as she regarded him. 'But I thank you anyway.'

Rob put the poker back in its place and straightened with a slight groan as the toil of the day made itself felt in his muscles.

'It was about to go out,' he told her, a smile playing about his lips and his dove-grey eyes softening. 'I couldn't let you get cold, now, could I?'

There was the briefest of pauses while Blodwen waited for the tightness in her old throat to go away. She was getting soft in her dotage, but this boy could bring a tear to her eye the way her lovely Huw could, without even trying. She found herself choking up, too, when watching the young one, Davy, struggling between boyhood and manhood, worshipping his big brother and trying not to covet their friend's wife.

'There's a nip in the air today,' she said after a clearing of her throat and a licking of her lips as she heaved herself more upright in the chair. 'It makes my old bones ache — and worse when the wind blows.'

'Then I did right, keeping you warm, eh?' Rob's smile, so bright and cheery, nudged her heart so that she had to cough and look away, feigning preoccupation with some thought or other.

'Get yourself cleaned up, look you,' she said with rust in her voice. 'There's hot water on the stove in the scullery. Put more on for Davy when he gets home — and Matt.'

Her voice had dropped at the mention of Matt's name, but if Rob had noticed it he gave no sign.

'Where's Dora?' he asked, as casual as could be, though she guessed he hid a lot of concern for the girl beneath an indifferent attitude.

'She'll be on the back step waiting for . . . ' She almost said 'waiting for Davy' and pulled herself up short. 'Just waiting — you know?'

With a nod to her, he took himself off into the scullery, where he knew she would have clean, dry towels waiting for him and a change of clothes, for she would not have any of them sitting down at the supper table with a bit of grime on them.

When Blodwen heard the big copper cauldron being emptied, she pushed herself up out of her chair and walked stiffly to the scullery. The latch on the door was faulty and it had blown open with the draughts coming down the passage. Blodwen pushed it further open and leaned against the doorpost, taking in the pleasing sight of Rob's taut young body.

Yes, she thought wistfully, *he's just like my Huw with his white skin like alabaster where the sun hasn't turned him brown.* She silently admired the fine delineation of his muscles, the broad back, the solid, rounded buttocks and the long, powerful legs. He was a fine specimen and no mistake, Englishman or not.

Rob, unaware of being spied on, turned to face her, busy with drying his thick, corn-coloured hair. He blinked in alarm when he saw her standing there, a small frown puckering up her face even more. In a swift, self-conscious movement, he pulled the towel around him like a sarong.

'Blodwen!' he exclaimed with an embarrassed laugh.

'Don't you worry, Rob,' she said. 'No need to be ill at ease, look you. I'm too old to be harbouring unclean thoughts and, besides, there isn't anything I haven't seen many times over in my long life. There's no excitement left for me now.'

She saw Rob gulp and search for something ordinary to say, but his face was flushed and his eyes troubled, as he stood there, half-naked before her.

'Were you wantin' something?' he asked, clutching desperately at the ends of the towel that were threatening to expose him and embarrass him even further.

'You have a fine body, boy,' she said, her head tilted in that characteristic way he was beginning to know all too well. 'It is my opinion that you will make some woman a good husband and I fail to understand why some deserving girl hasn't claimed you before now. You do like women, I take it?'

Another gulp from Rob and he was averting his eyes, not used to such intimate questions. His own mother would not even be that bold.

'I had a girl back in England, Blodwen,' he said carefully. 'We were engaged for three years.'

'So where is this lovely girl, eh? Why is she not here in Patagonia with you?'

'She had no fancy for coming.'

'Do you mean she had no fancy for Patagonia — or no fancy for you? God help her if that was so.'

Rob looked down at his bare feet, counting the toes on each of them. Blodwen watched and waited and felt a slight stirring of excitement somewhere beneath her breast-bone, but she could not say what it was that put it there. It would come to her later, in her head, no doubt.

'Never mind, Rob, my lovely,' she went on. 'There's a woman somewhere for you, I'm sure of it. A good woman, mind you. 'Tis what you deserve, so don't settle for anything less.'

'Yes, Blodwen — I mean — er — no . . .'

'Get dressed, son, and come and talk to me before we have supper. I feel lonely this evening.'

She went back into the living room and settled herself to wait. There was a rich, dark brown guanaco stew all ready to heat through when it was needed and Dora would see to that later.

When Rob appeared, looking all scrubbed and glowing and with his dampened hair parted and combed, she sucked in a long breath and afforded him one of her rare smiles.

'There's a time, Rob, when men look good unclothed, but mostly they look better dressed. Especially to an old woman who doesn't care to remind herself of her long-lost youth.'

'You're not old, Blodwen,' Rob said kindly and she gave him one of her girlish laughs. 'Even if you were a hundred you'd still have a twinkle in your eye.'

'Ouf!' She flapped a hand at him and

plumped up the cushions at her back as she felt heat arrive unbidden in her cheeks. 'You flatter me, Robert Barker, and your brother is following hard in your footsteps.'

'We'll stop if you don't like it,' Rob said, but didn't wait for her response because he knew she liked it well enough. 'And why are you calling me Robert tonight? You only ever call me that when you have something serious to discuss with me.'

'Aye, you're right.' Blodwen blinked into the glowing embers of the fire for a few seconds, then fixed him with an unwavering stare. 'Where is he tonight? He should have come home with you, should he not?'

He knew to whom she was referring all right. She saw his face blanch, saw him swallow and knew instantly that there was something wrong.

'Matt said to tell you he was working a double shift . . .'

'Pah!' Blodwen threw her head back in disbelief. 'Double shift, is it? Does he think I've gone senile, eh? There is no night shift at the dam, as well you know. Nobody can see to work in the dark. Where is he, really? Is he off womanizing again, eh?'

He looked shocked at her words, but not surprised that she had guessed right. Matt did little to hide the true nature of the beast that lurked inside him, like a bear lusting for honey.

'Well?' she persisted, her claw-like hands gripping the arms of her chair, her body leaning forward, ready to pounce on him if he gave her less than the truth.

'I'm not sure, Blodwen,' Rob told her. 'He might have gone off to McGinty's Tavern. That's where he usually goes, but . . . '

'But?'

He shrugged and spread his big hands that were roughened by the quarry work he was forced to do. She wished briefly that she could get him away from that. He was worthy of better things than breaking stones, like a criminal on a chain gang, ten hours a day.

'He simply said he had somewhere to go,' Rob said hesitantly. 'He didn't say where, but . . . '

'Go on, son. There's something bothering that head of yours. Better be out with it than let it sit there and fester.'

Rob shook his head and rubbed a weary hand over his face.

'On the way home,' he said, 'we passed a place. Matt had obviously noticed it before. About an hour out of here. There was a log cabin and a girl wandering about dressed in trews and feeding the guanacos. It was something to see, I can tell you. Blodwen?

Blodwen, what's wrong?'

Blodwen had felt a creeping finger of ice trace a pattern up and down her spine as he spoke, and now it was embedding itself in her heart.

'He's not gone back there, has he?' she wanted to know urgently. 'Please God, tell me he's not gone to that cabin.'

Rob's eyebrows shot up.

'Honest to God, Blodwen, I don't know, but he was certainly interested in that young woman. Do you know her? Ivor Jackson didn't have a good word to say about her.'

'Oh, Ivor Jackson! What does he know but what his mother tells him and her no better than she should be before she married his da!'

Blodwen banged a small fist on the arm of her chair as if smiting down evil. At that moment the door opened and Dora came in, all smiles and looking pretty as a picture.

'He's here,' she announced, biting her lip with girlish excitement as she turned towards the figure that came in after her. A figure that should have been her husband, but was not.

'Ah, Davy, boy!' Blodwen greeted the young, fair-haired lad with genuine affection. 'Did they work you well on your first day as a Patagonian farmhand?'

Davy's face crumpled and for a moment

they all thought he was going to break down and weep, but he simply sat down on his hunkers in front of the fire and groaned.

'A right lot of good I am as a farmhand,' he said through tightly gritted teeth. 'They don't think I should bother going back th' morrow.'

'And why would that be?' Blodwen had struggled to her feet again and was standing over him, one hand extended and hovering over his head like a blessing.

'Because I can't bliddy ride a horse!' Davy blinked around the room, then realized what he had said. 'Sorry, Aunty Blodwen.'

'Well,' Blodwen said, ignoring his expletive for once. 'We'll just have to teach you, won't we? And you too, Rob, for I don't like you working the way you do. If you want to be true Patagonians, you must learn how to ride. You're going to become *gauchos*, the pair of you, so there.'

'That'll be the day,' Rob said, scratching his head and laughing, the thought of becoming a cowboy tickling his fancy.

'Yes, it will,' Blodwen insisted. 'And I know the very person to teach you, if you don't mind taking instructions from a woman.'

8

Matt had gone to Irish McGinty's Tavern, where he paid for the luxury of a bath, but on this occasion had foregone the charms of one of Irish's girls. They would keep. Tonight, he hoped to score somewhat better, at a very different venue.

And with that in mind, he paid particular attention to his appearance, glad to see that the individual who returned his admiring stare in the fly-spotted mirror still had what it took to attract the ladies. Yes, he definitely scrubbed up good. Pity about the broken tooth, though. Still, it gave him a bit of a rakish air. He liked that.

'You must be ailing, laddie.' McGinty regarded him with a curious eye. 'Tis not like you to turn down a treat such as the virginal Virginia or the luscious Lucinda.'

'There's nowt the matter wi' me, bonny lad,' he said to Irish as the man peered curiously over his shoulder.

Matt continued to admire himself in the long mirror and smirked as he thought of the higher quality of delights that lay before him, if he played his cards right. And Matt Riley always played his cards right where women were concerned. He could turn on the charm like a quarry man pushing down the plunger that sets off the dynamite. *Boom!* She wouldn't know what hit her.

He fastened the buttons of his clean shirt up to the neck, musing on the fact that they wouldn't stay fastened for long. McGinty had proved himself to be a real mate. He kept a supply of clean clothes for Matt, just in case. Well, it was going to be one of those nights when they would be needed. He could feel it in his bowels.

'How about a taste of a nice young *Indios* girl?' Irish suggested, not wanting to let business slip through his fingers. 'I'll give you a special price.'

'I'm not touchin' no Indians, so save yer special offer.'

'Half price, just for you — and she'll do anything you want. How about it, eh? I can't say fairer than that.'

'No Indians, I said.' Matt pushed his face close to the innkeeper's and looked mean. 'Look, I'm in a hurry. Where can I hire mesel' a pony and trap?'

McGinty eyeballed him back with a disgruntled air, but he knew better than to argue with the best customer he had had in a long time. Whatever Matt was up to, he'd be back. The Tavern had become his second home, because of his craze for gambling and fist fighting in the back room, not to mention his predilection for ladies of loose virtue.

Matt livened the place up and that was good for business.

'If it's transport you're wantin', there's Mary Martha Harris — lives out on the Puerto Madryn road. Big house, painted white. You can't miss it.'

'What's she got, then, this Mrs Harris?' Matt pulled on his jacket, thinking that Patagonia was full of dried-up old widow ladies, who turned their prim noses up as soon as they looked at him.

'It's *Miss* Harris,' McGinty informed him. 'And afore the floods she had a family and a farm. Now, she hires out what little she has left to make ends meet. People around here respect her, so keep your nose clean.'

Matt gave the man a sidelong glance, laughing dryly. He didn't think he'd be likely to put a foot wrong with some elderly virgin. Not tonight, any road.

He found the Harris place without too much trouble, though he had to skirt Puerto Daffyd in order not to pass by the Widow Evans's house. It was a dark night, but he didn't want to take any chances of Rob or Davy coming out onto the veranda and catching him sneaking past.

He rapped sharply on the door of Miss Harris's house and stood back in the shadows in case a light should come on and illuminate him in all his glory for the world to see.

'Yes? What do you want?' The voice was high and thin like wind blowing through a crack in the chimney.

'I'm told you might have a buggy for rent,' Matt said to the invisible woman, though he thought he got a whiff of sweet violet scent floating out of the room beyond.

'Who sent you?'

'Irish McGinty.'

'I don't do business with that type of person.'

'Well, ye're not, are ye? Ye're doing business wi' me — that is, if ye've got something for hire and I didn't walk all this way fer nothin'.'

'You speak with a strange accent. You're not from the Old Country.'

'I come from a country just as old as yours, Miss Harris — from England, the North-east, where the River Tyne flows to meet the sea.'

'It's a strange accent, nonetheless.'

Matt was starting to lose patience and might have walked away, blaspheming to the sky, had his mission not been of such pressing importance.

'I'm right sorry about me accent,' he said,

'but will ye lend us a buggy anyway?'

The door creaked open even as he spoke and a figure appeared, a candle held aloft so she could see his face. He was surprised to find her quite young, though she had an old woman's look about her with a soft round face and a thickening figure. It was no wonder, he thought, she was still unmarried at whatever age she was, which was probably about thirty-five.

'There's a pony and trap in the barn,' she told him. 'You pay me now and bring them back in the morning, for late it is already.'

She was looking at him with what he took to be the half-veiled interest of a reluctant virgin. Matt made a mental note to keep her for a rainy day, but he'd have to be really down on his luck to turn to this one. Still, in the dark she would look just the same as any other. And she would no doubt be grateful to him for paying her such a compliment.

They quickly agreed on a price. He handed over the money and she clasped it tightly to her cushiony bosom before closing the door in his face.

The barn was behind the house, the key hanging on a nail for all to see, together with an oil lamp, which he lit once he was inside. The nag munching hay in the stall was a skittish bag of bones and turned a red, contemptuous eye on him. The buggy had seen better days, but there wasn't a choice. It was this or nothing, unless he was prepared to wait for a new shipment of horses and mules in a month or so. Patience had never been one of Matt's virtues.

It took a while before he could coax the old horse to stay still long enough to be hitched. Matt wasn't good with animals, unless they were cooked and sliced up on his plate, swimming in gravy.

'Come 'ere, ye skinny old bugger!' he snarled as he made a lunge for the nag's head, seeing the whites of its eyes and getting a whiff of its foetid breath.

Just as the front hoofs rose, aiming a good kick at Matt's groin, he managed to sidestep the beast, lashing it a few times with a whip he had picked up just inside the barn. He expected to have a fight on his hands, but the creature was soon beaten into submission and stood quivering and snorting softly, its head drooping miserably between its knobbly knees.

'That's more like it,' Matt said, though he was having sore doubts about arriving at his planned destination without the thing dying on him.

Thankfully, attaching the harness and then the buggy was an easy enough task. In fact, the silly creature seemed to come to life the minute they left the barn together, as frisky and as eager as a young colt and raring to go.

Matt went easy through the town, then with a few more lashings of the whip on the nag's bony rump, they took off like a steam train in the direction of the log cabin and its ravishing occupant.

★　★　★

'Easy, baby, easy!'

Gwyneth was hanging by one hand, clutching the length of rope she had fastened to a tree stump. With the other hand, she slowly reached for the tiny guanaco fawn lying on the crumbling ledge. Her body swayed gently to and fro, and she prayed that the tree would not uproot and send her crashing to the rocks below.

The fawn looked at her with big, scared eyes. There was nowhere for it to go, except down to certain death. As it was, a foreleg was undoubtedly broken and the poor creature was probably in shock. From the moment Gwyneth discovered the fawn it had never occurred to her that it might be better to leave Nature to take its natural course. The guanacos, like all the animals in this Patagonian province, were her friends. She could not leave it there to die.

'Now, now, baby,' she crooned to the distressed guanaco in a voice as soft as velvet. 'Don't move. I'm coming.'

Without warning, there was a sudden fall of earth and stones, probably dislodged by the friction of the rope. Gwyneth let out an involuntary cry, thinking that all was lost, but the rope held. The guanaco, however, was startled into frantic thrashing movements as it tried to get a purchase on the ledge, its three sound legs struggling, the fourth dangling helplessly at an odd angle.

Gwyneth propelled herself forward and managed to grab the animal at the last second before the ledge gave way. She held it tightly by one hind leg. It continued to struggle, bleating plaintively and she knew how it was hurting and she was adding to its pain, but she could not give up now.

Perspiration poured from her as she continued to dangle in midair, scraping against the cliff face as she tried desperately to find a foothold so that she could haul herself and the guanaco up to safety.

Just as her toe found a tree root that seemed firm, her ears picked up the sound of a horse's hoofs and the crunch of buggy wheels. Not stopping to wonder who was abroad at that time of night and passing her way, Gwyneth filled her lungs and let out a mighty yell.

'*Socorro*! Help me! Over here — oh, *please*!'

There was a gruff male voice that she didn't recognize, then the hoofs and the wheels skidded to an abrupt halt. She heard someone jump to the ground, heard the crunch of footsteps, but it was dark and he couldn't possibly see her.

'I'm here!' she called out again, speaking automatically in Spanish. 'Over here — in the crevasse! Oh, please be quick! I can't hold on much longer.'

More earth and stones showered down on her, then she looked up and saw a dim silhouette. A big man, by the look of it, for which she thanked the God that she did not believe in.

'Well, would ye look at what we've got here!'

He wasn't Spanish. Neither was he Welsh. His voice was rough, foreign almost. He leaned over the edge of the crevasse at an alarming angle. It didn't seem to bother him, but Gwyneth let out a breathy gasp of fear lest he fall down on top of her and take her and the fawn to the bottom with him.

'Be careful! If you fall you'll kill us all.'

'And who is 'all'? I can only see one

woman in deadly peril.'

'And she would be very grateful if you would rescue her!' Gwyneth retorted angrily, her patience wearing as thin as the taut rope that was between her and certain death. 'Here, take the fawn and I'll manage the rest on my own.'

He started to object, but she threw the tiny guanaco into his arms and as he staggered back with it, she used both hands to pull herself up, landing on her knees before him, her lungs bursting, her heart pounding and every muscle in her body trembling with the strain of the ordeal.

'What the hell! What's this you've given me?'

'It's a young guanaco and it's hurt.'

She struggled to her feet and stood before him, swaying unsteadily, her breathing ragged.

'Ye bugger, ye!' He threw the animal from him and it squealed out pitifully as its legs crumpled beneath it. 'It's just *shat* all ower me.'

'You might do the same in similar circumstances.' Gwyneth retrieved the fawn and cradled it in her arms, nuzzling her face into its soft coat and kissing the top of its tiny head. 'Who are you and what's your business out here in the middle of the night?'

'I might ask you the same question.'

'I live here. This happens to be my land you're on.'

'Oh, aye?'

'You're not Welsh, nor are you Scottish or Irish, though you sound like a mixture of all three. Where do you come from?'

She was walking, as fast as her shaking legs would carry her, in the direction of the cabin. Her mind was already working on how she could save the life of the guanaco lying calmly now against her chest.

'I'm a Tynesider — a Geordie. Me name's Matt Riley. I'm Welsh on me mother's side though.'

'Well, whoever you are, I suppose I should thank you for helping me just now, though you seemed reluctant to do so.'

She could see him more fully now in the light that poured out of the cabin windows and she thought no better of him for all that. He was too cocky by half with his swarthy good looks, and he had a strut like a prize rooster that she neither liked nor trusted.

'I would far rather have had *you* thrust in me arms, than that stinkin' animal,' he said as they reached the veranda of the cabin. 'Aa canna stand bloody animals.'

She could sense, the moment the words were out, that he realized his mistake, but he did nothing to rectify it. Not that she would have forgiven him had he even made the effort.

There was a long moment's silence between them that seemed to ring in Gwyneth's ears. Here was this perfect stranger, dressed *almost* like a gentleman, and his behaviour was just as obnoxious as the horny young lads who hung about McGinty's down in Puerto Daffyd — and a few other places with reputations that would set fire to the halo of a saint.

She stopped in the doorway of the cabin and turned abruptly to face him, not liking the closeness of him, like a second shadow. The door was not locked. She pushed it open a few inches with her heel and slid her hand inside, her fingers well practised in finding the rifle she kept propped there, ready for use if and when necessary.

'I thank you again, Geordie English,' she said, her mind not having grasped the name he had offered her as introduction. 'Without your help I would not have been able to save this poor animal.'

'Ach, what's one less when there are thousands of the things roaming the hillsides.' Matt's cockiness had returned in vigour. 'At least it's plump enough to make a good stew.'

Gwyneth felt the hairs on the back of her neck stiffen as a chill swept over her and settled in the pit of her belly. She did not take kindly to men, but this one had the air of Brin Johnns about him. A wild, lustful air like a bad spirit that needed to be exorcized.

'Animals are my friends,' she told him through teeth so tight that her jaws ached and the words came out strangulated and venomous.

Matt sniffed and gave her a lopsided grin.

'Are they, indeed? So what have you got cookin' in there, for that's the tastiest pot roast I ever did smell.'

Gwyneth's eyes narrowed suspiciously. She was not about to be backed into a corner while taking pity on a passing wayfarer. She had run into trouble before in much the same situation.

'It's a rhea,' she said.

'Is that one o' them ostrich-like birds I've seen?'

Gwyneth nodded. 'But I only kill to survive,' she rasped out, backing slowly into the cabin, her fingers tightening around the barrel of the weapon that more than one man had learnt to respect and fear in her hands. 'I do not kill for the pleasure of it.'

Matt smiled and his expression was full of charm and tinged with a plea for compassion.

'I'm wi' you on that. Sorry I offended you just now, but you scared the living daylights out of me. All I was doing was being neighbourly.'

'Then we'll call a truce,' she said, but felt insincere, for she wanted nothing to do with this man. 'Now, if you will excuse me, I have to care for this poor creature's broken leg.'

She backed away, but he was there, quick as a flash of lightning, his big foot wedged in the gap, his hand restraining the closure of the door.

'Aren't you even going to invite me in to warm up and have a bowl of something hot before I go on my way?'

'No, I am not!'

'I'd heard how inhospitable the Welsh are. I thought, maybe, that you might be different.'

'What do you know about me?'

'Nothing,' Matt removed the cap from his head and loosened the knot in his neckerchief. 'Nothing, except what I see. A good-lookin' lass who has compassion for injured animals, yet will shut the door in the face of the man who saved her life.'

Gwyneth tried once more to shut the door, but he was too strong for her. She did not want trouble with this man, whoever he was, and he had indeed helped her, however reluctantly. Maybe if she let him in to warm himself by the fire and take a bowl of stew he would go on his way and no harm done. But that was all he would get. One false move and any gratitude, sympathy or compassion would fly out of the window.

She let the door swing back and stepped away, the guanaco in one arm, the rifle now tucked neatly but visibly into her other side. The man hesitated, his eyes sweeping warily over the rifle. For a brief moment he stiffened, then his body relaxed and he sauntered into the cabin, heading straight for the wood-burning stove and the big black pot bubbling over it.

'There's a bowl and a spoon to the side, warming. Help yourself to a portion and then be on your way. I have work to do.'

He did as he was told. Gwyneth kept her eyes on him as she carefully laid the baby guanaco down on a blanket on the kitchen table and dressed its wounds, binding the broken leg tightly with hessian soaked in a mixture of bread paste and mud, wrapped around a wad of clean cotton. It would harden off and support the leg when the animal tried to walk. She then fed it on warmed milk and a drop of bourbon, letting it suck the end of her finger, which she dipped into a cup.

'That's a bliddy waste!' The Englishman exclaimed, horrified at the thought of an animal being given even such a small amount of alcohol.

Gwyneth slid him a sideways glance and her smile was sly as she said: 'You can finish it off, if you like.'

The man took the cup from her and stared at it. For a moment she thought he was going to drink the whisky-tinged milk left in the bottom. However, with an expression of disgust, he flung the contents of the cup into the flames beneath the stew pot.

Gwyneth made up a bed of straw in a corner of the cabin and laid the guanaco gently on it, covering it with one of her old woollen shirts. She caressed it gently, soothing its fears.

'You're quite a woman, aren't you?'

He had been enjoying her stew so much she had taken her attention from him, but now she got hurriedly to her feet as she realized he was standing over her. He was much too close for comfort and she didn't like the look in his eyes. The hunger in his belly might be appeased, but his eyes reflected a deep-seated hunger that would take more than a second bowl of stew to settle it.

'I'll thank you to leave now, English!' she said sharply, edging away from him and not liking the way he kept coming towards her.

'Not before I've claimed me reward.' He gave a serpentine smile and Gwyneth's insides turned to ice.

'You've had all the reward that's coming to you,' she informed him, her voice strong, her eyes fixed on him so hypnotically he stopped in his tracks. 'Go now, please. I won't ask you again.'

He didn't go and she kept her promise and didn't ask again. As he advanced on her, she swung around, swirling like a tornado, reaching for the whip she kept coiled on a nail in the cabin wall behind her. Her fingers closed on the leather-bound shaft. She lifted it from its moorings and let the thin coil of well-worn leather thong slice cleanly through the air between them.

The Englishman blinked, frowned at her and glanced down in amazement at the bright red colour seeping through the split in the front of his shirt at midriff level. He put his hands over it and the blood oozed through his fingers. He shuddered and gave a grunt, then raised his head and gazed at her in disbelief. As she watched, coldly, he staggered to the door, fumbled with the latch and wandered off into the night.

Gwyneth kicked the door shut behind him, shot the bolt, and replaced the whip on the wall before sitting down to eat her supper.

The guanaco gave a small moan, sighed and slept on peacefully. She would watch over it during the night. If it survived until morning she would know that she had done a good job and be pleased.

*　*　*

The wound wasn't serious, though Matt had been shocked to see his own blood oozing like that as if coming from a gaping wound. He hadn't even seen the whiplash coming. It was as if she had thrown a bolt of lightning at him, *the bitch*!

He stopped the horse after a few miles and sat beneath the moon and the stars, inspecting his midriff more closely. As his fingers probed tentatively, he winced, but was relieved to find that the cut was only skin deep. The blood had already stopped flowing and was beginning to congeal.

But he couldn't return to his aunt's house like this, covered in blood. She wasn't the kind of lady to put up with his shenanigans. Like as not, she'd throw him out and that stupid wife of his would have a fainting fit the minute she saw him. Wife, indeed! She didn't know the meaning of the word. Scared silly of him, she was. Aye, and just about everything else that moved, except that bloody lad, Davy.

It had been a mistake to let that one string along. What with him and Rob looking out for Dora like a couple of Dutch uncles, it made life just a tad difficult for Matt. No wonder he had to seek his pleasures elsewhere.

And thinking of his pleasures again, once he was sure he wasn't going to die from his whiplash injury, he felt the resurgence of manly desires stirring in his groin. The urgency he felt down below dispelled all other pain, so great it was and coming on him so frequent he thought it might do his head in if he didn't get satisfaction. He needed a woman badly, and a woman he would have, albeit not the one he married. That pathetic little wench was hardly woman enough for Matt Riley.

It was as he was drawing near to the town that he saw the red glow in the night sky. A mile or two nearer and he could smell smoke, feel the tang of it on his tongue and in his nostrils. Nearer still and he heard the clang of the fire bell and a cacophony of voices raised in panic. It seemed as if the whole of Puerto Daffyd was abroad, watching the fire.

The bad news, for Matt, was when he saw the flames leaping from the roof of McGinty's Tavern. Irish himself was in the line of volunteers passing buckets of water, while the band of uniformed firemen fought valiantly with the small, inadequate hose of their machine that seemed reluctant to spurt the water from the tank on the back of the horse-drawn wagon. In the larger towns they already had steam-driven fire engines, but a tiny place like Puerto Daffyd could, it seemed, afford only two retired drays and a hand pump that worked or not, depending on its mood.

Matt hung back, his natural reluctance to be involved taking precedence over his horror at seeing his favourite haunt being burned to the ground. Already, the roof had gone. Black rafters showed like skeletal ribs with scarlet tongues of flame licking the sky.

A rig, packed tightly with ill-clad prostitutes came careening towards him. Even in the dusky, rose-coloured darkness, Matt recognized every one of the girls and knew them all by name. He stepped out and waved an arm above his head as they came abreast. It was Mimi hauling on the reins. She was one of the older prostitutes and something of a mother hen. Matt had no liking for the woman. Every time he saw her she looked at him as if he were dirt under her heel.

'What happened?' he shouted at her as she reined in the horses and the gig skidded noisily on the dry, dusty track.

'You can't see for yourself, English?' Mimi sneered at him, tossing her black Italian curls and wiping the back of her hand across her sooty face.

'O' course I can, woman, but . . . ' Matt frowned as she clicked her tongue at the drays and they started off again.

'Somebody smoked in bed and fell asleep,' Mimi called over her shoulder. 'I was kinda hoping it was you they brought out of there looking like a stick of charcoal.'

'Sorry to disappoint you,' he shouted back. 'Where are you all off to, then?'

'Puerto Madryn. There's always plenty of work for the likes of us. They'll take us in like we were offering them gold. Hope you're not feeling horny, boy, for it'll be a while before Irish gets the place put back together.'

Matt swore loudly and kicked at a rock, the exertion tugging painfully at his wound. He looked down and saw that the cut had reopened and was bleeding afresh through his shirt. He had a good mind to go back and sort out the rotten female who had given him that.

He stood, looking uncertainly from right to left, wondering what to do for the best. After a minute or two, he saw Irish McGinty coming his way and hailed him. McGinty was not looking his jaunty best, with his clothes in tatters and his hair and eyebrows singed almost to the skin.

'Hey, Irish! Does this mean you're out of business th' night?'

McGinty scowled. 'Now if that isn't the daftest question I ever did hear. What do you think, eh? That the girls would stay around and give service in the open air, among the ruins of my tavern?'

'Just askin', like,' Matt said with a sniff and shoved his hands deep in his trouser pockets.

'It wasn't worth the bother. Are you blind that you can't see what state the place is in. Come back in a month or two, if ye can wait that long. Of course, ye can lend a hand to rebuild the place, but I've heard that ye don't cotton on too much to hard honest graft.'

Matt threw an expletive at the Irishman's back as McGinty walked away, his shoulders slumped, and full of dejection. He wasn't the only one to feel dejected, Matt thought selfishly. His gaze turned in the direction of his aunt's house. He could see the lights from where he stood. Indeed, there wasn't a house in the town that wasn't lit up. Every inhabitant seemed to be either on the street or hanging out of their windows, gawping at the spectacle.

He didn't seem to have much choice. Matt grabbed the lead rein of the old nag he had borrowed and turned towards a small cut that would lead around to the back of Miss Harris's place. He would return the nag and trap and go home. Dora wasn't much, but she was better than nothing.

He was just leaving the barn when a door opened behind him, shedding out a stream of flickering light. Matt turned and saw Miss Harris watching him, an oil lamp held high. She was in her night-clothes and he fancied he could see through to her bare legs, for the passageway behind her was well lit.

'Just returning your property,' he muttered gruffly and started to walk away, but there was something in her look that made him hesitate.

'The tavern's burnt down,' she said.

'Aye,' Matt replied, taking another step, but this time he was going towards her, a crazy idea forming in his head. 'So I see.'

'Best thing that could happen to this town,' Miss Harris told him with a narrowing of her small eyes and a prudish tightening of her mouth.

He noticed that for bed she wore her hair in a long plait, coming forward over her shoulder, the end of it resting on her breast. It taunted him, titillating his fancy. With a wicked smirk he wondered if she had ever had a man in her bed and what it would be like to bed her instead of the well-used whores to whom he was accustomed.

She realized, too late, what he was thinking. Before she could get the door closed, he had his foot on the threshold. With one hand, he took hold of that long plait. With the other, he squeezed her breast and pushed her back into the house. She was too shocked even to scream.

9

Rob and Davy had been in the line of people passing buckets of water that would never be enough to douse the flames of McGinty's Tavern. Most of the men of the little town and all of the women had stood back, only too glad to see the destruction of what was, for them, a den of iniquity. Rob and his brother did not frequent the place, but neither of them could stand by and watch while it burnt to the ground.

Irish McGinty was no saint by anybody's reckoning, but he wasn't a bad sort and proved it when he dashed in and out of the conflagration that had been his livelihood, dragging out men and women who were in varying stages of life and death. At the very last moment, when screams were heard coming from somewhere in the burning building, he had to be restrained, even though his face and his hands were singed red raw.

'But there's someone still in there!' he cried, struggling to free himself of the hands that held fast on to him.

'Not any more,' someone was heard saying

as the roof timbers gave way and the whole place collapsed like a bonfire on Guy Fawkes night.

It was hours before the flames died and even longer before Puerto Daffyd emerged through the lingering smoke, though it would be days before the smell of the inferno cleared.

Rob and Davy returned to the Widow Evans's house, black from head to foot, their muscles aching from all the hefting of the heavy buckets and smouldering timbers.

'Gawd, Rob, that was a bit of an experience, an all, was it not?' Davy gave a tired grin and shook his head. 'Poor old Irish. It's to be hoped he didn't stash his earnings under the mattress.'

'He's too canny for that, man,' Rob said, wiping his forehead with a damp hand and blinking at the black soot that came off onto his fingers. 'Look at that, will you? You'd think we'd been down the pit.'

They trudged on in silence, the crackling of cooling charcoal still ringing in their ears, the smoke still stinging their eyes and their noses and tasting bitter on their tongues.

Blodwen was hovering nervously on her veranda waiting for them. She held herself stiffly erect and her expression was stern, so they knew they could be in for a hard time from her.

'Well?' she asked as they approached her front step.

'The fire's out, Blodwen,' Rob told her and saw just the slightest twitch of relief in her face. 'There's nothing left of McGinty's, I'm sure you'll be pleased to hear.'

'And why should it please me, that a man should lose his livelihood? Even a man like Irish McGinty.'

'I thought you didn't approve of such things as taverns, Blodwen,' Davy piped up, giving a great sneeze and blowing black mucus into his handkerchief.

'I don't say I approve, but then I don't totally disapprove either,' Blodwen fingered the lace frill of her nightcap. 'You men have to have somewhere to go to get rid of the fire in your heads and your bellies — and other places. Mr McGinty was simply providing a service to meet the demand and he ran a clean house. The Elders saw to that.'

'Aye,' Davy grinned, his teeth showing a startling white in his blackened face. 'I bet they did, for they weren't averse to paying the tavern the odd visit or two themselves. I've seen them . . .'

Blodwen gave him a severe look and Rob knocked his arm surreptitiously. Davy stopped in mid-sentence and looked beyond the old woman into the house, which was lit

182

up as if it were the middle of the afternoon instead of the small hours of the morning.

'Were there any fatalities?' Blodwen asked, her jaw firmly set in expectation of bad news.

'Yes,' Rob said with a nod. 'They carried three bodies out of the flames and they're still sifting through the rubble for more.'

'Who were they? Do you know?'

Rob shook his head. 'I didn't recognize them.'

He didn't like to tell her that there hadn't been much left of the bodies to recognize.

'One was a woman — I think,' Davy said, screwing up his face at the memory of that rigid corpse with the flesh burned down to the bone on the upper part of the torso, but with a frilly petticoat still intact and a pair of satin slippers on tiny feet. They could have belonged to a child, only there were no children at McGinty's.

'It is to be hoped the others got away. I do not approve of their occupation, but it is a necessary evil, I'm thinking, and death by fire is not the way I'd wish even my worst enemy to go to his Maker. You said three bodies, Rob. Could Matthew be one of them, do you think?'

There was a long silence while the three of them regarded one another. They all knew that Matt frequented the tavern, but now that it was out in the open, it seemed more shocking somehow. Blodwen waited patiently for an answer, her eyes fixed on Rob's face.

'No,' he told her and saw her chest rise and fall, though it was not evident what it signified. 'Has he not come home then?'

'He has not, and that poor wife of his is inside wringing her hands because she thinks she is to be a widow woman and her not yet twenty.'

Rob had to stop himself thinking that it would have solved a lot of problems had Matt been caught in that fire. Dora would be better off without him, as would a lot of people, for there was a constant stream of complaints against him. Even the men he consorted with did not have a good word to say about Matt Riley.

'Come on, my lovelies,' Blodwen was suddenly waving her hands at them as if she had only just noticed the state they were in. 'Round the back with you and wash off that soot before you set foot in my clean house. 'Tis fortunate it's Saturday and you can lie longer in bed the morrow, though 'tis already morning.'

It was as Rob and Davy were washing themselves down, sharing the ice cold water in the rain barrel at the back door, that Matt came round the house, whistling softly to himself. He stopped short, and coloured slightly when they looked up and saw him.

'Where've you been, then, Matt?' Rob asked, his expression stony, his eyes dull.

'Aye, Matt,' Davy said, grabbing a rough towel and briskly towelling his fair hair, then tossing the towel to his brother. 'You missed a fair bit of excitement th' night.'

'Who says I didn't have some excitement of me own?' Matt said, looking about him and avoiding eye contact.

'And did you?' Rob couldn't help himself. He had to ask. If his suspicions were correct, he wasn't sure he was going to like Matt's answer.

Matt licked dry lips and fingered his midriff. Rob's eyes were drawn to a tear and a dried bloodstain on the front of Matt's shirt. He waited for Matt to speak, wondering what kind of trouble the man was in this time.

'Not exactly the kind of excitement I was expectin',' Matt said eventually. 'It's right what they say about that half-breed. Devil's blood, that's what she's got. A wild hellcat and best left alone — and that's from the mouth of an expert.'

'Did she give you that?' Rob nodded in the direction of Matt's wound and saw his friend flinch.

'Aye, she did, and it's a miracle I came out of it alive.'

'What did she use, Matt?' Davy, too, had noticed the blood. 'A knife?'

'A knife I could deal with, Davy, lad, but she used a bullwhip. Flailed me good from across the room. I didn't stand a chance and all I wanted was a bowlful of her stew.'

And some, Rob thought. He said: 'You're talking about that girl we saw earlier? The one surrounded by guanacos, beside a log cabin.'

'Aye, that's the one. Be warned, mate. Don't touch hide nor hair of that one.'

'I've heard she killed a man and nobody did anything about it,' Davy said as he remembered the gossip about Gwyneth Johnns. 'Makes ye think, doesn't it?'

There was a creak of a wooden floorboard behind them and Blodwen appeared with two sets of clean clothes for Rob and Davy. On seeing Matt there too, she gave him a roll of her eyes.

'So, you're home at last,' she said sharply and squared her shoulders, giving him the benefit of her small but imposing stature.

'Sorry to disappoint you, Aunty Blodwen, but here I am, like the proverbial bad penny.'

'He's hurt, Blodwen,' Rob said and saw the old woman's eyes grow large, then squint as she followed the line of his pointing finger. 'It seems he met a girl with no taste for brash Geordie lads.'

'So, she dealt with you good and proper, my Gwyneth, did she?' Blodwen took a fistful of Matt's shirt and lifted it, revealing his whiplash wound. 'You'll not die from that, more's the pity, and God forgive me for saying it. Come inside and I'll see to you, though how you're going to explain it to Dora I do not know.'

Matt made a noise like a stallion blowing hot air down his nostrils, but he followed his great-aunt meekly enough into the house where Dora was already on her feet, her hands to her face, expectant and fearful.

'You can stop worrying, girl,' Blodwen said to Dora as she entered the main living room. 'Your man's had a little accident. Go you and fetch my first-aid box. We need to put some alcohol on this wound to stop it turning septic.'

Dora drew in a sharp breath when she saw the blood-soaked shirt and the wound beneath it as Matt stripped off. He threw the shirt on the smouldering embers of the kitchen fire.

'What happened?' Dora asked in a small, shaky voice.

He gave her a disparaging look and ignored the question.

'Get me a glass of that medicinal brandy Aunty Blodwen hides in the cupboard under the sink, will ye? Now that McGinty's Tavern is gone there's going to be a lot of thirsty men in this town for a while.' He turned to Rob and Davy: 'I don't suppose old Irish managed to save some of his bottles?'

'He was too busy saving lives,' Rob said.

'Aye,' Davy added. 'And getting burned for his trouble. 'There's hardly any skin left on his hands.'

'Well, I'll just have to pay me respects to the ladies of his tavern in Madryn.' Matt smirked, but the expression soon turned to one of pain as Blodwen dabbed something strong-smelling on the place where the whip had bit in deeply.

'Where've you been, Matt?'

Dora's timid voice made them all turn and stare at the girl as she advanced carefully, holding out a glass containing a good measure of brandy. Matt grabbed it from her and swigged it back as if it were water and he a thirsty man.

'Never you mind, Dora,' he said, his voice already slurred. 'Get me another one o' them there brandies and then let's go to bed, eh?'

'Oh, no!' She looked shocked.

'Whaddya mean, no! I'm your husband and don't you forget it.'

'I'm not able to forget a thing like that, Matt,' Dora said and they were all surprised at how she spoke out in front of them all, for she was such a quiet, timid little mouse at the best of times.

Matt pushed Blodwen aside, spilling the raw alcohol she was putting on him.

'And what's that supposed to mean, missy?'

Dora's courage instantly left her as he fixed her with a mean eye and gripped her fragile wrist in his big paw.

'Nothing, Matt. It's just ... ' She swallowed hard and looked wildly about the room. 'It's almost time to get up and — and make your breakfast. I — I'm sure you must be hungry after ... '

'Aye? After what? What d'ye think I've been doing, then?'

Dora's chin dropped to her chest and Davy took a protective step towards her, which didn't exactly please Matt, though he kept mute. In fact, he laughed. He laughed a little too loud for Rob's comfort.

'Here, Dora,' Matt delved into the pocket of his jacket, which was slung over the chair he was sitting on. 'See this? I bought you a present. Had to go a long way to find it and it cost me near enough a week's wages, but I thought you would like it, being as how you're a female and all females like a touch of romance, now don't they?'

What he held in front of Dora's astonished nose glinted in the light of the oil lamps. It was a small silver pendant, ornately engraved. Dora reached for it with a tentative hand and he whisked it away, grabbing her and pulling her in to him.

'Later!' he said and her cheeks burned crimson as he kissed her full on the mouth. 'First, you have to give me my reward for thinking so kindly of you. Eh? Eh, Dora?'

Dora blinked up at him, her expression of surprised pleasure turning to rigid fear.

'Leave it be, Matt,' Rob muttered, his quiet words seeming loud in the silence that pervaded the small kitchen.

'But — but Matt,' Dora stuttered. 'You're hurt. You need to rest.'

'Like hell I need to rest,' he replied and shot a lopsided smile all round the room. 'I'm hungry, I'll give you that, but it's not for me breakfast. I had neither supper nor dessert last night, so I think I'll have mesel' a good helping of that right now, if ye don't mind, *Mrs Riley*?'

Rob thought Dora was going to faint, she had turned so pale. Davy moved closer to the girl, but stopped when he received a look from Rob. They might not like what went on between Matt and his wife, but they had no right to interfere.

The two brothers exchanged glances, then looked at Blodwen, but she was steeling herself against what they all knew was going to take place in that extension at the back of the house.

'I'll make a pot of tea,' Blodwen said. ' 'Tis the answer to all ailments, hurts and disasters. Rob, will you fetch the water, my lovely? And Davy, stir up the cinders in the fire. There's a sudden chill in the air.'

Rob went out to the well and hauled up a bucket of water. As he turned with it, he saw a glimmer of light flickering through the thin curtains of Matt and Dora's quarters. He saw moving shadows, thought he heard a small, wretched cry. Something like a heavy fist hit him in the stomach. Every instinct in his mind and body was telling him that he should go in there and put a stop to Matt's cruel game, but as long as the pair of them were married, it was none of his business.

'Here you are, Blodwen,' he said as he hefted the bucket up and poured water into the old copper kettle she kept on the stove. 'Make it strong and put in plenty of sugar, for I think we all need a little sweetening this night.'

'Aye, son,' Blodwen said softly, her old eyes

caressing him and Davy. 'Aye. How right you are.'

★　★　★

Blodwen was singing softly to herself as she weeded her garden. The sun was out and warming the land, the temperature high for the time of year, for it was winter. It was probably the last time she would spend working the land until the following summer, if she lasted that long.

'Guide Me O Thou Great Redeemer . . . ' she sang the hymn, only she sang it in the Old Language, for that was the only way she could remember the words.

She bent low with a slight groan as the pain of her ever-present rheumatism gripped her, plucked a handful of weeds and transferred them to the old bucket she carried with her. It was a satisfying feeling, getting rid of worthless weeds that cluttered up the life of her garden. She wished she could do the same with her own life. There was one *weed* in particular she would gladly get rid of.

'*Arglwydd, arwain trwy''r anialwch,*' she sang and out came a clump of something or other she did not recognize, but knew instinctively that it was of no medicinal use. '*Fi bererin gwael ei wedd, Nad oes ynof nerth*

192

na bywyd, Fel yn gorwedd yn y bedd: HollalluogYdyw"'r un a"'m cwyd i"'r lan . . . '

She plucked enthusiastically at the weeds and every time she thrust them into the bucket she had a mental vision of Matt going in with them and, for once, guilt bore no part of it.

'That's a fine, rousing song you're singing, Blodwen,' said a voice from over the fence.

Blodwen looked up, red in the face from her exertion, and saw Gwyneth regarding her inquisitively. She straightened her back with the utmost care and hung on to the white picket fence, panting slightly and longing for a sit-down and a sip of *maté*.

'Gwyneth, girl. You surprised me.'

'Were you not expecting me?' the young woman said, pulling the red kerchief at her neck so that it slackened and allowed her glistening skin to breathe more freely.

'You got my letter, then?'

Gwyneth nodded solemnly. 'I got your letter and I came at your bidding, but I don't know why you sent for me so urgently. They need me up at the *estancia*. With winter coming on there is a lot to do and some of the hands have left to find work in the cities.'

'Ah! Then it's providence that has prompted me to send for you.' Blodwen wiped her hands on the long piece of sacking that she always wore about her when she gardened.

'Providence? How do you mean?'

'Let's go inside, girl. I have things to discuss with you.'

A few minutes later, when they were both sitting toasting their toes in front of a roaring fire in Blodwen's small living room, Gwyneth asked again what the song was that her old friend had been singing so lustily.

'Ach, 'tis a hymn from the Old Country,' Blodwen told her, slurping a little noisily from her cup, and cringing at the sound her old mouth was making. 'I was asking God to guide me, for I'm feeling the need for guidance right now, the way I've never done before.'

She closed her eyes, struggling to remember the English words to the hymn she had learnt at her mother's knee back in Prestatyn, for wasn't her mother a touch English, though nobody knew it?

'Let me see now . . . Open now the crystal fountain, Whence the healing stream doth flow; Let the fire and cloudy pillar . . . lead me all my journey through . . . '

She stopped abruptly and fixed Gwyneth with a hypnotic eye. 'And so on,' she said, folding her hands in her lap.

'Well, it's all very brave and spiritual,'

Gwyneth said with a small smile, 'but it doesn't tell me why you sent for me.'

'No, I suppose it doesn't,' Blodwen glanced at the clock that ticked solemnly on her mantelshelf and heaved a sigh. 'They will be home soon — the men folk. You know, of course, that I have family living here with me now?'

'You did mention this in your letter,' Gwyneth said, her forehead creasing. 'A nephew, you said.'

'And his wife — and two friends, brothers. Nice boys, Rob and Davy. The girl doesn't have a brain between those pretty eyes of hers, but she's a delight to have around and I wish she were mine to keep.'

'And . . . ?' Gwyneth leaned forward, eager to know more.

'They have work, digging and breaking rocks to build more dams, but I want them to do better for themselves,' Blodwen stared off into the distance, her mind taking her back to her unfulfilled dreams of having children. 'When I'm gone, they will have money to share between them. They can buy land, invest in a future better than any they could have back in the Old Country.'

Gwyneth's frown deepened. 'I don't understand. They can do all that without me.'

The old lady stared up at the ceiling and

rocked to and fro. This was proving more difficult than she had envisaged. Gwyneth would give her life to help a poor animal, but when it came to men . . .

'Gwyneth, my lovely,' she said, finally lowering her chin and staring full-face at the beautiful half-breed. 'Have I not done well by you all these years and not asked for a thing in return?'

'Indeed, Blodwen, you have, and I am eternally grateful. I'm sure you must know that without my saying so?'

'Yes, but . . . ' Blodwen drew out her hesitation and sighed. 'Oh, perhaps it is too much to ask, even of you.'

'What? There's not a thing you can ask of me that could possibly be too much. Blodwen Evans, you have been like a mother to me, a girl nobody would look at, without condemnation.'

Blodwen reached out and gripped the girl's hands in hers, squeezing them tightly.

'My dear girl, will you teach my boys to ride — teach them everything you know?'

Gwyneth smiled and there was a trace of amusement on her face and twinkling in her amazing eyes.

'Does that include lace-making, Blodwen?' she asked and gave a rare, melodious laugh. 'I'm not sure that your *boys* will take to that.'

Hearing the clatter of boots on the pavement outside, Blodwen gave an impatient 'tch', though it was accompanied by a short chuckle at the thought of any of those three sitting behind a cushion of bobbins and weaving fine lace for the ladies of Puerto Daffyd to trim their Sunday frocks with.

'They have never been on a horse before,' she said quickly. 'They do not know how to handle a rifle, or lasso a cow, or herd a flock of sheep. They know nothing of the land, except how to break it up. Rob is good with his hands, an excellent carpenter. His brother hasn't lived long enough to see daylight outside the pit in which he hewed coal. The other . . .'

Gwyneth's eyebrows shot up. 'The other?'

Blodwen sighed again, deeply. 'He is the one who is my kith and kin, but . . . 'tis the other two I'm concerned with. They are good boys. I want you to turn them into good men — good ranchers. Can you promise me this, Gwyneth?'

Blodwen's eyes darted quickly to the door, the approaching tramp of feet getting ever closer. There was urgency in her request, yet she knew that Gwyneth could so easily refuse, and she would not blame the girl for that.

'Of course, Blodwen,' Gwyneth said, surprising her. 'You know I'll do my best to carry out your wishes, whatever they are.'

Relief spread warmly through Blodwen. 'Good. That is settled then. I can go to my grave when my Redeemer calls me and leave nothing undone.'

'Oh, Blodwen, you'll be around for a long time yet . . . ' Gwyneth's words were blown away with the wind that rushed through the little house as the door opened and two burly figures marched in.

★ ★ ★

'And where's that nephew of mine?' Blodwen demanded, getting to her feet and going to the kettle that was singing merrily on the stove.

'It's all right, Blodwen,' Rob answered her quickly, his eyes shooting like magnets to the widow's visitor. 'He's gone straight around to the back.'

Rob had built on another entrance to the part of the house occupied by Matt and Dora so they could have some independence. It was mainly for Matt, so he wasn't forever upsetting his aunt with his comings and goings at odd hours of the day and night. Dora still preferred to come through the main part of the house, where she liked to sit companionably with the old lady when the men were at work.

He looked around now, missing Dora's presence, and being self-consciously aware of the green-eyed young woman with the shining black hair who had turned her attention full on him, with barely a glance for Davy.

He nodded at her, recognizing immediately the woman he had seen on occasion working the land and tending her animals around the log cabin out on the wild plains.

Blodwen poured scalding water over fresh tea leaves in the big earthenware teapot. It splashed onto the hot red coals of the stove, hissing and spitting like an ill-tempered cat.

'This, my lovelies,' she said, turning with the pot in her hands and bringing it to the small table in the centre of the room, 'is Gwyneth Johnns. She has just promised to turn you into *gauchos* of the highest calibre, and when the job is done, I can die in peace.'

Davy's mouth dropped open with a small, unintelligible sound. Rob simply stared, feeling his heart lurch and trip over itself at the sight of this much-talked-about woman with the reputation of a hellcat. So this was the one who had dealt severely with Matt. He hadn't expected her to have such a presence. She made every other woman he knew pale

199

into insignificance.

'Miss Johnns,' he said with a stiff little nod, which she returned, not taking her eyes from his for one second.

'I'm Davy,' Davy stepped forward, hand outstretched.

It seemed a long time before Gwyneth noticed him. She rose to her feet and briefly shook hands with both of them.

'Which one of them is your nephew, Blodwen?' she asked, looking at Blodwen, who was busily pouring out tea in her best china cups.

'Neither of these two lovely boys is my nephew, though they will inherit their share of my estate jointly with Matthew.'

'Matthew?' A note of doubt was creeping into Gwyneth's voice and Rob noticed it.

'You will meet him in good time,' Blodwen told her, her cheeks and throat suddenly growing hot, for didn't she know there would be a problem when Gwyneth realized who this *Matthew* was.

'She can meet him now,' said a voice from behind them and into the room strode Matt himself.

There was a moment's silence, then Gwyneth, turning to look at the newcomer, gasped, stumbling backwards into the table. Rob darted forward to steady her, but she recovered herself quickly and moved closer to the outer door.

'We have already met,' she said, her head held high, her eyes throwing poisonous darts at Matt and his sly smile. 'And I do not care to meet him again.'

'Gwyneth, my lovely . . . ' Blodwen put out a hand towards the dark-haired girl, who shook her head vehemently.

'No, Blodwen. You cannot make me do business with this . . . this animal! My business with him is closed and he has the scars to prove it.'

A small cry was heard and, for the first time, they saw the tiny childlike figure of Dora peering around her husband.

'It was a mistake,' Matt drawled. 'I saved the woman's life and she turned on me thinking I was wantin' my way with her. She's as crazy as they say she is.'

'I apologize for my friend, Miss Johnns,' Rob said quickly. 'When he's had a drink or two he isn't responsible for his actions.'

Matt gave a sneer and shrugged off Dora who was tugging at his arm.

'Tell them,' he said to Gwyneth. 'Tell me aunty Blodwen how we met.'

Gwyneth tore her attention away from Matt and turned to Blodwen.

'*This* is your nephew?'

'I'm afraid so, Gwyneth. Does this mean that you will not now keep the promise you have made me?'

The girl licked her tongue about her dry lips, her gaze passing from one to the other of them, coming to rest on Dora with her large, moist, frightened eyes.

'You are really married to this man?' she asked pointedly.

'Yes, miss,' Dora whispered and gave a loud sniff.

Gwyneth placed the flat of her hands together in prayer mode and pressed the index fingers to her mouth. They heard her sigh, could see her mind working, mulling over the situation.

'I have only ever made three promises in my life,' she said slowly. 'I have kept the first two, but they were easier to keep than this one I've just made to you, Blodwen.'

'Oh, aye, and what promises were they, then?' Matt asked in a loud, belligerent voice.

When she spoke, she did so softly and there was more menace behind her words than if she had screamed them at him.

'I swore I would kill the man who violated me,' she said. 'And I did.'

'And the other promise?' Davy got a warning nudge from Rob, but treated it with a shrug. 'Well, I thought we'd better know, just in case . . . '

'I also swore I'd never let another man touch me — not like that, anyway. And none has. Blodwen, will you release me from my promise?'

Now it was Blodwen's turn to lick her lips.

'He'll be no trouble as long as he's with the other two. They'll see to that. And now, with a bairn on the way he'll no doubt settle down like the man he's supposed to be.'

Her words didn't immediately sink in. It was Rob who cottoned on first and reacted, darting a concerned look at Dora. He heard Davy beside him give a groan of despair and saw how startled Matt was at the news Blodwen had just imparted. However, it was Dora herself who appeared to be the most startled of all.

10

The sight of Blodwen gathering driftwood and pampas grass along the shore was not unknown to the townsfolk of Puerto Daffyd. She was always to be seen at this time of year, stocking up on the free winter fuel that lay there just for the taking. And anyone who got there before the Widow Evans would find themselves taken severely to task.

She placed a sodden tree branch in her barrow, the weight of it almost too much for her, and straightened her back with a groan. At the water's edge, where the foaming wavelets crept up the sandy slope beneath the rocky breakwater, Dora was standing, staring out to sea as if expecting her personal boat to come in at any moment. The dear child did not understand what was happening to her. To be so far away from her roots, even if those roots were tenuous, as they were in Dora's case, it was hard on the poor girl.

'Dora! Dora, my lovely, leave that dream and come and give me a helping hand, will you?'

It was some moments before Dora reacted and Blodwen was opening her mouth to shout a second time when the girl gave a shudder and looked quickly over her shoulder.

'Aunty Blodwen, I don't want there to be a baby inside me,' she said with a little, spasmodic jerk of her blonde head. 'Are you sure about — you know, what you said?'

'Don't you know anything, girl?' Blodwen put her hands behind her, rubbing her tender spine and stretching it back into an upright position. It took longer these days to get herself straightened up. 'And don't you go shouting those words so that the whole of Patagonia will hear you.'

She saw the rise and fall of Dora's flat chest, and the nervous fiddling of her fingers as she turned and walked back to the barrow, a single piece of shipwreck timber in her hand.

'I'm sorry, Aunty Blodwen, I really am, but I can't seem to get things straight in my head. A baby!' Upon which, she scrunched up her face and closed her eyes tightly, squeezing out tears like drops of glycerine to her pallid cheeks.

'You'll be telling me next that you can't be pregnant because that husband of yours has never kissed you!'

The pallid cheeks flushed pink and the watery eyes returned quickly back to the sea where the wind was driving fret before it, almost invisible as it fell, but as wet as any real shower of rain.

'You think I'm stupid, don't you, Aunty Blodwen.' Dora's words came thickly and ended in a sobbing intake of breath before she clamped her lips together. 'I know how a baby is made. It's just that — that . . .'

Blodwen placed a hand on the girl's thin shoulder and squeezed hard, which brought forth more sobs.

'There now, child. No tears. It's wet enough I am already with the salt water that's in the air today. Besides, you're a married woman and 'tis no business of mine, except . . .'

'Aye, Aunty Blodwen?'

'Except I'm worried for your well-being. We all are.'

A small smile broke through the tears like a half-hearted rainbow and Dora blew her nose on a scrap of a handkerchief.

'I don't think Matt was pleased,' she said, fingering the silver pendant around her neck. 'And I — oh, Aunty Blodwen, I don't know how I feel.'

'Is that in your belly or your head, girl?' It was a harsh question, but the old woman spoke softly and as she did so she pushed back a strand of hair that had escaped Dora's bonnet and patted her cheek, like a kindly grandmother. 'Don't answer that. I have eyes in my head as well as a brain and I know how you suffer.'

'But you've never had children. How would you know?'

'I'm a woman, aren't I?' Blodwen felt the prick of a tear in her own eye now and got on with the task of moving the barrow further up the beach, leaving Dora to trudge after her. 'Come on, or I'll be late for my meeting with Jenkins the Co-op.'

★ ★ ★

From the small jetty, Rob had watched the two women as they walked off into the distance, the spume from the sea and wind acting like a wraith of mist, making them look like ghosts disappearing into another time. He stayed where he was, drinking in his surroundings, thinking how he would miss it all.

Today was the last Sunday he and Davy and Matt would have here in Puerto Daffyd. On Sundays not even Gwyneth forced them to continue the rigorous training programme she was relentlessly putting them through. It was only a few days before they were due to make the long trek to the Gomez-Pan *estancia* with her. All three of them had been curious about Gwyneth Johnns and sceptical about her ability as a teacher of predominantly masculine occupations. But it took only a short while for her to prove to them how good she really was.

Matt, seemingly forgetting the harsh reception she had given him, had made some ribald comments about the situation, until Blodwen gave him the benefit of another kind of lashing. With her tongue. She had made him promise, before all of them, that he would be on his best behaviour and would heed everything Gwyneth told them.

'*And touch her like any man touches any woman, you shall not, Matthew Riley, unless you want to find yourself in serious trouble.*'

There had been a short stand-off when Rob worried what Matt was going to do or say. They both knew the power Blodwen still retained over the Committee of Elders, as well as the townsfolk. However, Matt wisely compressed his mouth, narrowed his eyes and nodded his agreement.

'Hey, Mister! Are you Mr Rob Barker?'

Rob didn't know how long he had been sitting there inside his thoughts, but when he heard his name he looked up and found that the light had faded considerably to the opalescence of early evening.

The scruffy little urchin, carrying a sack full of rattling seashells, stood a few feet beneath Rob. He looked tiny among the crab-infested rocks and the minnow pools with their brilliant emerald seaweed and mosses. He strained his neck to look up, shading his eyes from the white light of a pale sun and sniffing back columns of mucus that ran down from his nose to his mouth.

'Aye, lad? What of it?'

'The *Indios* was asking for you. Told me to run and fetch you, she did. They've opened up the Co-operative Store especially so you better get on down there quick. Mr Jenkins, the manager, is blowing a gasket he is.'

'In that case, I'd better be off, like you said.'

'Aye, you can't keep people like Mr Jenkins waiting, look you! And she said you'd give me a peso.'

Rob gave a lopsided smile. 'She did, did she? Generous with other people's money, isn't she?'

'She hasn't got any money of her own, is why,' the boy said, suddenly looking quite mature and serious, and much older than his twelve years. 'They say she's evil, but I don't think she is. I seen her do good things.'

'What kind of good things?' Rob enquired, smiling indulgently and trying to deny to himself that he was curious to learn more about the girl the locals called the *Indios* or, at times, the half-breed.

The boy sniffed and hitched up his pants.

'With animals and such,' he told Rob. 'She saved my baby brother's life once too.'

'Did she now?'

'Aye. The doctor said he wouldn't live another day, but she came and looked at him and gave him magic potions.' The lad's eyes grew wide as he remembered. 'Stayed with him until what ailed him passed, then walked away. Never asked for a peso. Not like the doctor. Mam's been grateful to her ever since, though she doesn't let on to the other womenfolk around here. They'd like as not run us out of town just like they did her.'

Digging in his pocket, Rob drew out a few shiny new pesos and threw them down to the lad, who caught them expertly, inspected them closely and bit each one in turn to make sure they were real.

'Thanks, mister. You want me to take a message back to the Co-op?'

Rob's smile broadened, recognizing a businessman when he saw one, albeit his tender years.

'No, I'll go on over there myself and see what it's all about.'

He gave the lad a nod, then strode back to

the road, shaking the sand from his shoes and the bottom of his trousers, feeling some grains of the stuff install themselves in his socks, chafing his skin. It was a whole lot worse than coal dust, he thought, but cleaner.

It wasn't evident that the Co-operative Wholesale Society was open, for the blinds were down and the shutters shut, which was fully expected on what his mother would have described as a 'good Sunday'. But then, a lot of things in this country went on behind locked doors, and he could not help thinking that it was the influence of the Welsh, for everywhere you looked there were signs of the League of Temperance and the power it wielded.

The Puerto Daffyd Tea Room was the only place that was exactly as it said it was with its great brown shiny teapots pouring strong Welsh tea. There was an array of foodstuffs to be enjoyed and it had surprised the Geordie lads to find that it was pretty much the same as their mother had produced for the table every Sunday afternoon. Scones dripping with strawberry jam and cream, bread and butter, egg custard tarts, sponge cake, gingerbread and so much more. The tearoom, of course, did not open on Sundays.

Rob pushed on the closed door of the Co-op, expecting it to open, but it didn't, so he rapped on the glass panel with his knuckles and heard the scuff of a footstep inside.

'Who's there?' demanded a deep, male voice.

'It's Rob Barker. I was told to report here.'

The door blind twitched and a beady eye with a hawk nose appeared. The eye gave him the once-over, then the door clicked and opened a few inches to allow him sufficient room to squeeze in.

'What's this, then?' Rob asked, blinking in the darkened area of the shop front as he tried to get his bearings. 'Is it some kind of secret society?'

'It's all right, Rob, I'm here too!'

He felt strangely reassured to hear Davy's voice and there was no trace of apprehension in it. Rob knew his brother well enough to read every nuance in the lad's tone as well as his glance. If there were a problem, he would have been warned by now.

'Where's Matt? Shouldn't he be here too?'

'Aye,' Davy told him. 'He had something else to do.'

'This way, laddie,' the man at his side said and Rob recognized the voice now as that of the store manager, Mr Jenkins, who looked more like a Spaniard than a Welshman with all those fine black whiskers he sported.

Rob followed the manager through a heavy, curtained archway into the back shop where the stock was kept, neatly packed away in boxes up to the ceiling, until it was needed. The overhead lamp was lit and it shone down a yellow glow on the heads of the people gathered around a large table.

The first person he saw was Gwyneth Johnns, the light from the oil lamp turning the blue sheen of her black hair to tarnished bronze and her skin to ochre. She was standing at the shoulder of a seated Blodwen, one hand resting lightly on the old woman's shoulder. The two women were so different, and yet Rob perceived a likeness that came not from facial resemblance, but from something that went much deeper. Strength of character came to mind, but he thought it was even more profound than that.

Davy was standing on the other side of the widow, but further apart. His forehead was creased and he was giving his brother a wry smile, but as yet Rob sensed nothing untoward, despite the bizarreness of this clandestine meeting.

'Please . . . ' The manager came forward, brandishing a tape measure and looking as if he expected disaster to strike at any moment. 'I would like to get this over with as soon as possible. Mrs Jenkins thinks I'm exercising the dog.'

There was an answering, disgruntled moan from a shadowy corner of the stock room and Rob caught a glimpse of an old, overweight bulldog who looked as if a walk might finish him off.

Rob, forever the animal lover in the family, went to stroke the dog's bald and wrinkled head, but Davy gave a sharp warning cough, making him stop warily.

'I wouldn't go near him, if I was you, Rob,' Davy said. 'He's a right little bleeder and no mistake.'

'Language, Davy!' Blodwen said and the lad looked suitably chastised. 'However, Rob, your brother is perfectly correct in what he says about the poor animal.'

'Taffy's a good watchdog,' Mr Jenkins affirmed, but withdrew his own hand before Taffy could sample the ends of his fingers with sharp, snapping teeth. 'Now, shall we get on? Come along, Mr Barker. I've already done your brother. It's your turn now.'

Rob looked at him in puzzlement, then glanced in Gwyneth's direction. She had removed herself from them and was standing at another counter dreamily fingering a fancy trinket box. He saw her open the lid and look embarrassed when the thing played music at her. She put it down again quickly, but then picked it up again and gazed at it as if she had never seen anything quite so beautiful.

'Go on, Rob,' Davy encouraged with a mischievous grin. 'Mr Jenkins only wants to take your measurements and he's very thorough, especially with the inside leg.'

'Davy!' That was Blodwen again, but she was having difficulty controlling a smile.

'Can I ask what the measurements are for?' Rob wanted to know.

'Aye, ye might well ask, Rob,' Davy's grin was spreading even wider. 'We're goin' to be kitted out with new clothes and them hide things the cowboys wear ower their trews.'

'Chaps,' Gwyneth said. 'They're called chaps.'

It was the first word she had spoken since Rob's arrival. Now he looked at her and their eyes met and it wasn't the first time that Rob felt an invisible fist wallop him in the gut and send reverberations scattering like bolts of lightning to every part of his body.

Gwyneth had been teaching the boys to ride and lasso steers in the pastureland behind her cabin for three weeks now. It had been as difficult for her as it had been for them. Davy took to it like it was second nature and Matt, despite the ill-feeling between him and the *Indios* girl, wasn't far

215

behind. He liked to prove how manly he was and was determined to show off his newly learnt ability, no doubt in order to impress her.

It had not worked. Gwyneth ignored Matt in favour of spending more time with Rob, who was grateful for the extra tuition. The training sessions were hard on all of them and for the first few days they couldn't sit down comfortably, limping about the place like old men with haemorrhoids. But Gwyneth had no sympathy, as he found when he kept falling off the young and vigorous gelding she had picked out for him. The animal was as feisty as she was and the third time he flew out of the saddle and landed in the hard dirt he was ready to throw in the towel and admit defeat.

'Get up, English!' Gwyneth had shouted at him, cheered on in the background by Davy and Matt. 'Prove that you are a real man and not a weakling. You look like a man. Go on! Prove it to me!'

'Aye,' Matt had shouted from the sidelines, taking no notice of Davy pulling on his arm and telling him to shut up. 'Gan on, bonnie lad. She's askin' for it so ye'd better give her what she wants and good luck to ye!'

Rob had seen Gwyneth's spine go rigid as she looked across the grassy plain where she had erected a makeshift corral near her cabin.

'*He is so stupid, that one!*'

Rob heard her mutter the words under her breath as she stared coldly at Matt. She coiled the long thong of her bullwhip, wrapping it slowly in equal loops, making sure it did not tangle. Then she did the same with the stiff rope lasso. As she did so, she gave Rob a searing glance.

'Maybe I should give up now before I make a bigger fool of myself,' he said, heaving himself to his feet, feeling every muscle in his body as if it had been trampled by a herd of cows instead of the one small bullock they were practising with.

'Go home now,' Gwyneth said softly. 'And make sure you take your friend with you. I do not care if he never comes back. A man who does not have respect for his horse does not get my respect.' Her eyes were blazing, the setting sun flickering in them like green fire. 'Or the respect of any other person. It does not matter how good a rider he is. He is vile.'

Rob brushed himself down, sending out clouds of fine red dust. He had not responded to her angry words, but he tended to agree with her. How had it taken him so long to realize just what kind of man his friend was?

Now, in the stockroom at the back of the

Co-op, he felt her eyes on him as Mr Jenkins slipped the tape measure around him just beneath his armpits, then measured his arms and his hips and leg length.

'The Widow Evans told me you were a big man,' he said eventually, studying the measurements he had written down. 'However, I'm sure I will be able to find something that will do.'

'As long as we're not talking burial caskets,' Rob said with a sardonic smile and a wink in Davy's direction.

Blodwen leaned forward, her white hair looking yellow, her face young in the lamplight, made even younger when she gave him one of her special smiles.

'You are being rigged out like a new ship ready to sail in search of the New World, Rob. If you are to live the life of a *gaucho*, you must feel and look the part.'

'Aye, well, we're all feeling our parts right now,' Davy grimaced and tentatively rubbed his backside.

'Don't worry,' Gwyneth said with an unexpected smile that flashed on and off so quickly that they would never have seen it had they not been watching her closely. 'There is always plenty of horse liniment at the *estancia*.'

'Nice thought,' Davy said with a rise of his

eyebrows and Rob was glad Matt wasn't there or he would have made some bawdy comment about who was going to rub it on him.

'The smell at least keeps the flies at bay — and other insects.' Again the hint of a secret smile as she turned for the door. 'I'll leave you to it, then, Mr Jenkins. You know what is required. And Rob — Davy . . . '

'Aye, Miss Johnns?' Davy was quick to respond politely, though she had already instructed them to call her by her first name.

'We leave early in the morning. Come by the cabin at six. I'll be waiting with the wagon and some extra horses. Blodwen has a list of what you should bring with you.'

And then she was gone, leaving a vague whiff of musky perfume in her wake, a product of leather, lavender and female perspiration all mingling. Rob breathed it in, felt it stir something in the pit of his stomach. He had to clear his throat before he could trust himself to speak.

'So what's the rush all of a sudden?' he asked, looking from Davy to Blodwen. 'I thought we had another week yet before we headed for the Andes.'

Blodwen reached up and wagged a crooked finger of warning under Davy's nose and the boy remained silent for once, his head bowed and his eyes staring at his shoes.

'I'll explain everything later, back at the house,' Blodwen said in a low voice, her attention on Jenkins the Co-op who was at the far end of the stockroom choosing underwear from a stack of variegated cardboard boxes.

Within half an hour Rob and Davy had their arms filled with packages containing all the things needed for a *gaucho* on the job. There were heavy-duty riding coats to keep out wind and rain, hide waistcoats, woollen shirts, red flannel underwear with more buttons than an accordion and great, flapping leather chaps to protect the trousers and the legs. What Rob and Davy treasured most of all, however, were the calf-high riding boots, and the real *gaucho* hat in black, stiffened woollen felt with its low crown, wide brim and shiny ribbon band.

'Just a minute, will you,' Rob said as an afterthought struck him and he collared Mr Jenkins about to lock up the store. 'Mr Jenkins. There's something else I want, if you would be good enough . . . ?'

'What is it?' Davy asked, a few minutes later as Rob jumped up beside him, clutching a small parcel wrapped in brown paper.

'Just a bit of a present,' Rob told him.

'Oh, aye? Who would that be for? Margaret?'

'Yes, maybe. Thought she might appreciate it . . . well, you know . . . '

He shrugged his shoulders and grinned inanely at his younger brother. Margaret hadn't exactly been in his mind, but he supposed, if he were sensible, it was a better idea than the one which had prompted him to buy it. When he got the chance, he would send it to her.

Back on the street, with the Co-op door locked firmly behind them, Blodwen took up the reins of the trap as soon as they were aboard and clicked her tongue at the two mules, who set off at a trot and with a great jingling of harness down the road to the little white house with the red roof.

Davy and Rob exchanged a look that confirmed how they felt about the adventure that lay ahead of them. They were both excited at the prospect of doing something so entirely different. Even Rob, who now rode as well as the other two after an uncertain start, was looking forward to his arrival at the *estancia*, where Gwyneth had secured them jobs as *gauchos*. He no longer wasted time on thoughts of returning home to England. Patagonia was, as yet, a foreign land to him, but he now felt he owed the place time to grow on him. It was no coincidence that he had changed his mind the first time he laid eyes on Gwyneth Johnns, for she was a sight that would grow easily on any man.

'Now then, Rob, my lad,' Blodwen said as they pulled up outside her house. 'No need to unpack this lot. You and Davy take the rig around to the back and mind you look after my mules well, so they'll be fresh to take you on your journey tomorrow. Then I want to see you both. There are things you must know that are weighing heavily on my conscience because maybe I've done wrong and I will live to regret it — or you will, one day, and I'll be mightily sorry for that, I can tell you.'

They did what she asked of them and found her, a few minutes later, sitting by her fire in the kitchen, rocking to and fro so gently, her eyes staring so hard into the flames, that they thought she had passed away and gone to that other place she spoke of so often when she was being maudlin and telling them that she did not have much longer for this world.

'Sit you down,' she said without opening her eyes. 'I will speak quietly so as not to disturb Dora who is resting.'

'Is it about Matt?' Rob asked. 'What's he done now?'

'You don't need worry about him,' Blodwen said, opening her eyes wide as she spoke, and glaring at them so hard it was like she was stabbing them with burning pokers. 'He's gone.'

'Gone?' Rob was on his feet, looking about the kitchen as if expecting Matt to walk in any minute with those merry eyes of his and that wicked smile that had deceived the heart of many an innocent young lass.

'How do you mean, gone, Aunty Blodwen?' Davy asked.

The old woman rocked more precariously now and they feared she would topple herself onto the floor in the ashes of her own fire.

'The sheriff came round today wanting to talk to him,' Blodwen said, her voice growing rough about the edges. 'It seems they found a dead person and they think he may have had something to do with it.'

'A — a dead person? Who?' Rob sat down again, heavily, the chair creaking beneath him.

'Miss Harris it was they found.' Blodwen took a deep breath and her chest seemed to rattle with the emotion that it dislodged.

'But what's that got to do with Matt?' Rob had to ask, though he was fairly sure he knew the answer, or part of it.

'Was she sick?' Davy said, though his quick glance at his brother conveyed his own real fears about Matt.

'She wasn't a well woman,' Blodwen told

them. 'Not after she lost her parents. She was a timid soul, not given to mixing well. She had no friends, you see, which is why she wasn't found until this morning when a boy kicked a stone through her window and saw her lying there. Or what was left of her, for the rats and mice had devoured a good part of her flesh and she was running with maggots. The police think she was murdered and somebody saw Matthew in the vicinity. The night of the fire at McGinty's Tavern, it was.'

'Aye,' Rob said, remembering. 'He was high on something that night all right.'

Davy just stared, shocked into silence. Rob's head fell into his hands and he groaned like a man in great pain.

'Dear God,' he said. 'I should have known something like this would happen. I saw it coming, but I didn't think he would go this far.'

'What do you mean, Rob?' Davy said, a worried treble in his voice.

Rob lifted his head and fixed him with a haunted stare.

'Remember how we got our tickets for the boat to come here, Davy?' he said. 'After they told us there wasn't a place to be had? Then there was a fight of some sort and a man died. His attacker left him lying in the road and ran off. We ended up with that man's tickets — for him and his family. They were going to build a new and happy life for themselves and . . . ' Rob swallowed back a mouthful of bile as he thought of it and said out loud for the first time the words that had bothered him somewhere at the back of his mind since they had left Wales. 'It was something he said, the way he acted. It made me suspect that he was involved in the man's death. I brushed it aside. I mean, how can you believe your best mate of a lifetime can happily kill somebody?'

'Aye,' Davy said, remembering. 'He was sitting there whistling and looking pleased with himself and all the time . . . '

'Where is he Blodwen?'

Blodwen stopped rocking. She pushed herself to her feet and rested on her hands, leaning over the table, addressing the two brothers.

'It's not for you to worry,' she told them firmly, though her eyes betrayed the hurt she was feeling in her heart. 'There is no proof that he did these terrible deeds. He obtained the dead man's tickets, yes, but that does not say that he murdered him in order to do so. He may have visited Miss Harris — though, knowing her, I doubt he got past her front door without a struggle.'

'Where is he, Blodwen?' Rob persisted.

'I don't know, son, and that's God's honest truth. The police knocked on my door. He was here beside me at the time, but by the time I answered the summons, he had gone. He did not even stay long enough to say goodbye to Dora. I can only say, good riddance, and I hope the Dear Lord keeps him away from this place.'

'Amen to that,' Rob said and Davy stared at them both, blinking and not daring to say that he hoped the Good Lord would send Matthew Riley directly to Hell.

11

Dora was pale-faced, but dry-eyed when she emerged from her room. They did not speak of Matt. Blodwen had warned them well to keep off the subject, but their silence was short-lived when there was a loud knocking on the door.

The sheriff and a representative of the Committee of Elders entered the room, looking as if they meant business.

'Mrs Matthew Riley?' Sheriff Dawson said, a menacing look in his eye that made poor Dora quake visibly. 'That necklace around your neck. It's been identified as that belonging to the murdered woman, Miss Martha Harris. How did you come by it?'

Dora licked her lips and looked at Davy before replying.

'Matt gave it to me.'

'Give it here, ma'am.' The sheriff was a brusque North American, efficient at his job, but lacking in any sensitivity.

Dora quickly removed the pendant with shaking fingers and handed it over.

'I don't want it anyway,' she said in a tiny, quivering little-girl voice. 'Matt said he bought it for me, but if he stole it, I don't want it no more.'

'It's not yours to keep, ma'am. The owner was killed and it was ripped from her neck.'

Dora looked horrified.

'Oh, please! Don't!' she cried.

'Leave the child alone,' Blodwen admonished. 'She knows nothing.'

Sheriff Dawson then turned to Rob and Davy, but after brief questioning seemed satisfied with the answers they gave him. Blodwen fairly threw the two lawmen out of her house when they began probing more deeply into the affairs of the three Geordie lads from the time they had stepped off the boat. Matt was already well known for his drinking and brawling, so there was nothing to deny there. However, she would not have them say a wrong word about Rob and Davy and they took the hint.

'You're not of our people,' Glyn Morgan, the leader of the Committee of Elders said as he turned on the widow's doorstep and fixed his eye on the two brothers. 'However, I've heard nothing but good of you and I'm told that you have found yourselves ranch work. All power to your elbow, I say. But if Riley turns up, wherever you are, you tell him to report to me — or to the sheriff here. He's a rotten apple and he'll taint everything and everyone he touches.'

Rob heard a small gasp from behind him, where Dora was hiding, pressed up against his back. He could feel the tremors of fear rippling through her. Rob knew that his brother was hurting for the lass too, perhaps more than anybody, for he didn't want to leave her behind.

In the early hours of the next morning, Blodwen, who had not slept a wink, shook their shoulders and ordered them to be up and getting their belongings together.

'Come, be off with you now, look you,' she said, hugging them both when they had dressed and sipped the hot herbal tea she had prepared for them together with great wedges of bacon sandwiches and apple cake for the journey. 'I daresay I shall miss you, but it will be nice to call my home my own again.'

'Does that mean you don't want us to come back, Aunty Blodwen?' Davy asked and she gave a little chuckle and touched cold fingers to his cheek.

'I didn't say that, now, did I?' She clucked her tongue at the pair of them and shook her head. 'No. You'll be back, and welcome you will be, but mind you make the most of your opportunities, whatever they are. And just remember, you can always come back here if you want to.'

She wagged a mocking finger at them, not daring to say another word lest she show them the emotion that was welling up in her ancient breast. She had not felt quite so emotional since her beloved Huw died in her arms, and here she was filling up with tears for two English boys she hardly knew. She must be older than she thought.

Davy hugged the old woman and felt the tightness of her love for him in those stringy arms of hers. Then it was Rob's turn. He towered over her, shyly offering his hand, which she took in both of hers, and she pulled the back of his fingers to her soft pink lips, kissing him as she would a lover who had chosen to go his separate way.

'Goodbye, Blodwen, and thank you for everything you've done for us.' He bent and kissed her flaccid cheek, whispering as he did so: 'And I'm sorry that Matt was not the nephew he should have been.'

'Sorry? What have you to be sorry for, Robert Barker? There's bad blood in every family, if you look hard and long enough.'

'Take care,' Rob said gravely, his eyes sliding over to where Dora was standing on anxious tiptoes at the front door, watching Davy mount on the trap that was piled high with carpetbags and trunks and boxes. 'And take care of Dora for us, eh?'

Blodwen nodded. No need for words of assurance on that score. They had found some common thread that bound them together, despite the great difference in their ages.

Rob squeezed Dora's arm as he passed through the doorway, heading for the trap and the restless mules that danced on the spot, anxious to be away. 'And when we come back, you'll . . . '

He got no further. Dora, as if catapulted from the house, threw herself bodily at him, though it was Davy her eyes sought out as she pleaded with them both.

'Take me with you! Oh, please, don't leave me!'

Blodwen came to her, touched her shoulder. 'Come now, girl, none of that. How can they take you with them?'

She had not reminded Dora that she had a husband out there somewhere, hiding from the law. Nor did she remonstrate with the girl for preferring to be with her husband's friends rather than wait for the return of the man she married, however long that might take.

'Ach, man, Rob,' Davy shouted from the high seat on the trap, where he already had the reins held tightly in his hands. 'Can we not take her? Where's the harm?'

The four of them fell into a heavy silence that seemed to last an eternity. Rob looked at Davy, whose eyes were full of pleading, then at Dora, then finally at Blodwen. The window's lips fell apart and she breathed deeply as she tried to stem the words that forced their way to the surface, words she knew the Elders would criticize her for. But then, she was well used to their criticisms. Hadn't she had a lifetime of them? They fell on her like rain on a fathomless ocean, making hardly a ripple.

'It would be selfish of me to say that I would prefer her to stay,' she told them kindly. 'Dora, my dearest, most lovely girl — do you truly want to go with these two and take your chances on the *estancia*?'

Dora turned to face her, eyes wide and brimming with tears.

'Oh, Aunty Blodwen, how can you ask? You, who know how it has been with me. I love you, you know that too. I always will. But . . .'

'Then go. These boys will look after you. Gwyneth Johnns too. She is not the she-Devil people say she is, though she sometimes acts the part. She, too, has had a taste of Matthew Riley and — forgive me for saying this, Dora — she did what you should have done and spat him out.'

Dora looked down at the ground, humiliated, but it was a momentary thing. At the sound of an impatient braying from one of the mules, she spun on her heel, ran into the house and reappeared, half in and half out of her woollen cloak and shawl and dragging a canvas bag with items of clothing escaping from the fastenings. Davy was down from his seat like a flash. He stopped long enough to gaze into her eyes. She smiled up at him, then he took the bag from her and threw it onto the trap before lifting her up with a quick look to Rob for approval.

Rob felt it would not have mattered a jot what he said at that moment. What he was sure of was that it was the correct thing to do. If ever a girl was right for his little brother, Dora was that girl. It was a pity, however, that she had married Matt. One day, no doubt, the bastard would turn up and claim her back, as was his lawful right.

'Best be off, and quick about it,' Blodwen said, her voice a faint croak in the pre-dawn silence. 'My blessings go with you and I shall expect a letter or two to let me know how you are faring.'

Rob nodded, too choked for words. He climbed up beside Davy and took the reins.

'You look after Dora,' he said to Davy, trying to sound nonchalant and finding it nigh impossible. 'Don't let her fall off. It's a rough track between here and Gwyneth Johnns's shack and it'll still be dark when we get there.'

He set the mules off at a brisk walk, looking briefly over his shoulder. Blodwen was standing stock still, one hand raised in a farewell gesture. As he looked, the moon came out from behind the dark night clouds and he could have sworn he saw tears glistening on her cheeks. A hard woman, she had told them she was. Aye, and maybe she was for some things, but underneath she was as soft as butter and her heart was as warm as the summer sun.

★ ★ ★

The light was playing about the ridge of the foothills as they reached the shack with its yellow-lit windows and a thin spiral of smoke rising from the one narrow chimney. Gwyneth was already outside, saddling up the horses. Close to her a group of guanacos were grazing. They lifted their heads and scattered at the sound of the approaching party.

'So, you have come at last!' she called to them in a voice that was not too pleased. 'I expected you half an hour ago. We are losing precious daylight.'

Then her eyes found Dora and she stared uncomprehendingly at the girl, before seeking out Rob's attention.

'What is this? I expected three men, not two men and a girl.'

All three on the trap spoke in unison.

'I'll explain,' said Rob.

'It's a long story,' said Davy.

'I'm sorry!' said Dora.

Gwyneth approached them, her sharp gaze scouring the three new arrivals and their luggage.

'Your friend — the ugly one. He is not with you?'

Rob shook his head. 'No. It seems he had other plans, but we have brought Dora because . . . '

'I'm sorry, Miss Johnns,' Dora apologized yet again. 'It's not their fault. I made them bring me.'

'We couldn't leave her,' Rob said quickly, seeing how Gwyneth drew in a deep breath and straightened her shoulders, which made her look tall and intimidating.

'Aye,' said Davy, his chest expanding proudly. 'If you don't take Dora, then you don't get us and that's all there is to be said about it. Isn't that so, Rob?'

Rob suppressed a smile. Davy was still playing at being a man, but he wasn't doing

235

such a bad job at that. He nodded his agreement.

'Yes, I'm afraid so.'

'I'm not afraid of hard work,' Dora said. 'I'll do anything, but I won't go back to . . .'

'To Puerto Daffyd?' Gwyneth asked with a toss of her fine head. 'Or to that husband of yours?'

Dora's chin dropped onto her chest. She plainly did not know what to say to this bold and larger than life female. Rob thought he understood a little of how she was feeling. Gwyneth scared him too a little. Or was it something inside him that unnerved him?

Rob cleared his throat and laid a protective hand on Dora's shoulder.

'Matt's got himself into some trouble,' he said. 'It seems he's wanted by the sheriff — for murder.'

Gwyneth's fine head shot back. 'So! He's on the run?'

Rob nodded, then inclined his head towards Dora. 'We thought she would be safer with us,' he said softly, his eyes pleading with Gwyneth to understand.

He needn't have worried. Like old Blodwen Evans, Gwyneth was quick to comprehend a situation, even without words.

'I don't doubt that for one moment,' she

said. 'Are you sure this is what you want, girl?'

'Yes,' Dora whispered, blinking fiercely.

'Let's be off then, shall we?' Gwyneth said determinedly.

Fortunately, for Dora, they were taking a wagon full of supplies back to the *estancia*, so there was no question of the pregnant girl having to ride a horse. Not, Rob mused, that he thought she had ever been on one. He himself had done no more than ride a donkey along the sands at South Shields when he was a child before Gwyneth had put him through his paces. That same boy would never have believed, in all his dreams, that he would one day be a *gaucho* riding the plains of Patagonia. If his pitmen friends could see him now, they would never believe their eyes.

A ripple of excitement gripped him as they started forward. He could see Dora gripping the iron rail of the seat she was sharing with Gwyneth, her eyes wide and her rosebud mouth tight as she tried not to show her fear. The Welsh-*Indios* girl sat erect as she guided the wagon mules competently over the rough, bumpy track, heading towards the Andes.

Rob's thoughts wandered back to Gateshead and the girl he had left behind. How Margaret would have hated all this. He felt guilty about her every time he thought of the way he had presented her with his plans for the future, which in no way could have included her, he knew that now. She had broken off the engagement without a moment's reflection and he had walked away lighter of heart and spirit than he had been in a long while, glad that she had set him free. No wonder he felt guilty.

The horse beneath him stumbled and almost jettisoned Rob out of his saddle. He managed to right himself, feeling more than a little foolish, especially when he caught the look Gwyneth gave him.

'What were you thinking of just then?' she asked him as the mules pulled up, unable to pass until he moved on.

'Just dreaming,' he told her, pulling his *gaucho* hat down low over his eyes, for the sun was on the rise and the glare was blinding him.

'A girl, no doubt,' Gwyneth said, her eyes narrowing. 'Someone from the Old Country? Or is it someone you have met here?'

'I don't know anybody here,' he said, urging his horse to go forward, though it was intent on seeking a particularly luscious clump of grass on the low side of the track.

'Hey, Rob, were you thinking about Margaret, then?' Davy said with a grin, then he winked at Gwyneth. 'I'll bet he's missing her at last, is that not so, Rob?'

Rob scowled at his brother, willing him to shut up. He wished his horse would behave too so they could continue on their long trek. Most of all, he wished that Gwyneth would stop looking at him the way she did. He couldn't figure out that look of hers. There was mistrust in it, aye, and curiosity too, but there was also something else. Whatever that something was, it scorched him to the root of his being and made him more than a little uncomfortable.

'Get your horse under control, Rob,' Gwyneth said with stern authority. 'You are both too excited and that can be a dangerous thing.'

By God, Rob thought, she can read minds too.

'I'll do my best, but he seems to have a mind of his own this morning.'

She tossed him a half-smile that almost softened the hard expression in her blue-green eyes.

'You stallions are all alike. Gelding is the only cure, but the horse you are on is good for breeding.'

'What's gelding mean?' Davy asked.

'It's what Gwyneth here will do to you if you don't behave,' Rob said, trying to keep things light and he saw Gwyneth's eyes grow large, then she laughed, a wonderfully joyful sound.

'Come on. Enough talk,' she said, the laughter drying up and her face once more a mysterious mask. 'We have many miles ahead of us and a pass to negotiate before we set up camp.'

★　★　★

It had been a good idea to hide in that stupid bitch's house. The dumb sheriff would never think to look for him here. Matt stretched out on Miss Harris's bed and crossed his feet at the ankles. He would keep his boots on. There was no telling when he might have to flee, though he felt perfectly safe here in the house of the woman he had murdered.

He frowned down at the toecaps of his work boots, and then stared up at the ceiling. It was a strange feeling, being a fugitive. He had often escaped by the skin of his teeth back in England, but from leaving the North-East, life and the way he lived it had changed drastically. It had never been in his head to kill anyone, but it had happened. He had beaten up that fella in order to get his hands on the boat tickets. He had thought that maybe the man would have handed over the tickets without too much fuss, but he had put up a god almighty struggle. Matt hadn't expected him to die like that.

Then there was the woman. Miss Harris ought not to have fought him off like that, as if he were some kind of leper. No, she should have been nicer to him and she would still be breathing right now, instead of buried in the local cemetery alongside the rest of her family.

'Stupid bitch!' he said to the air that was rapidly chilling around him. 'Served her right.'

He tried to sleep, but somehow it wouldn't come. His head was full of jumbled thoughts. If it hadn't been for that half-breed girl whipping him like that, he wouldn't be in this situation. And if it hadn't been for the fire that destroyed McGinty's Tavern, he would have been able to appease himself with one of the girls and there wouldn't have been the need to seek out that dried-up old virgin. And if . . .

Ah, God, he thought. There were too many 'ifs'. And now he had missed out on going with Rob to that *estancia* and he felt all chewed up about that. Rob was going to have a fair crack at the *Indios* girl. His mate might pretend not to be interested, but he'd seen the way he'd looked at Gwyneth Johnns. Crafty beggar! He'd soon be trying to get his feet under her table. That Rob knew what he was doing, casting off all ties with his girl back home. It was a pity he, Matt, had lumbered himself with a wife, but he had thought there might not be any decent female flesh for the taking over here. How wrong he had been.

Matt's thoughts flashed onto Dora. She was useless as a wife, and no better than any of the other daft lasses he had bedded in his time. In fact, she was worse. She didn't even enjoy him. All she could do was screw her face up and squirm the minute he put his hands on her. That old hag, Blodwen, had said that Dora was carrying a bairn. Matt shuddered, though he wasn't sure whether it was his fear of being tied down to responsibilities of the family kind, or whether there was some deep-seated pride inside him. At least he wasn't firing blanks.

Matt's lips pulled back, showing a self-indulgent grin. Unless every girl he had impregnated in his time ran off to some back street abortionist, he was at least populating the earth with a sprinkling of little Matthew Rileys that would grow up and be just like him.

With a grunt and a long sigh, Matt turned on his side and pulled the coverlet up over his head. Might as well get some rest while the law was looking for him. As soon as things cooled down he'd be off, heading into the mountains where nobody would ever find him. The place was too vast. He'd heard talk of great glacier fields and floating icebergs as big as houses. It shouldn't be too difficult to get lost in among that lot.

It would be lonely though, unless he had a bit of female company. Well, if he played his cards right, that could be taken care of too. He licked his lips like a bear dreaming of honey. The vision in his head changed from Dora to Gwyneth Johnns. Now there was a prize not to be ignored. Separate her from her rifle and her whip and she'd be putty in his hands, especially if she couldn't call on anybody to come to her rescue.

With a soft groan of anticipation, he sank down further into the bed, smelling the perfume of the dead spinster and delighting in the soft warmth of her feather-filled mattress and eiderdown. Soon, he thought. He would catch up with them soon.

He was on the verge of sleep when he remembered the silver pendant he had removed from Miss Harris's thick neck as she lay, gasping her last, on the floor beneath him. He didn't know why he had done that, but it seemed like a good idea to give Dora a little present that might sweeten her up some.

'Jesus!' Matt sat up with a jerk, the eiderdown flying off him and slithering down to the floor.

That necklace was the one thing that would prove, without a shadow of a doubt, his guilt. If anyone recognized it, they would guess that he had been the one to choke the life out of Miss Harris. No amount of lying and prevaricating on his part would get him out of that. Right now, they just wanted him for questioning. They had their suspicions and no man was hanged on suspicion alone. With the pendant as prime evidence, and that stupid bitch Dora telling all and sundry that he had given it to her only hours after the death of the other woman . . .

Matt was on his feet in a trice. He pulled on his overcoat and went to peer through the closed curtains. The road outside was empty and silent, but for a cat gliding along, tail held high, in search of prey. It moved stealthily, a small black silhouette. He followed its progress. When it reached the middle of the road the animal seemed to sense that it was not entirely alone. The feline head lifted, the moonlight turning its eyes into almond-shaped, iridescent orbs. It looked directly at Matt and, as if he had looked into the eyes of Satan himself, he jumped back, letting the curtain fall.

'Bliddy moggy!' He swore in a rasping whisper as he hurried down the stairs and let himself carefully out through the back door, checking every direction before turning his feet towards Widow Evans's house.

* * *

Blodwen was sleeping in her usual light fashion, waking and dozing and thinking that she hadn't slept at all, for didn't she look at the clock, or so it seemed, every hour on the hour. And her mind wouldn't let her be, so busy it was with the events of the last few weeks. Round and round her head the images played themselves out, sometimes the same, sometimes changing and making her wonder if she was getting senile in her old age.

She was certainly very tired, so she asked the Good Lord to give her mind a little peace to allow her to recuperate. However, the fourth time she looked at the clock above the mantelpiece, with the little night candle glowing beside it, she decided that God must be busy elsewhere and so she must make do with her inadequate snatches of sleep.

Of course, the minute she did fall into a deeper, more comfortable sleep, there was a noise that disturbed her and set her heart beating like a trapped butterfly in her chest.

She had been dreaming that Huw was there with her and she was marvelling on how young and handsome he still was. And he, in his way, was joking with her and telling her that he was half a century older and so was she.

It was on his laugh, that lovely mellow sound, that the noise filtered through to her subconscious mind. Had it been a knock, some heavy hand beating on her door? Something falling? She struggled to sit up, propping herself on one elbow and showing only her eyes and her nose to the darkness of the room, the night candle having snuffed itself long ago.

'Rob? Davy?' Her voice echoed thinly through the emptiness of the house. 'Is that you?'

When there was no reply, Blodwen remembered that the boys were no longer with her. They were somewhere out there on the plains, heading for the *estancia* with Gwyneth. Not even Dora was here to keep her company. She would miss that girl, especially now that the winter was drawing in and the hours would be tedious, stretching into the dark at both ends of every day.

Something grated or scratched in the corner of the room. She swivelled her head in the direction of the noise, willing her old eyes to adjust to the blackness that surrounded her. It could be a mouse or a snake or even a cockroach, though they weren't usually to be found in her house. She was far too fastidious still with her house-hold chores.

Another scratching sound and, at the very moment when she saw a flame leap into life only feet from her nose, she recognized it as the scrape of a match on a flint. Just for a second, her heart stopped beating and a weak cry escaped her lips as Matt's face was illuminated in an eerie yellow light that flickered and made him look evil and unreal.

'Don't make a sound, Aunty Blodwen,' he said and his voice grated on her nerves. 'Not a sound, do you hear?'

'I hear you all right, Matthew Riley,' Blodwen blurted out and then took a gulp of sulphur-tinged air before she could go on, thinking that any minute now she would breathe her last. 'What are you doing here? Don't you know that the law is after you.'

'I came to get my belongings,' he said, ignoring her words and lighting the oil lamp that sat on a table near the door. 'You stay where you are and I won't hurt you.'

'I should think you won't hurt me,' she said, thrusting her chin at him and fixing him with a piercing stare. 'Why would you be wanting to harm a helpless old lady anyway?'

Blodwen drew the covers more tightly about her, holding them bunched up in her fists under her chin. She watched his every move, but he did not meet her gaze. Perhaps he could not meet her gaze for the guilt he must be carrying inside him.

He had entered through the scullery at the back, she guessed, since why else was he standing there in her kitchen when she was respectably tucked up in bed with her hair in braids and her nightdress wound tightly around her haunches, so turbulent her sleep had been?

Matt gave her a cursory glance over his shoulder as he opened the door that led into Rob's room. He put his head in, then returned to her, standing over her, lamp raised. He was unshaven and she could smell the rancid odour of his perspiration and alcohol-tainted breath. How any relation of her Huw could give life to a creature like this, she could not fathom.

'Where's Dora?' he asked gruffly. 'The place is all locked up. I had to break in through the scullery. Where is she?'

Blodwen shook her head. She was having difficulty finding her voice. He looked so big and mean and ugly he frightened her.

'She's not here,' she told him, trying not to show him her fear, for she knew better than to show fear to any wild animal since it would like as not provoke even more aggression.

'Where is she, I asked?' Matt's free hand rose and she thought he was going to strike her, but it hovered there above her face, threatening, demanding a reply that would satisfy him.

'She went with Rob and Davy,' she told him. 'After all, what is there here for the poor little mite?'

This time, Matt's hand did come down, with force, catching Blodwen a blow across the temple and one eye. She fell to the side with a gasp of pain and curled into a small ball in the middle of the bed.

'You old witch! This is all your doing. You encouraged her to keep company with those two. Well, I'm going after her, do you hear? But if you whisper a word of this to anybody I'll be back in the dead of some night and finish you off. Now, where's this *estancia*, eh?'

When she did not respond immediately, he punched her, splitting her lip. She felt the fragile skin break open and tasted the salt of her own blood.

'I don't know where it is,' she said, her voice muffled as she attempted to staunch the bleeding.

'Of course you know where it is, Aunty

Blodwen! You know what they say about you, the Widow Evans? She knows everything there is to know and more. That's what they say. Now, where is this bleedin' ranch?'

Blodwen shook her head and held a hand up in front of her face to protect herself from his next blow. But it didn't come. He just stood there, glaring down at her, his eyes small and mean, his mouth firmly set.

'It's the truth,' she muttered. 'I don't know. Gwyneth works for people called Gomez-Pan. It's way out in the foothills, somewhere to the west of here. I swear, that's all I know, may God help me.'

He stared at her some more, but she relaxed, for his anger was spent. He was a dangerous man; he had killed now more than once, so she could not understand why he was going to leave her clinging on to what threads of life she had left in her. That was between Matt and his god, if he indeed had a god.

'Where's your money, Aunty Blodwen?' he asked, his eyes skimming the room.

Blodwen blinked at him through a blur, for her left eye had closed and her head was swimming and throbbing with pain.

'Don't call me that!' she said with all the feisty spirit she could muster. 'You are no nephew of mine, great or otherwise.'

'I know you keep money in the house. Where is it?'

Blodwen slid her hand beneath her pillow and drew out her day purse, which contained enough money to pay for food and any other necessary items. Thankfully, the bulk of what money she still had was safely deposited in the bank above the Co-op, and there it would stay until she died, but this ruffian would get none of it, she would make sure of that. She thanked Heaven that she had lied when she sent money to England, claiming it to be her life savings.

'Here! Take it and get out of my house. You are not fit to set foot in here, so don't ever think of coming back, look you!'

Matt grabbed the purse, weighed it in his hand, looked thoughtful for a moment, then, putting it in his pocket, he left the house the way he had entered it.

Blodwen felt a little of her life escape in a hot waft of air as she breathed out and realized she had been holding her breath, fearing the worst. Shakily, she got out of bed and staggered feebly to the scullery to make sure that Matt had, indeed, gone. She was relieved to find that she was alone, though he had left the door wide open, hanging off its hinges where he had forced it, probably with a kick from his big foot.

'I shall have to get Morgan the carpenter to look at that tomorrow,' she said, regretting the fact that Rob was no longer there to take care of things, though if he had been, there might have been a rare fight between him and his old friend, with young Davy joining in for good measure. She would not have liked that. Oh, no. She hated the thought of her two lovely boys being hurt.

As best she could, she pushed the door closed and pulled her old poss tub in front of it, dragging it inch by painful inch. It took a long time and at the end of it she was exhausted, but satisfied that she had done all there was to be done to keep out any likely intruders.

She was too nervous and her face hurt too much to allow her even to contemplate sleep, so she wrapped herself in a quilt and sat in her chair by the fire, which she rekindled. And like that, she waited for the dawn and daylight to make the situation better. Tomorrow, she would report Matt to the authorities. What a fool the boy was, to think that she would keep silent about his visit. He had threatened her, yes, but she was sure he would never again show his face in Puerto Daffyd. If he did, he would be for the hangman's noose and no mistake.

Gingerly, her shaking fingers traced the

contours of her misshapen face, remoulded by Matt's fist. What a pretty sight she would present to the Elders when she made her report. No doubt she would have an endless stream of visitors. All the ladies of the town would be down on her like a ton of bricks, finding fault, but being secretly glad that they had something to keep their tongues busy for weeks to come. She would have to buy in a larger than usual supply of tea and make scones and cakes as soon as she was able to see well enough. She might be old and infirm, but she still knew how to be a good hostess.

12

They had been travelling for days before they were able to see mountains rising through distant mists. Days turned into weeks before the ghostly shapes were transformed into solid masses of granite as the plains gradually gave way to undulating foothills and small, frozen lakes.

The Andes themselves were like no other mountains Rob had ever seen. He remembered looking at photographs and paintings of Scottish mountains like Ben Nevis with its rounded hump and those of Switzerland with their snowy peaks, but these great fingers of rock pointing vertically to the sky were far more breathtaking.

'Gawd almighty!' Davy breathed every few hundred yards as the scenery changed at each bend in the dirt track on which they were travelling.

'Oh, it's lovely!' Dora kept exclaiming, though Rob noticed that she kept holding on to the side of the wagon with one hand, while the other gripped Davy. 'But it's awful scary.'

Gwyneth gave a smile and urged her mount forward, joining Rob up front. She had handed over the wagon to Davy and was having a spell on horseback. Rob thought she looked an absolute natural sitting there astride that great black stallion that he would not have the nerve to ride. The two seemed to be moulded together as one entity.

In one graceful motion she swept off her wide-brimmed hat and wiped the back of her hand across her glistening forehead. They were riding into the sun and although the year was well on through autumn and winter was already declaring itself, it was warm work. They had been on the move since dawn, which is how it was every day, after making camp as soon as darkness fell.

Rob and Davy had a small tent to sleep in and the girls shared what little space there was in the covered wagon. Gwyneth was always the last to bed down and the first to rise in the morning. So far, she had kept herself to herself, not showing any interest in conversation or closeness of any sort. Rob supposed he couldn't blame her for that, but it would be more cordial to get to know her better. Or, as well as she would allow him to know her, and he suspected that this would be more than a little difficult.

'How far now, Gwyneth?' he asked, falling in beside her as she kicked her horse into a slow gallop over a flat, grassy plain.

'We're almost there,' she told him, her eyes fixed on the way ahead. 'There's a pass a few miles on. There'll be ice and snow and it'll be very cold until we get to the other side. I hope you have warm clothes with you.'

Rob nodded, smiling to himself as he remembered the red flannel underwear they all had packed in their valises, not to mention the heavy leather and canvas overcoats and thick woollen shirts and socks. Well, it might get a bit cold out here, he thought, but it would have to go a long way to beat the damp coldness of the north-east of England.

'I'm worried about Dora,' he said as he saw the terrain changing, making their progress more difficult. 'She doesn't complain, but the lass doesn't look well.'

'I hear she is carrying a child,' Gwyneth said and he saw her cheek muscles twitch.

'Aye, that's right.' He thought he saw her face set, but when she turned her gaze on him, she had recovered her bland expression.

'I assume it's the seed of that husband of hers?' she said, her eyes narrowing perceptively.

'Yes, of course! You don't think for one minute . . . '

'I try not to think. Nor do I judge.'

Well, Rob thought, though he kept his

opinion to himself, you might say that, but by God I don't believe it.

'She's better off without him,' he told her, having to raise his voice because there was a sudden gusty wind that was surging over the planes, flattening the grasses and bending what few trees there were.

The horse beneath him pulled at the reins, wanting to turn, wanting to get away from *El Pampero*. The animal tossed its head, showing him the white of an eye and teeth that chewed and slavered at its bridle.

'Keep control!' Gwyneth shouted. 'Hold him steady.'

But Rob had already lost the reins and his balance. When a huge, rolling ball of pampas grass came rolling past them, his mount rose on its hind legs with a great whinnying and Rob tumbled out of the saddle. Just before he hit the ground he saw the whole scene go upside down, heard anxious shouts from Davy and Dora. Then he landed, winded and seeing stars.

There was a thunder of hoofs as Gwyneth rode by him after the escaping horse.

'Take care of your brother!' he heard her shout and then everything went black.

When he came to, it was Gwyneth, not Davy or Dora, who was sitting by him, her arm about his shoulders, a flask at his lips.

257

He tasted brandy, hot and fiery, the way the *gauchos* liked it.

He pulled a face and struggled to get up, but she held him down with a hand flat upon his chest.

'Look at me,' she ordered in a voice that was low and supposed to be unfeeling, but he thought he detected a tremor in it as if she might be worried about him after all, though she was not about to admit it. 'What can you see?'

He blinked up at her, then looked from her to Davy and Dora, both of whom looked shocked and white-faced. Then he looked beyond them to where his wayward horse was tethered and quietly grazing alongside that of Gwyneth's stallion.

'Well, I can see where your priorities lie,' he said with a grin that turned into a grimace of pain as he felt the bump on his head.

'You hit your head on a rock,' Gwyneth told him. 'As for my priorities, had I not gone after your horse we would have lost him and a lot of good that would have done us, unless you fancy walking from here to the *estancia*. I'm trying to find out if you have concussion. How many of me can you see?'

'One,' he said, rubbing his head where it hurt. 'And that's more than enough for any man.'

She quickly removed her arm from around him and got to her feet, surveying the landscape and the sky above them.

'Then let us get on. I think it will snow tonight. You had better replace Davy in the wagon.'

Rob struggled to his feet and was in time to see Dora's fleeting look of disappointment at having to give up holding on to Davy. It was a cosy sight, the two of them snuggled up close together. He wondered if Blodwen, had she been there, would approve. Somehow, he thought, she would not see too much wrong in it.

He was about to argue, but the fall had shaken him up and he had no fancy for remounting a skittish horse just yet. Besides, Gwyneth was already tying the young gelding to the back of the wagon and Davy was jumping into the saddle of the docile mare they had brought with them.

Just before they set off, Gwyneth came round to the front of the wagon and placed a gentle hand on Dora's knee.

'Are you all right, Dora? The road is going to get rough from now on.'

'Oh, yes, I'm all right,' Dora said with a brave little smile and her hands went protectively around her stomach.

'Good, because I don't want us to have to

stop yet. There's another range of high hills to cross, but the pass is short and not too difficult. On the other side, we will find shelter and can bed down for the night.'

'I'm fine, really, Gwyneth.' Dora nodded gravely and glanced at Rob, who was now beside her, holding the reins to the two mules pulling the wagon. That look told him that she thought anything was preferable than being left at the mercy of her husband were he to return to Puerto Daffyd.

Rob wondered, as they started off again, what Matt was doing right at that moment. He hoped to God the law had caught up with him. And yet, another small part of him, the part that still held on to their shared boyhood friendship, felt a stab of pity for Matt. Because of his stupidity, Matt had given up the chance of a good life. What price his dream of a golden-paved future now?

'Get them moving, Rob!' Gwyneth yelled at him through the howling wind. 'Davy, ride ahead with me and keep an eye out for hidden boulders.'

Davy's cheeks were rosy. The wind was making his eyes water, but he gave her a cheeky grin and touched a finger to the brim of his hat that was tied tightly under his chin with a plaited cord. He gave Rob a wink.

'Yes, ma'am!' he said with a wink at Rob,

then he turned the mare to follow Gwyneth, who was already galloping away on Diablo.

Dora leaned into Rob as they trundled and bounced their way over the rough track, following in Gwyneth and Davy's dust cloud.

'I know they call her names,' Dora said, pursing her lips as she thought seriously about what she was trying to say. 'You know, they say she's wild and wicked and all that. But I think she's nice, don't you?'

Rob smiled down at her and nodded.

'Yes, Dora, I do.'

★   ★   ★

Blodwen looked at the semicircle of faces aligned in her living room. They looked back at her in a brooding silence while they waited for their leader to arrive. If she looked above the stiff, unyielding expressions of the Committee, she could see the purplish-black sky, storm-ridden and threatening. Rain spattered relentlessly on the windowpanes and despite the added warmth of so many bodies squashed elbow to elbow in her little house, the room felt cold and cheerless.

Between her and the Elders, a table groaned beneath the weight of her hospitality and she, for one, hoped they would not be kept waiting for too much longer, for she felt peckish, having not stopped to eat since breakfast and she had made a very special custard tart for the occasion.

The kettle had been boiled more than once, but the tea would not be made until Mr Hughes the Elder of all the Elders, and minister at the chapel, appeared. He had a wedding and three funerals to conduct today and would undoubtedly turn up a little the worse for forbidden wine, but never mind that. She just wanted this business, this unofficial court, to be over and done with.

There was the sound of quickening footsteps, light on the timber sidewalk that lined the street, a new and great improvement to ankle-deep mud when it rained and knee-high dust when it didn't.

'Ah!' Winifred Jenkins, who considered herself the unwritten dowager duchess of Puerto Daffyd, raised her long nose and one finger into the air. 'I do believe that Mr Hughes is about to descend.'

Blodwen gave her a stony look, the kind she reserved for people she considered to be more stupid than the rest.

'Well, it is to be hoped he uses the front door and doesn't try to come down through the chimney,' she said, and one or two of the group let go their stern expressions long enough to titter behind their hands.

There was a timid tap on the door and everyone sat to attention as the door creaked open and the minister's bony face appeared, followed by his long and equally bony body. Oh, but he was a poor specimen of manhood, Blodwen thought with a frown as Mr Hughes sidled into the room with a series of nervous nods that finally got around to Blodwen herself.

'Widow Evans,' he said in his weedy voice, and as he bowed over her extended hand she caught the whiff of something stronger than tea. 'I trust that you are well and fully recovered from . . . ' He cleared his throat, unable to pronounce the words that truly described what had happened to Blodwen. ' . . . from your little accident.'

'Sit you down, Mr Hughes,' she said austerely. 'And before I make us some tea to go with my cakes, I want you to know that my 'little accident', as you put it, was neither little nor an accident. My great-nephew beat me up and threatened me with my life, and the lives of others if I reported it. However, I was never one to fall foul of blackmail. The boy needs catching and, may the Lord forgive me, stringing up. I had no hand in the creating or the raising of him, so I'll thank you to remember that.'

'Oh, Widow Evans . . . I . . . oh, really . . .

I . . . ' Mr Hughes' hands were fluttering about before his face like pale moths, so profound was his agitation.

'Well, what have you to say for yourself in front of this brave Committee of yours? Am I to be condemned? Banished from Puerto Daffyd? I should think well before you do such a thing, Branwell Hughes, for I was here in this town of ours before your star began to twinkle in the firmament. And I will say this. Let him who is without sin cast the first stone. There now. What do you have to say to that? Eh? Eh?'

There was a grand clearing of throats, much discreet coughing and furtively exchanged glances. The minister looked uncomfortable and she saw a telltale rosy hue creep up from his collar to his ears, which were as big as jug handles and she had even seen them once flapping in the wind.

'Please, Widow Evans,' he said at last, gathering up his courage and facing her with hands clasped in supplication an inch under his long chin. 'This is a difficult task, which should have been carried out by the sheriff, but he was persuaded to leave the nasty business in our more caring hands.'

Blodwen gave him a sideways glance, wondering what the Devil he was on about, but she held her tongue, for maybe she had said enough already.

'It's about that nephew of yours,' Mr Hughes continued, and heads nodded, eyes swept the floor and not a crumb yet to be found there.

'What about Matthew?' she asked, her back teeth gritting together tightly, for she had a feeling she was not going to like this, whatever it was.

'Well, you see . . . '

'Get on with it, man!'

'The thing is . . . Oh, dear me, how difficult this is.'

'It will not be so difficult once you spit it out,' Blodwen said rigidly and saw Mr Hughes, the Elder of the Elders, blanch. However, he did at least take her advice and spat out his words, making her blood run cold.

'Some *gauchos* brought in a dead body. They found it somewhere in the foothills not so far from Gwyneth Johnns's property. Looks like it's your nephew, Widow Evans.'

'Are you sure that this dead person is Matthew Riley?' Blodwen asked.

She did not like death, felt it was too big a price to pay for anybody's sins, but she couldn't suppress a certain relief flooding through her old veins at the thought of her little world being rid of such a nasty character. Her thoughts strayed to Rob and Davy and, in particular, Dora. Poor, sweet little Dora who had been too innocent to know what she was getting mixed up in when she plighted her troth to that black-hearted Devil.

'The thing is, Widow Evans,' Mr Hughes said, one hand busily smoothing down strands of hair on his otherwise shiny bald pate. 'The body is in such a state . . . well, we cannot identify it for sure and the law needs a positive identification before it can draw a line through the case.'

Blodwen's eyebrows shot up and she gave a little involuntary gasp, realizing what he was about to ask her.

'You want me to identify this person?' she said, looking from one to the other of them.

'It would help and you are the only one left who knew him well enough, I'm thinking.'

She was a wise and an experienced old woman, who always had words of advice and wisdom for all and sundry, but there were two things she had never done. One was to help in the birthing of babies. The other was to see a dead body other than her beloved Huw, and that had been enough to make her never want to see another lifeless person, though there had been opportunity aplenty in the last half century.

She stood and drew herself up to her full height, which was just below five short feet, but she was a daunting figure of a woman nonetheless, and with a noble bearing.

'If it will settle the matter once and for all, Mr Hughes, I will do it. Where is he?'

'Why, he's at the funeral parlour, Widow Evans, but he is not a pretty sight, look you.'

'Nevertheless, it is necessary, isn't it? I want to be able to write to my lovely boys and his wife Dora and tell them the news. I can't do that if I haven't seen his body for myself, now, can I?'

'No, indeed. Perhaps we can go down to the parlour a little . . . erm . . . later, you know . . . ' His beady little eyes were on her cakes and, in particular, her fruit loaf, which she always baked especially for him, though she didn't know why she should.

'We will go now and be done with it,' she said unwaveringly and led the way to the door, followed by Mr Hughes and the Committee of Elders, who no doubt were wishing that they had eaten their tea before parting with the bad news. After viewing this dead body they spoke of, she doubted that any of them would have the stomach for even one fairy cake.

★ ★ ★

Rob, feeling the need to pass a few moments in solitude, left Davy with a lovesick glint in his eyes for Dora, who was bundled up in a heavy blanket as the two of them sat warming themselves at the crackling fire, feeding it the dry twigs they had gathered before making camp. Every now and then, their eyes would meet and they would exchange secret smiles. It did Rob's heart good to see the pair of them in love like this, despite all the difficulties it brought with it. Davy was a kind, soft-hearted lad. He would never do anything to hurt Dora or any other girl, for that matter — unlike that damned husband of hers.

He walked down to the edge of the lake. In the dark it would be dangerous to do so, but tonight there was a moon and the sky was sprinkled with stardust so bright that the light on the land was a mystical grey-blue.

Now, all was tranquil except for the odd tinkling of the moving iced water, a plop here, a tiny scuffle there. Even *El Pampero* had calmed down to a soft breeze, though there was a bitter chill in it that made Rob shiver and draw his long, leather coat more closely about him.

'You like my paradise, yes?'

Gwyneth appeared suddenly at his side, sounding very Spanish tonight, he thought.

He gave her a swift look, then let his eyes return to the lake. When she was like this, all soft and feminine, he was afraid of giving himself away. It was all right for Davy to wear his heart on his sleeve, but Rob had been keeping his hidden for days, weeks even, not daring to show any feeling of warmth when he was around Gwyneth, who seemed so tough on the outside, yet was, he felt sure, quite fragile within.

'It's like nothing I've ever seen,' he told her, 'except in children's fairytales.'

She laughed and it was such a natural, liquid sound, which he found particularly attractive. He wondered how many people, men especially, had heard that laugh.

'You read fairytales, Rob?'

'I did, when I was a bairn. I remember this book that Matt gave me . . . ' He broke off, realizing that he was about to go on a nostalgic journey which, had Matt not fouled up, would have been a happy one.

'You were close — you and Matthew Riley?'

'Aye . . . yes, yes! We grew up together, went to the same school, got sent down the pit at the same time and worked shoulder to shoulder digging out the coal.'

'Black gold,' she said to the ground at her feet.

'Yes, well, there's nothing golden about working underground, I can tell you.'

'So, you really were friends?'

'Best mates . . . until . . . ' Rob broke off, thinking back. He couldn't make up his mind when things had started to sour between him and Matt. He suspected it went further back than he had realized. It was too easy to shut oneself off from the faults of others, perhaps not wanting to believe that they actually existed.

'I'm sorry.' She was standing there and her fingers were touching his arm. 'I'm sorry that you have been hurt by your friend. It's not good to lose people you trust in such a way. Better that they die and leave you mourning for them, rather than have them ruin your life.'

He guessed she was talking, in some way, of her father, Brin Johnns.

'That's one thing that will never happen,' he told her. 'Matt will never ruin my life. I won't let him. Or Dora's or Davy's.'

'You are lucky to have people to love.'

She looked over her shoulder wistfully. Rob followed her gaze to where Davy and Dora were sitting, talking quietly, their heads close together, holding hands, he suspected, beneath that blanket.

'But you are loved, Gwyneth,' he said

270

suddenly and saw her flinch and lift her eyes to him questioningly. The words gave him a strange lift inside his ribcage as if he were about to blurt out the truth — that he had fallen in love with her, far more deeply than he cared to admit.

'Who?'

'Why, Blodwen, of course.'

'Ah, yes . . . ' Was that relief shining in her eyes? 'Blodwen loves the whole world, though she acts as though she doesn't. And I will admit to you, Rob, that when I am with that old lady, I do feel loved. I feel safe.'

'That's not hard to imagine. Underneath that steely exterior of hers, she's a warm-hearted soul.'

Her smile lit up her eyes and showed teeth so strong and white they were brilliant against the ochre of her skin.

'I won't tell her you told me so,' she said. 'Shall we go back? It's growing cold and we must be up and away early in the morning if we are to make good time.'

Rob gave one last lingering look at the lake and then followed her back to the campfire. Dora was on her feet, stretching and yawning wearily and looking pale but happy.

'I'm going to bed,' she announced, then turned to Gwyneth, her brow furrowed. 'Is the rest of the way like it was today?'

'It's pretty rough, yes,' Gwyneth con-firmed, and they saw the younger girl's face fall as she gave a groan of discontent. 'Why? You are all right, aren't you, Dora?'

Dora hesitated, just a fleeting moment, then shook her head before climbing into the back of the wagon.

'There's nothing wrong, honest. I'm fine.' They heard her muffled response.

'Do you think she's telling the truth?' Davy said. 'She's been awfully quiet today.'

'She's pregnant, Davy,' Gwyneth said a little abruptly. 'Maybe she's having problems coming to terms with that . . . and with the fact that her husband is a murderer and on the run.'

'Aye, well, we're all having problems with that one,' Davy said grumpily and crawled off into the tiny tent he shared with his brother.

Rob took Davy's place at the fire and threw another handful of sticks and dry brushwood on the dying flames. It leapt back into life, crackled merrily and sent sparks shooting up into the darkening sky. He had expected Gwyneth to join Dora, but instead she lingered, walking to and fro for a minute or two, then settling herself by his side. He reached behind him and retrieved the blanket Dora had dropped as she left. Gwyneth sat perfectly still while he draped it around her shoulders.

'You are a very thoughtful man, it seems to me, Rob,' she said after a moment's silence. 'I do not meet many thoughtful people in my life.'

'You're not so uncaring yourself, but like old Blodwen, you don't like to admit it.' She gave him a curious glance. 'Oh, I've heard how you charm animals and heal sick children.'

She gave a short laugh and drew in the dust with a twig that had escaped the fire.

'The White Witch of Patagonia, that's me,' she said, lightly.

After a few minutes more in silence that had started out as being companionable but ended up something of a strain for Rob, he got up and stretched his long legs.

'Aren't you going to bed, then?' he asked pointedly. 'I thought you said we had to be away early in the morning.'

'I prefer to wait until Dora is asleep,' she said, staring at the stick and the pattern she was drawing with it. 'She tosses and turns a lot. I'm not used to sharing my sleeping quarters. Not with anyone.'

Message received, Rob thought, if message there was dressed up in her words.

'You seem sad tonight, Gwyneth. Is there a

problem that I should know about?'

Her dark eyebrows rose in his direction.

'No. I'm always sad at this point. Puerto Daffyd seems so far away. For some reason it makes me morose.'

'I thought you liked being at the *estancia*.'

'I did . . . I mean, I do, but . . . ' She jumped to her feet with such vigour that it startled him and he half expected to find a rattlesnake or something equally lethal slithering at their feet. 'You would not understand. I think I will go to bed now.'

'No, wait!' Was he mad, tempting fate like this? But he had to make this one gesture. It had been on his mind to do so for days. Now was as good a time as any. 'Don't go. I have something for you.'

She blinked at him through the darkness as a heavy cloud masked the moon. She had forecast snow, but it had not yet arrived. Only a few showers of icy rain thrown in their faces like needles in the wind.

'What is it?'

'Just wait, I tell you.'

She waited. In fact, she had not moved a muscle by the time he had rummaged around in his valise and returned to the spot where he had left her, a small parcel in his hands wrapped in stiff brown paper and tied with string.

Gwyneth looked immediately suspicious as he held it out to her.

'What makes you think I want to accept this?' she asked.

'Because it's for you. A small token. A present to say thanks for all you've done for me . . . and for my brother, and are doing for Dora. Go on. Take it. It's not much.'

Gwyneth tentatively took the package, weighed it, felt it. She pulled off the string and the wrapping, dropping them to the ground, where the wind captured them and whisked them away down to the lake.

'Oh!' Her exclamation of delight was spontaneous, then she became suspicious again. 'But why are you giving me this? I thought you bought it for your girl back in the Old Country.'

They were both staring at the little music box. He had indeed thought of buying it for Margaret, as a peace offering. But the moment he saw the look on Gwyneth's face when she fingered it in the Co-op, when she thought no-one was looking, he knew he had to offer it to her.

'If you don't like it, I'm sure the shop will change it.'

'Oh, no! I mean, no, thank you, Rob. It . . . it's beautiful, really. I'm just not sure how to react. You see, apart from Blodwen Evans, nobody has ever given me a present of any kind. It's such a . . . an unexpected thing for you to do.'

Rob felt suddenly very shy and awkward. He gave her a quick, lopsided smile and shrugged his shoulders.

'It's nothing,' he said.

'Oh, but it is . . . '

She ran her fingers over the polished pebbles that were embedded in the pewter box. She ever so slowly opened the lid and the tinkling music of the old lullaby filled the night air.

She likes it, Rob thought, content that she did not throw the thing back in his face.

'Goodnight, Gwyneth,' he said and she simply smiled, then returned her attention to the box, taking it back to the wagon with her, where he could hear the music going on and on until it wound down and silence fell on their little camp.

13

'Now prepare yourself, Widow Evans.' Rhys Jones, the town undertaker, looked like an underfed raven with his funereal black clothes and the only thing white about him being his alabaster face and hands.

'I've been prepared all the way down the street,' she told him stiffly, hoisting up her shoulders and pulling the edges of her shawl more warmly about her, for it was as cold in this deathly place than the frozen wastes of this vast, wild land. 'Now where is he, this body that the whole town thinks is my great-nephew?'

He led her into a back room, through a purple velvet curtain with golden silk tassels, which she thought was a little tasteless, considering. It was probably the choice of Mrs Jones, who had no taste in anything, including husbands, for Jones the Coffin was her fourth and word had it he wouldn't be her last.

'Here we are, then.' Rhys Jones spread out his hands, indicating a corpse on a trestle covered with a white sheet. 'As I'm sure Mr Hughes has warned you, it is not a pretty sight.'

'Death, Mr Jones, is not pretty, but we all come to it sooner or later, when the good Lord calls us, though in this man's case, it wasn't the good Lord who called him, but a killer with a taste for blood, I'm thinking.'

'Shall I reveal the deceased, Widow Evans? Are you ready?'

'As ready as I will ever be. Go ahead and somebody get ready to catch me if I faint away at the sight. Go on, then!'

With practised slowness, the undertaker peeled back the sheet to reveal a battered corpse, the face of which was unrecognizable and would not be known even to his own mother, if he had one. Blodwen took a little gasping breath and willing hands shot out, ready to break her fall, but she fooled them all and stepped forward for a closer look.

'Is this your nephew, Widow Evans?'

'Great-nephew.'

'Yes, yes, of course . . . is it . . . um . . . ah . . . Mr Matthew Riley?'

'They are certainly Matthew Riley's clothes, but the head is nothing but mush. Let me see his feet, to be sure.'

'His feet, Widow Evans?'

'Don't stand there with your mouth hanging open, Rhys Jones. Let me see his feet.'

He was slow to respond, so she brushed

him away, unveiled the corpse's feet and stared down at them long and hard.

'Hmm.' She took one trouser leg between finger and thumb and raised it a few inches, showing a thin, hairless leg, the top of a blue sock and a suspender hanging loosely about the ankle.

'Well? Does that help you identify him, Widow Evans?' It was Mr Hughes, the minister, who spoke and she found him crowding her elbow, so she gave him a little dig to make him give her room to breathe, for she was all of a sudden feeling faint.

'No, it does not, look you.'

There were intakes of breath behind her, like steam escaping from a hissing kettle. She would give anything right now for a cup of good, strong Welsh tea with plenty of sugar.

'I . . . I don't understand . . . ' Mr Hughes was looking as faint as she felt.

'No, I don't suppose you do, but I can tell you that this is not Matthew Riley.'

More breath parted company with the agape mouths in the room. She turned her head and looked at them all.

'It's not him,' she affirmed. 'And if any of you had anything about you, you would have known better than to come and distress me like this.'

'Well, I am terribly sorry, Widow Evans,'

Mr Hughes was flapping his hands and his eyes were standing out like organ stops. 'But how can you tell for sure?'

Blodwen sucked in her mouth and prepared to give them one of her famous lectures, but changed her mind, for all she could think of was to get out of this place, smelling of lilies and the sickly sweet, almondy aroma of the embalming fluid.

'Matthew Riley was a great hairy brute and he had feet that would fit into those boots there, but the feet inside at the moment are not the feet of Matthew Riley and that is all I'm going to say on the matter.'

'She's right,' said the sheriff who had just arrived and was pushing his way to the front. 'Look at that, would you? Well, that settles it. We're still looking for that murdering bastard, Matthew Riley. Looks like he's ensuring himself a place on the scaffold.'

As he spoke, he pulled off one boot very easily without unlacing it. The foot, thus revealed, was at least three sizes smaller and the sock flapped emptily at the toes.

The crowd in the small, stuffy room parted to let Blodwen leave. She got to the street and gulped in a lungful of fresh air. Her legs were giving out beneath her and she hoped she would be able to walk back to her house unaided, and without making a fool of herself. And probably because she was in a weakened state, she felt a tear sting the corner of her eye.

There were things she had to do. Things that she would have preferred to defer until she knew better how the great plan of life was going to turn out. However, she could not leave things too much to chance. More than ever before, Blodwen felt the end of her days beckoning on some close horizon.

The beating she had taken at Matthew Riley's hands had seen to that. She would be damned if she left her all to the likes of him. Family ties were all very well, but she was far removed from any family that she had ever known. Rob and Davy were her family now. As were Gwyneth and Dora.

Blodwen stopped to rest at the bench outside the chambers of William Davis & Son, the only solicitor firm that Puerto Daffyd boasted. William Davis, the father, had long since gone to push up the daisies and good riddance, since he was always robbing his unsuspecting clients and charging enormous fees that nobody could afford to pay. The son, another William, was far less corrupt, she had heard, and his reputation as an honest man was growing.

After a few minutes to catch her breath, Blodwen knocked on the door to the small block of offices and went in. A heavy jawed female in a starched white blouse and black felt skirt sat behind a desk and peered at her over tiny pince-nez. She had the square face and clotted cream complexion that spoke to Blodwen in volumes of stern Welsh ancestry, but she seemed amicable enough when she came forward with hand outstretched and a welcoming smile.

'Widow Evans! How nice to see you. What can we do for you?'

'I'm here to see Mr William Davis,' Blodwen said, struggling to recognize the woman and failing, which irritated her for the person before her obviously knew her.

'My brother is speaking long-distance on the telephone right now, but if you would like to wait, I'm sure he'll be delighted to see you.'

'Your brother? Good heavens, girl, you cannot be little Miriam Davis!'

'That's exactly who I am. Do you not recognize me?'

Blodwen shook her head in disbelief. 'Why, girl, the last time I saw you I seem to remember that you were knee high to a guanaco and sucking your thumb.'

'That was a long time ago, Widow Evans,' the woman said. 'More than thirty years. I went back to the Old Country with my mother, but when Dada died and I had no strong commitments in Wales, I came back to help William. Ah, here is my brother now.'

'Widow Evans? This is an honour.'

William Davis stood before her in all his portly glory, looking the spitting image of his father, which was no recommendation, but his eyes were kindly.

'You used to be a skinny youth with spots,' Blodwen told him as he shook her hand firmly.

'As you can see,' he laughed heartily, 'I've grown and the spots have departed. What can we do for you?'

'I need to make out a new will. The one your father drew up for me is no longer of any use. I have different priorities these days.'

He bowed respectfully and indicated the open door of his office. Blodwen marched through it, feeling much more settled in her mind. Things were going to be taken care of, whatever happened after today, she was sure.

* * *

The long journey in the wagon was taking its toll on poor Dora. She was being sick all the time and they had to make frequent stops to let her rest from the constant jolting. Careful though Davy and Rob were to miss boulders and potholes when they were driving the mules, it was still a rough ride. They made her as comfortable as possible, but with each passing day she seemed to grow weaker. Not a word of complaint did she utter, but her grey, drawn face and suppressed groans told them without a doubt that it had been a mistake for her to come.

'No, please, go on. I'm all right. Honest, I am. It'll be fine when we get to the other side of the ridge.'

She said the words over and over again, but Rob was beginning to doubt that she would stay the course. As thin as a sparrow already, she got rapidly thinner, for she couldn't eat and when she tried to force herself to swallow the food they gave her, it didn't stay down for long. It was as bad as the seasickness she had suffered on the voyage from England.

'Gwyneth! Hold on, there!'

He rode out from the wagon and caught up with Gwyneth. She always rode on ahead and seemed to prefer her own company most of the time. Now and then, however, she would drop back and ride with him, though words were few between them. It was, nevertheless, a comfortable improvement since their first meeting when she seemed ready to cut his legs from under him if he so much as looked her way.

Gwyneth reined in the big black stallion and the animal stood there, snorting and pawing the ground, impatient to be off. And that was a sight to behold, seeing horse and girl fly over the flat terrain, as if they didn't even touch the ground.

'Gwyneth, Dora's getting worse and worse. How long is it now?'

'Not long. Three or four days.'

'I don't think she'll make it. Not without proper rest and food.'

Gwyneth gave a solemn nod. 'Yes, I have seen that too.'

'What can we do? These wide open spaces are no place for a pregnant girl.'

'If she can hold out until the next rise, there's a cabin. I know the people who live there. They will let us stay a while until Dora can face the rest of the journey.'

'How far is it?'

'Only a few more miles . . . It's a little off the beaten track, hidden in a wooded valley, but it's the best we can do in the circumstances.'

'You know these people?'

'Yes. It's all right, Rob. They're good people, though there are some who would disagree, or so I hear.'

Rob hoped she was a good judge of

character, for he couldn't see why any god-fearing person would choose to live in such isolation. They had travelled for days now through the Patagonian pampas, largely deserted, apart from a few ubiquitous guanacos, hare-like maras and ground-burrowing owls. Gwyneth shot a rhea, which they roasted, feathers and all, and they found it more than palatable, but not quite as good as turkey.

They came to the valley as the sun was sinking in the west, turning the green plains to pink-tinged gold. There was a small dense wood spreading halfway up a hill in the middle of a patch of land that was rocky and barren. From the centre of this cluster of conifers rose a thin plume of grey-white smoke.

'Ah! They're here!' Gwyneth pointed, looking pleased.

Rob thought she was probably as relieved as he was that they could rest Dora for a while before continuing the arduous journey.

'What do they do, these friends of yours?' he asked as they descended to the edge of the wood.

She seemed to hesitate before answering, which made him suspicious, but she was the kind of woman who thought deeply before speaking on any subject. In that way, he felt, she was not about to say something she might regret.

'At the moment, they are hunters . . . trappers.' When she saw his sharp glance, she added, 'They only take enough to keep them alive. They eat the meat and sell the pelts.'

'You said 'at the moment',' Rob queried. 'What do they do other than hunt?'

They were entering the wood, along a narrow, bumpy track. Davy and Dora were following cagily with the wagon. It was dark inside the wood where the setting sun did not infiltrate. When Gwyneth looked his way, Rob could not make out her expression, but he sensed a certain reticence to reply to his question.

'It is of no concern of yours,' she said eventually. Then, 'I don't mean to be difficult, but it is best you do not know who they are. Their lives have been ruined by people who thought the worst of them, but the world isn't always the best judge.'

Rob shrugged his shoulders and allowed her to go on ahead up the steep, overgrown track. He didn't care who or what these people were. His only concern was to find some respite for Dora.

The track grew too narrow to take the wagon, so they left it, hidden among the trees. Davy carried Dora in his arms while

Rob and Gwyneth led the horses and the mules through fern and bracken and low conifer branches that stretched out across their path like arms barring their entrance.

The cabin was bigger than Rob had expected, having seen Gwyneth's tiny abode. It was solidly built and a dull, yellow glow flickered in the steamy windows.

Gwyneth rapped on the door with her bare knuckles. It took a while before the door was opened and Rob felt that whoever was inside knew exactly who was standing there before he appeared.

'Hi, there!' The young man was bearded and dressed in a woollen checked shirt with denim trousers, which set him apart from the Welsh Patagonians Rob was used to. 'Good to see ya! Come on in.'

'It's good to see you, too, Harry,' Gwyneth said. 'I have some friends with me. We were heading for the *estancia*, but the girl is pregnant and the journey has been too much for her. Can we rest up here for a day or two?'

'Don't see why not.' The man moved back and beckoned to them to enter, then shouted to someone over his shoulder. 'Hey, Etta! We got company. Ladle out some stew. These people look like they need it.'

A young woman with a large soup ladle in her hand and a broad smile on her face came to greet them. From a pot over a log fire in the grate there drifted over a delicious meaty odour, so rich and brown that Rob felt his taste buds ooze.

'Come on in and get warmed,' she said, then turned to a second man huddled by the blazing fire. 'Bobby, move over and let these folks feel the heat.'

'Sure thing,' Bobby said, then turned his attention on the weary Dora, nestling in Davy's arms. 'Put the li'l lady on the couch over there, my friend. She looks all done in. I'll warm her some milk and lace it with brandy. That'll put the colour back in them pale cheeks of hers.'

'Oh, please, I don't want a fuss, sir,' Dora was heard to mutter as Davy tucked her in on the sofa amidst soft cushions and crocheted coverlets.

'Now don't you worry, none, missy,' Harry was now standing over her, feeling her forehead, testing for fever. 'Yor gonna be just fine after a li'l rest. And the name's Harry Longabaugh. This wild female here's Etta and my hairy buddy over there's Bobby Leroy Parker.'

'This is good of you,' Rob said, not quite knowing what to think of these two men, for they were like no-one he had ever met. Backwoodsmen, no doubt, though they didn't act as wild as they looked.

'Shuck, tis nuthin', fella. Say, you've got a mighty queer accent. Where you from, eh?'

'He's English, Harry,' Gwyneth said, smiling at the two cowboys with unbridled affection.

'We're Geordies,' Davy added, his cheeks growing pink with the warmth of the blazing fire he was standing close to, rubbing his hands, thawing out his posterior.

'It's like English, but different,' Gwyneth said, and Rob thought he saw the shadow of a mischievous dimple appear at the side of her mouth. 'These two you can trust.'

'Well, that's good news. We couldn't trust the last Englishman who came by here a couple of days gone.' Harry spat into the flames. 'He was a bad lot and no mistake. Near got hisself killed coming up here and actin' tough like he didn't care two hoots fur nuthin'.'

Rob felt a sudden twinge in his gut, though he didn't want to believe his suspicions. There were plenty of Englishmen here in Patagonia and not all of them were good.

'What did he call himself?' It was Gwyneth who asked the question that was echoing in his head, but couldn't find its way out.

'Damned if I remember, but we sent him tailing out of here. Seems like he'd heard of us and wanted to be pardners, if ye please.' Bobby gave a raucous belly laugh. 'As if!'

'He said he was English,' Harry said, his eyes narrowing. 'But he had the same strange accent as your friend here, only thicker. His name was an Irish one, I'm thinkin'.'

'Yup, Harry's right. Lemme think, now.' Bobby's forehead furrowed.

'Matt Riley,' Rob said softly and they both looked at him, eyes wide and bright.

'That's the one,' Bobby said. 'Nasty bit of business. He a friend of yours, is he?'

'Not any more,' Rob said. 'But maybe you won't be so ready to give us hospitality now that you know.'

'Ah, shoot! You look like a decent sort, you and the young'un. And that li'l lady of yours sure needs to rest, bless her heart.'

Dora had fallen asleep and they could hear her heavy breathing across the room.

'We're very grateful,' Davy told their hosts.

'Think nuthin' of it, young fella. Besides, Bobby and Etta and me are off at sun up. It's time to move on and settle down some. We've just bought ourselves a ranch in the Cholila Valley. Stay in the cabin as long as you like. There's provisions aplenty and a stock of firewood out back.'

'Thank you, Harry.'

'No, Gwyneth Johnns, thank *you*.' Harry

turned to Rob and inclined his head towards Gwyneth, who was looking slightly embarrassed. 'This here female saved our lives a while back when we was poisoned from eatin' somethin' bad. And she patched me and Bobby up good when he took a bullet, and I got a foot caught in my own stupid trap.'

'As you say yourself, Harry,' Gwyneth said with a coy smile. ''Tweren't nuthin'. I would have done the same for any furry friend.'

She gave a playful tug at his beard and they all laughed. All, that is, except Dora, who went on sleeping peacefully.

★ ★ ★

From his makeshift hide not a mile from the wood, half hidden among rocks and by a burbling stream, Matt huddled, shivering in his blanket. The blanket smelled strongly of the Indian he had taken it from, but the old man had no further use for it now. Matt also had the Indian's horse, a skinny palomino that wasn't much in the way of horseflesh, but was better than no transport at all.

He had been tracking Rob's party for days, always making sure that he was far enough away for them not to see him. He had no particular plan in his head, but he felt that he had to stick close. Something would transpire.

A few days ago, he had found himself way ahead of the little group, having taken a circuitous route that was quick, but no good for a wagon. That was when he came across those two cowboys holed up in the woods. He really thought he had fallen on his feet there. They were a rough twosome and at first they welcomed him like an old friend. Then he'd got a bit too clever for his own good when he found a 'Wanted' poster with their faces plastered all over it.

Dead or alive, it had said. Butch Cassidy and the Sundance Kid, otherwise known as Robert Leroy Parker and Harry Longabaugh. Well, that had made his mouth water, thinking of the money that was offered as a reward. Of course, the minute he held them at gunpoint with one of their own guns, he realized his mistake. By the time he figured out how to fire the damned thing, they had overpowered him. It had been as easy as taking candy from a baby.

He only got away when some other fellow came snooping around, claiming to be a Pinkerton man. They sent the agent away, too, with a load of buckshot in his behind. Matt had stayed around long enough to see that happen, then he had hightailed it back into the hills.

A couple of days later, he picked up the wagon's trail again, and this time he didn't try any shortcuts, but kept well behind, following their dust cloud. And now they were actually holed up in that very same shack with those two wanted individuals and he intended to sit it out until they decided they'd had enough.

The palomino was restless. It shuffled its feet and pulled at the tethering rope, the movements interrupting Matt's sleep. He picked up a stone and hurled it at the stupid creature, catching it on its bony flank. It was enough to make the animal fraught. It pulled and pulled until the tether gave way, and then it was galloping away from him in the dark. He made to run after it, but after a few yards, hobbling in his socks over the stony ground, he gave up and went back to his shelter. It was going to be a long walk tomorrow and he hoped to God the tracks of the wagon and the horses would stay fresh until he caught up with them, wherever that was.

* * *

They had been at the cabin in the wood for three days and Gwyneth was beginning to feel claustrophobic with dense trees on all four sides of her. Harry and Bobby had been generous hosts, but they were now gone on their travels, seeking out new lives for themselves as ranchers. She didn't believe all the bad things that were said about them. They admitted the robberies, yes, but they had been young boys hungry for adventure. They were not wanton killers.

The boys, as she liked to think of them, had swapped her wagon for theirs. Theirs was bigger and more comfortable, so Dora would be able to ride the rest of the way without too much hardship. Thankfully, the girl was looking a lot better and her sickness was only minimal in the mornings rather than spread throughout the day.

'Do you think you'll be able to manage if we leave tomorrow, Dora?' Gwyneth asked her, seeing that the girl was eating her supper with surprising relish and laughing with Rob and Davy.

'Oh, yes,' Dora replied. 'I'm sure I can do it. You shouldn't have stopped just for me.'

'Don't worry about that,' Gwyneth said, feeling a sympathetic warmth spread through her at the thought of this fragile creature putting on such a brave face.

'When do you think we'll arrive at the *estancia*, Gwyneth?' Rob asked.

When their eyes met across the table something strange passed between them that disturbed Gwyneth so much she upset the salt she was reaching for. Davy and Dora grabbed for the pot together, laughing. The girl threw some of the spilled salt over her left shoulder, saying it was to break the bad luck spell.

Gwyneth drew in a deep breath and broke a piece of stale bread into her guanaco stew.

'We should make better time with the extra mules that the boys gave us. I'd say another two, maybe three days and we'll be able to sleep in proper beds and eat proper food.'

'And have a proper wash, I hope,' Davy said, pulling his red flannel vest away from his skin and sniffing at himself in disgust.

'All that and more. The *estancia* is isolated, but they have everything they need to exist without too much hardship. It's a good life, but they do need extra hands and they aren't always easy to find.'

'If the life is so good there,' Rob said, 'why do you leave the place so often?'

She dragged her gaze away from him and concentrated some more on her stew. Guanaco stew was fine, but eating the same meal three days running got a little tedious. She was looking forward to some of Therese's chicken cooked over charcoal and the fresh vegetables they grew in the *estancia* kitchen garden.

'I don't know,' she told Rob quietly, and it was the truth. 'I like to see Blodwen and, as you know, I make lace for her . . . ' She gave a small laugh. 'That is, when I'm not bullying *gauchos.*'

'Gee, Gwyneth, I can't imagine you making lace, somehow!'

They all laughed at Davy's remark, which sounded more like Harry or Bobby than the young, inexperienced Geordie lad he was. Gwyneth rose from the table and smiled at him. She smiled a lot these days, and it was something that sat well on her, and felt good.

'Just for that, Davy Barker,' she said over her shoulder as she stepped out of the cabin into the soft darkness outside, 'you can clear up tonight.'

There was a groan from Davy, a laugh from Rob.

'I'll help you, Davy,' Dora said, already on her feet and stacking dirty plates.

Outside, the air was chilled, but there was no wind here in the wood. Gwyneth walked towards the nearest chink of light shining through the dark silhouetted trees. Branches spread out across the track, like arms wishing to block her way. She pushed them aside and headed for the plain beyond. She needed

297

some space, needed to see beyond the trees.

The moment she broke from the cover of the wood, she felt better, less stifled. And as the moon came out from behind a dark cloud, she saw the way they would travel tomorrow lit up with silvery traces. She gave her thoughts free range. It would be good to see Therese again . . . and Miguel. Maybe he would have forgiven her by now for refusing to dance with him. Oh, how she had loved dancing like that, before Miguel grew too demanding. Now that she knew the make of the man, knew that he was not for her or, indeed, for any other woman, she did not lust after him. It would be good if they could be friends, though he had given no sign that this could be possible.

But the lusting had not stopped. The fire still burned bright in her body and she could not understand it. Perhaps she did not want to understand it. It was her personal torture, and she would have to learn to live with it.

A rustle of leaves and snapped twigs alerted her that she was not entirely alone. Her heart stopped beating, then leapt in her breast, racing and pounding as if it was out of control. As she saw something dark move towards her she wondered if it might be Matt Riley, coming back to claim his desserts.

Those desserts she had robbed him of when they first met.

Gwyneth looked wildly about her, wondering if she could run from a man as big and as strong — and as desperate — as Matt? And she had come out without rifle or whip, which proved that she was turning into some kind of weak-headed fool.

With her hands pressed to her chest in an attempt to control her heartbeat, she backed away, not taking her eyes from the silhouette of the man coming towards her. She opened her mouth to shout for Rob and Davy, hoping they weren't making too much noise to hear her through the thick timbers of the cabin.

'Gwyneth? Are you all right? Here, I brought a coat for you. It's cold out here.'

Rob stepped out into the moonlight. She gave a little half-suppressed cry and took a few deep breaths as he approached her, inspecting her with anxious eyes.

'What's wrong?'

Her shoulders had slumped and she was shaking visibly. He draped the coat around her. It was Rob's coat, not hers. It smelt of him, impregnated into the rawhide. She pulled it more tightly around her and, as he rubbed his hands up and down her arms from the back, trying to warm her, she laid back against him with a sigh.

'Thank you, Rob,' she said in a very small voice because her throat was too tight. No man had ever touched her like this. No man had ever got this close.

He slid his arms about her, hugging her for a few seconds, then turned her gently to face him. They were standing so close they might be joined as one. It both frightened and excited Gwyneth and she almost broke away, but something stopped her. Maybe it was her own confused heart, or the gentle expression in Rob's grey eyes. All she knew was that she liked it there and didn't want the feeling to stop.

'I think I'd better get you back to the cabin,' Rob said, pulling away from her with a jerk that was so sudden she almost overbalanced.

Gwyneth didn't speak. She couldn't. The moment was gone, maybe never to return, but Gwyneth knew she would hold on to it, perhaps cherish it for a very long time.

'Come on, then. They'll be wondering where we've got to.' Rob still had one arm draped around her shoulders as they walked slowly back.

'Somehow,' Gwyneth told him, her voice still hoarse with hidden emotion, 'I don't think they'll be too worried.'

His thumb was on her cheek, caressing it

with slow movements that made her catch her breath. Suddenly, he leant down and kissed her temple. She held her breath, waiting for his lips to descend and find her mouth, suddenly longing for his kiss.

But it didn't come.

'Maybe I shouldn't have done that,' Rob said a little stiffly.

Gwyneth gave a small shrug and disengaged herself from his arm. She strode out ahead of him and was back in the cabin before he reached the front stoop.

Neither of them was aware of a pair of malevolent eyes watching them through the darkness. Matt Riley spat out some vicious expletives as he was gripped with a deep, dark jealousy, seeing his best mate getting cosy with the woman Matt himself intended to have.

14

They reached the *estancia* three days later, having negotiated a tricky pass in a range of high hills that was almost blocked by snow. However, within hours they were back on the green plains and finally, with great relief, they pulled up on a ridge and gazed down on the wide valley where the ranch nestled. It was late afternoon and the light was turning mellow.

'There it is. *El Estancia Paraiso.*'

Gwyneth pointed out the cluster of red-roofed buildings with their white walls, in startling contrast to the surrounding green countryside. There was a large square of blue, shining water, and little twinkling streams that ran from it, irrigating a patchwork of crops, mainly cabbages and root vegetables at this time of year, it being winter. There was also a small rose garden that would be a blaze of colour, no doubt, in the spring.

There were white-fenced corrals where horses were grazing and in one special enclosure a man sat astride a stallion that leapt up vertically in the air. The man stayed miraculously in the saddle, holding on to the reins with one hand, while the other hand waved his hat in the air and one or two spectators shouted their encouragement.

'Gawd! Would ye look at that, Rob!' Davy exclaimed, his blue eyes standing out from his head, his mouth dropping open. 'Hey, I hope we're not expected to do that.'

'No, of course not,' Gwyneth chuckled and led the weary group down the hillside. 'That's Buck. He's an expert at breaking-in wild horses. He comes once a year and people from miles around bring their difficult animals for him to tame.'

'There are other people living here in the valley?' Rob asked, for on looking around he could see nothing but rolling hills and plains as far as the horizon.

'Our nearest neighbours are about fifty miles away,' Gwyneth said and he whistled, not sure that he would like this sort of isolation for too long.

Closer to the *estancia* the complex opened up and seemed almost like a small village with its cottages and outbuildings all surrounding the large main ranch house. The wheels of the wagon rumbled and crunched over the dry ground, clouds of golden dust rising from the plodding feet of the horses and mules. At their approach there was a shout of recognition.

'Hey, Gwyneth! Hola!'

A well-built Spanish woman hailed them from the veranda. She had hair as black as the local Indians and skin darker than Gwyneth's. She was no longer young, Rob noticed, but she still retained her Hispanic good looks and the smile she offered them was spontaneous and genuine.

The two women greeted one another like sisters and it was interesting to see a different side to Gwyneth, one that was not dark and brooding over a past she carried around with her like a heavy burden.

Introductions were made, and after a swift conversation in Spanish, Therese fussed over Dora like a mother hen. It warmed Rob's heart to see Dora's pleasure at being treated so amicably.

'What did you tell Therese?' Rob asked Gwyneth as they were off-loading the wagon with Davy and a couple of the resident *gauchos*.

'I told her everything. She will be good to Dora. Therese has always wanted a child to mother. Now she has two . . . or will have when Dora's baby arrives. I think it will be good for both of them.'

The wagon emptied and the goods deployed, mostly in the direction of Juanita's spacious kitchen, they were shown to their quarters. The men were to share some bunkhouse space with the other *gauchos*. It wasn't ideal, from Rob's point of view, him being such a private person, but Davy seemed to welcome the idea of keeping company with what could only be described as wild, but jolly ruffians. For Gwyneth and Dora, there was a surprise, for a new wing had been built on to the house, much as Rob had done for Blodwen. There were three rooms and, to Dora's amazement, a small, connected water closet, so they could enjoy their ablutions without disturbing the hormones of the men in the general wash house.

When they all gathered in the big, communal living room, called there by Therese for pre-supper drinks, Dora's face was beaming.

'Eeh, isn't it lovely!' Dora enthused to Rob and Davy. 'I can even go to the lav without going outside!'

'I don't believe you!' Davy grinned.

'Come and see!' She grabbed his sleeve and beckoned Rob to follow. 'Look! A room of my own and we've even got our own sitting place if we don't want to be with everybody else. And this . . . ' She threw open another door. 'This is Gwyneth's room.'

Fortunately, Gwyneth was not present at that particular moment. Rob caught a glimpse of white-painted walls and a red terracotta-tiled floor. The bed and one comfortable chair were covered with bright *Indios* rugs in heavy, dyed, lambswool, stitched together in assorted rectangles.

Rob felt vaguely uncomfortable as if he were spying on Gwyneth. He was about to back out, but then his eye alighted on the small trinket box he had given her. It seemed to be the only thing she had had time to take out of her bag, apart from some fresh clothes to change into after the journey.

'She loves that box you gave her, you know, Rob,' Dora was saying.

'Does she? I'm glad.'

Dora was nodding solemnly. 'She cried when she brought it back to the wagon that night.'

'Cried?'

'Aye, Rob. Not loud like, you know, but she had tears streaming down her cheeks and she sat there half the night looking at it and turning it over and over in her hands and playing the little tune.'

'Well, I'm sorry if I made her cry. It wasn't meant to make her sad.'

'Oh, she wasn't sad. She was happy. That's what made her cry.'

Rob frowned. The idea of tears spurting from the eyes of a woman known for her toughness was strangely touching.

They both spun round at the creak of a floorboard and found Gwyneth standing there, wrapped in a thick dressing-gown five sizes too big for her and towelling her gleaming wet hair. Her cheeks were flushed and her eyes blazing as she pushed past them, smelling cleanly of soap.

'Sorry, Gwyneth,' Rob muttered. 'We didn't mean to intrude. Dora was just giving us a guided tour of your new premises.'

Gwyneth sat down on the edge of the high bed and, taking up a brush, slowly drew it through her long hair.

'Tonight,' she said, her tone a little strained, 'Therese is organizing a party. Tomorrow you will start work. I suggest you do not touch the raw rye whisky. It's lethal and takes many years' practice before even a drinking man can get used to it.'

'Hey, a party, that's great!' Davy enthused, giving Dora a quick hug and she smiled up at him radiantly. 'I don't suppose they have Newcastle Brown ale, do they? No? Silly question, I suppose, eh, Rob?'

Rob shook his head at his brother.

'Yes, it was, lad, but don't you go sampling the stronger stuff. I don't want to have to carry you around on my shoulders the first day at our new place of employment.'

'By God, our Rob, it's a long time since you were able to do that!'

Rob slapped him on the back and pushed him and Dora out of the room. He gripped the door handle and started to close the door after him, but then he hesitated and gave Gwyneth a smile.

'I like your *estancia*, Gwyneth,' he said. 'And Therese seems like a nice woman.'

'You'll meet the rest of them this evening at supper,' she told him. 'Miguel should be back by then.'

'Miguel?'

'Therese's brother.'

'Ah, yes. The dancer.'

She gave him a sultry look and continued brushing her hair. He went out, closing the door quietly behind him.

★ ★ ★

Miguel Gomez-Pan appeared halfway through supper, which was taking a long time because everyone seemed to be in a festive mood. Therese said it was in honour of Gwyneth's homecoming, not to mention that of her 'little' brother, who had been visiting Buenos Aires.

Rob couldn't help but stare at the tall, arrogant Spaniard with the good looks and the tight-fitting black outfit that seemed to belong on a stage rather than in a working ranch house.

He noticed, too, how Miguel stared at Gwyneth with a curious expression, and how the girl seemed to avoid his eyes and any close proximity. There had to be a bit of history there, Rob thought, with a twinge of jealousy that he would rather be without. Gwyneth was a free spirit, free to choose any man she wanted and who wanted her. If this was her choice, he could hardly blame her. The man had looks and style and, if he and his sister owned this *estancia*, they must be rich. It would be foolish to even try to compete against him.

However, as the dessert was served, it was Gwyneth who moved so she could sit next to Rob. Her conversation was unexpectedly animated as she told him stories from her times at the ranch and the histories of the men who worked there.

'It is a good life, Rob,' she assured him as his eyes roamed around the table, sliding from one coarsened face to the next, and finishing on the smooth countenance of Miguel Gomez-Pan.

'Yes, maybe,' he said slowly. 'But one day, my dream is to own a piece of land, just like this . . . only not so isolated.'

'This country is vast, Rob. Isolation comes with every parcel of the land that's for sale. You have to like being lonely. Out here, there are less than two sheep to every acre and although each landowner has thousands of acres surrounding his homestead, the land itself is poor.'

'Well, maybe I'll change my mind after a taste of the life here. Who knows?'

'Gwyneth!'

Gwyneth's head snapped around at the sharpness of Miguel's tone and the snap of his fingers in her direction.

'Yes, Miguel?'

'We will dance, *si*? Antonio, music if you please . . . you too, Fernando. Where is your fiddle? This is a grand celebration. We must have music and dancing. Come, Gwyneth!'

Rob noticed a slight hesitation before Gwyneth rose and took to the floor with the handsome Spaniard. His heart sank to see her go so eagerly into the man's arms as the music began to play. There was a loud burst of applause, some tapping of feet and clapping of hands in time to the music. The sight of Gwyneth, now dressed in a swirling skirt, whirling and wrapping herself in Miguel's arms was almost too much to bear.

One of the *gauchos*, with too much Bourbon in him, staggered over to where

Dora was sitting, engrossed and shyly keeping time to the music with little nods of her blonde head.

'Hey, *señorita*, you dance with me, eh?'

'Oh-oh!' Davy was immediately on his feet and ready to put up a fight to save Dora's honour if necessary. 'She's with me, cowboy!'

The man gave Davy a sour look and drifted away. Dora looked at Davy with an expression that oozed love and affection. It was not surprising that she got up and the pair of them jigged around the room, locked together in a dance that was neither waltz nor *tango*, but they didn't seem to care, and neither did anyone else.

'Rob!' Therese was down upon him and pulling him up to his feet before he could do anything about it. 'Come on. I've lost my partner to Gwyneth.'

'I can't dance,' he told her, but she wasn't having any of that.

'I will show you, *caro*,' she said as she pulled his arms around her thickening waist and moved them both onto the floor.

Over her bare shoulder he could see Gwyneth, dancing with the fervour of someone at the mercy of a great, undeniable passion. So, that was how it was, he thought miserably. She had talked of Miguel, but had never mentioned the fact that they were in any way a 'couple'. And yet, he had formed the idea that there was a spark of something taking hold between Gwyneth and himself. What a fool he had been to build up hopes on that score. He didn't have much to offer any woman.

The *gauchos* were up on their feet and stomping about, like donkeys that had partaken of too much rancid barley. There was a lot of hollering and whooping and they hooked arms and swung each other off their feet, all to the rhythm of the *tango*. Outside, the dogs were barking. Nobody took any notice. They had been acting like mad things all day.

'You are right, *gringo*,' Therese laughed after five minutes. 'You cannot dance, but you will learn. You will never be another Miguel Gomez-Pan, but you at least do not have two left feet. I will give you lessons, like I did with Gwyneth. It will be fun.'

Rob wasn't sure about that, but he was willing to try anything if it got him bonus points from Gwyneth.

'I wonder which one of us will regret it first,' he joked with her, finding her easy company.

As he spoke there was a great crash and a howling of wind as the shutters were caught in a sudden gust and blown back and forth. A pane of glass had shattered, scattering shards over the floor and making people rush for cover. The music stopped and so did the dancing. Even the dogs were now silent.

A hoarse cry of alarm came from Gwyneth. Everyone turned to look in her direction. Rob was nearest to her. He thought maybe she had been hit by flying glass, but it wasn't Gwyneth who was hurt. It was her dancing partner, Miguel. The Spaniard toppled forward and Gwyneth tried to support him, but she wasn't strong enough. He slithered to the ground and lay there, face down, unmoving. Rob stepped forward and turned him onto his back. There was a gasp all round at the sight of a red stain spreading across his crisp white shirt just above the heart.

'He's been shot!' somebody shouted out and it prompted great confusion in the room.

Juanita, the housekeeper, came running with a bowl of water and cloths to staunch the blood. Therese bent over her brother, stunned by what had happened. Rob and Gwyneth looked on, as grey-faced as the rest of them. Rob was surprised at how calm Gwyneth was, in the circumstances, but then shock had many ways of manifesting itself.

'It's all right,' Juanita announced. 'He is not dead, but the bullet is still in him. Carry him to his room so I can care for him.'

Four *gauchos*, suddenly sobered up, picked up their *patrón* and carried him off, with Antonio and Fernando following, their faces creased with worry. Rob bent and helped Therese to her feet and she leant against him, breathing heavily and looking about her wide-eyed.

'Who?' she asked weakly. 'Who would do that to my brother. He has no enemies.'

A couple of *gauchos* who had immediately run outside to investigate the origin of the bullet that had felled Miguel, came back inside shaking their heads. 'He got away,' one of them said. 'It was nobody we knew.'

'Perhaps somebody from Buenos Aires,' suggested the other and they exchanged glances, then lowered their eyes to the floor. 'Jealousy, perhaps.'

'The bullet was not meant for Miguel,' Gwyneth whispered to Rob, her fingers digging into the flesh of his forearm.

He gave her a puzzled look. 'What? How do you know that?'

'I know that, Rob, because the very moment that bullet shattered the glass, you were the chosen victim, but you stumbled and almost fell. Miguel and I were directly behind you.'

'What? But who would want to kill our Rob?' It was Davy who had overheard her

314

words. As soon as he spoke, both he and Rob knew the answer to his question. 'Oh, Gawd! It must have been Matt.'

'But why would he want to kill you, Rob?' Therese demanded.

Rob looked directly at Gwyneth, saw an anxious flicker appear in her eyes. He gave a shrug and spread his hands. He had given up trying to put reasons to Matt's behaviour. Even so, he couldn't help wondering if it had anything to do with his tentative relationship with Gwyneth.

There were men now scouring the land surrounding the *estancia*, and the shutters were being nailed shut across the broken window to keep out the winter cold and *El Pampero*.

★　★　★

'How is he?'

Gwyneth was standing just inside the door to Miguel's room, watching the still, pale form lying so motionless in the bed as Juanita cleared up the bloodied towels and the bowl full of pink-tinged water.

'I do the best I can,' Juanita said as she made to leave the room. 'The bullet is out, but he has lost much blood. I think he will survive, but he must rest. No dancing for

Señor Miguel for long time, I am thinking.'

'Will it be all right if I sit with him a little?'

The housekeeper's suspicious eyes swept over her, but then the woman's expression softened and she nodded.

'Why not. He will need someone beside him when he wakes up and his sister has gone to her room exhausted with emotion at the thought of nearly losing him.'

Therese had been by Miguel's side all through the delicate operation, holding his hand, feeding him sips of raw Bourbon against the pain of the knife digging into his already mangled flesh. Miguel had borne it all with stoic pride, but Therese had been close to collapse at the end of it.

Gwyneth sat by the bed of this man who had held such fascination for her for so long. She didn't think that she had ever loved him with her heart, and for that she was grateful. Even without the terrible affliction he carried, he would not have been the man for her. He was too volatile, too demanding and insensitive.

Miguel stirred restlessly and made a small groaning noise. Gwyneth reached out and took his hand gently in hers. After a while, his eyes opened and he peered up at her, a crease appearing in that faultless face of his.

'What happened?' he asked in a voice no

more than a painful whisper.

'You've been shot, Miguel, but it's all right. Juanita was able to remove the bullet.'

'Who would want to shoot me? Your new boyfriend, the Englishman?'

She shook her head and gave him a half smile. 'No, he was dancing next to us at the time. I think the bullet was meant for him and I think I know who fired it.'

'Who? Nobody from the *estancia*!'

'No, of course not. It's no-one you know, Miguel. He used to be Rob's friend, but now . . . '

'He has strange friends, your man.'

Gwyneth licked her lips and wasn't sure how to reply.

'He . . . he's not my man, as you say.'

'But you like him. I saw that and . . . I saw also that he is in love with you.'

'Don't! He can't be. He . . . I . . . '

'We are the same, you and I, *cara*,' Miguel's fingers squeezed hers and she could tell how weak he was by the lack of brute force he usually employed when he danced with her.

'The same?' She gulped, not understanding what he was trying to tell her and afraid of what it might be, if it were proved to be true.

'Yes, Gwyneth Johnns, daughter of the terrible Brin. You see, I was abused also by my father . . . ' He stopped, gripped by the pain of his raw wound beneath Juanita's expert dressing.

'I didn't know that, Miguel,' Gwyneth said. 'I'm sorry.'

'What it did for me was to rob me of my manhood and turn me towards members of my own sex. For you it was different. It turned you against men. But that almost makes us the same, deep down, does it not?'

'We are both victims of the same crime,' she said. 'Yes . . . but . . . '

'I have something to say to you, *cara*. No, please do not interrupt. I have to say it. If I could love any woman, you are that woman. I was so hard on you because I felt myself falling under your spell, despite everything. I would never have been able to love you fully, but I came so close that it frightened me. And it frightened my poor Antonio. We have been together for so long. I do not like to hurt him, but I know he has been hurt ever since you came to the *estancia*. *El Paraiso* has never been the same since you rode in here that very first time.'

His flow of words was arrested by a bout of coughing and he clutched at his chest, his face twisting in pain.

Gwyneth got to her feet, gave him a sip of water, holding the glass to his lips. He

318

nodded his thanks, too weak to speak any more. She bent to brush her lips over his glistening forehead and saw that he was already asleep. She turned to leave the room. That was when she saw Antonio standing there in the open doorway, his eyes full of tears.

'Antonio . . . ' she said, her features softening. 'Miguel will be pleased to find you beside him when he wakes up again.'

Antonio nodded, then slowly and silently replaced her at his friend's bedside. He would no doubt stay there for as long as it took.

★   ★   ★

Matt was clinging on, for dear life, to the neck of the Indian pony, having lost his reins in his panic to get away. And now his right foot was out of the stirrup and he could feel himself slipping and sliding, now falling, now being dragged like a limp rag doll over the rough, bumpy terrain.

At last the pony slowed to a walk and stopped, its breath coming in raucous gasps as it put its head down low and grazed on the short, wiry tufts of grass and moss. Matt eased his foot out of the second stirrup, feeling every battered part of him and thinking that it was a miracle he had survived.

He couldn't believe all this was happening to him. He couldn't believe anything any more. It was almost as if he had been taken over by some demon spirit set on destroying him. It had started back in England, he was sure of that, but when or how, he could not begin to guess. Then in Wales when he had beaten up that fellow who had refused to sell him his tickets. He couldn't believe he'd had the gall to go, later on, to the new widow and offer to buy the damned things.

Everything seemed to have gone downhill from that moment on, with his best mate, Rob, gradually distancing himself until there was no friendship left at all between them. And the sight of the *Indios* girl snuggling up willingly to Rob, and then the Spaniard, when she would have none of him was too much to take.

With what he thought was infinite courage, he had lured the dogs away with poisoned meat. Nobody noticed because they were enjoying themselves too much. He had then returned to the ranch with murder burning hotly in his heart.

The bullet he had shot through the window when the shutters blew wide open was meant for Rob, but the plan had been to kill all of them indiscriminately. When he saw the Spaniard fall, his courage suddenly deserted him and there seemed nothing for it but to run.

What the hell had pushed him to such extremes? He asked himself the question over and over. Rage had surged through him, seeing them all so happy and knowing that all he had to look forward to was the hangman's noose. Rob, the silly sod, had tripped over his own feet while dancing with that fat Spanish bitch. The bullet had missed by inches. After a moment of stunned silence, the ranch hands were pouring out of the building, ready to string him from the nearest tree.

Matt sat now, his aching bones propped against the rough bark of a cedar tree. He sank his head in his hands, too beaten and weary to weep, though he felt full of tears inside for the things he had done and for those he might be driven to do in the future.

A stone rattled a few yards away and he looked up, fearfully, but it was only a lone guanaco crossing the track, the outline of its thick brown coat appearing like a halo of golden threads in the moonlight. It stopped and looked at him with large, doleful eyes. Even the animals seemed to be accusing him.

'Garrn! Away wi ye!'

He threw a handful of grit and dust at the animal and it bounded off. He listened to the pattering of its hoofs as it crashed through the undergrowth, crushing stiff grass fronds and snapping branches as it went. Then a heavy silence fell all around him and he sighed, sinking down even lower.

The *gauchos* had not chased him for very long. The old horse he had been on had been pretty nippy, but now it looked as worn out as he felt. He edged carefully over to the animal and gripped the dangling rein, tying it to a low branch. It wouldn't do to wake up in the morning and find that his only means of transport had fled.

He dosed fitfully, then decided that the ground was too hard and frozen, so he spent some time painfully gathering a supply of dry pampas grass to make himself a bedding. He lay down on it, too fatigued even to think of pulling a blanket over himself, but his leather coat was thick, as were the clothes he was wearing underneath. By morning he would be strong enough to crawl away into hiding, until he could put his plan into action, and next time he would get it right.

★ ★ ★

Gwyneth checked on Therese and found young Dora sitting by the older woman, stroking her hand. It was good that the girl could feel useful. It would take her mind off her own wretched situation. Going quietly through the big house, she noticed that one or two of the *gauchos* were stationed strategically about the place, their hats pulled down low over their faces, but all of them fully awake and alert. If the would-be killer came back, they would be ready for him.

Out on the veranda, she found Rob and Davy sitting on the steps, talking together in low mutters. Davy jumped up as she approached.

'Well, I'll be off to me bed,' he said, giving her a nod and another one to his brother. 'Goodnight, Gwyneth.'

'Goodnight, Davy,' she said wearily and looked down at Rob. 'Do you mind if I join you, Rob? I don't want to go to bed just yet.'

He patted the step beside him. She pulled a cushion from a seat and put it beneath her to absorb the cold, then she sat silently for a while, her hands clasping her knees, staring out into the starry night.

'I'm sorry about Miguel,' Rob said after a while and she blinked at him through the glow of the single oil lamp that was flickering yellow through a nearby window.

'He's going to be all right, I think,' she said with a deep sigh. 'Antonio will look after him, make sure he doesn't overdo things.'

'Antonio? The guitarist?'

'Yes. They are . . . friends.'

'Friends? As in . . . ?'

'Lovers . . . yes.'

'But that's not what . . . I mean, I thought that you and he . . . Miguel, I mean . . . were . . .'

She smiled at his wide, innocent stare, then looked back again into the nothingness of the endless plains that stretched out into eternity.

'Don't you have that kind of thing in the Old Country?' she asked and felt him stir uncomfortably. He was obviously not accustomed to discussing such matters, especially with women.

'Aye, we do . . . yes, Gwyneth.' He was stuttering, floundering over his words. 'But it's all kept very quiet. Men have gone to prison for that kind of thing.'

She nodded. 'Yes, but the physical side apart . . . well, it's still love, isn't it? And maybe it's the only love they can find.'

She told him then what Miguel had said about his father and he shook his head in sympathy.

'Poor bugger! And I thought my father was bad because he was too strict with Davy and me. But he never did that to us. Never.'

'You're lucky, then.'

She felt his hand searching for hers through the darkness and she liked the feel of it as it gripped her so tightly that it seemed to warm her soul.

'Tonight, when I saw you dancing with Miguel and saw the way he seemed to look at you . . . I thought I was the most unlucky man alive.'

She turned and frowned at him, though he probably couldn't see it, because the lamp had finally gone out and the moon was hiding behind a cloud. There was only the twinkling of a scattering of stars above them. She felt his free hand touch her throat, tilting up her chin and stroking her cheek. Leaning towards him she felt his heat and the faint soapy, leathery smell that he always had about him.

'Gwyneth,' he said huskily. 'If I kiss you, you won't take a whip to me or shoot me or anything, will you?'

Her chest was heaving as her breath came short and fast. She left her reply for so long that he must have thought she hadn't heard, for he said her name softly, as his lips brushed hers and waited, poised.

'I think I'd like you to kiss me, Rob,' she whispered and felt his mouth press down, but she pulled away, scared.

'It's all right, Gwyneth. It's just a kiss, between friends.'

His head descended a second time and then he was kissing her much more surely and her whole being seemed to open up to him. It's not just a kiss, she thought, her head swimming and her heart pounding with the sheer ecstasy of it. And, dear God, I hope that we are more than just friends.

15

'Ah, Gawd!' Davy groaned as he staggered into the bunkhouse looking like he had been born with rickets. 'I think I've just put paid to me manhood.'

Rob laughed at his brother, but he felt much the same way after a week's hard riding in the saddle rounding up sheep. And he was hoarse from shouting to get the poor brainless beasts to go where they were supposed to go. Sore though he was, however, it had been an exhilarating experience, made even more so by the blossoming relationship between Gwyneth and himself

Davy too, it seemed, was having the time of his life, despite his complaints. He and Dora were no longer trying to hide their mutual feelings and Rob felt it was all to the good. There was no point in Dora acting the prim married lady, not when she was married to Matt, at any rate. And that bloody husband of hers might be swinging from some high gibbet by now, after all he had done, and well deserved it would be.

It was amusing, really, to see them openly advertising their love through a thin veil of discretion. Had they been back in England, they would have been ostracized for such flagrant behaviour. Well, chances were that the two of them would be able to tie the knot one day and settle down to a proper married life, raising children.

He had never asked Davy what he felt about Dora carrying another man's child. No doubt the lad had given it some thought, but there was no outward sign that it bothered him. Things might be different when she started to show. If that were the case, then Rob would be ready to support his little brother, do whatever it took to ensure the young couple's happiness.

'You still sweet on Gwyneth, then?' Davy asked as they sank down in their adjacent bunks and other *gauchos* bedded down for the night all around them.

'Need you ask, lad,' Rob said, closing his eyes and seeing Gwyneth's face smiling at him through a swirling fog of encroaching sleep.

'She's special, isn't she?'

'Mmm. Very special.'

'You going to marry her, our Rob?'

Rob's eyes shot open and he sat up on his elbow. 'Not so loud, eh? We don't want these cowboys to think we're a pair of softies, do we?'

The men were largely single. Being a *gaucho* wasn't the ideal job for a married man. They were on the move a lot of the time, living rough, drinking hard. But they weren't slackers. Most of them could turn their hands to anything and complaints were kept to the minimum.

'Are you?'

'Hold your horses, Davy,' Rob lay back down and turned his back to his brother so that Davy couldn't see the eager flush on his face, creeping up from his neck. 'We hardly know each other.'

'You kissed her on Sunday and she looked pretty willing to me.'

He had indeed kissed Gwyneth on Sunday, their day off. They had been walking by the river and suddenly their hands joined as if in mutual accord. She had smiled at him and he had pulled her out of sight of the *hacienda*, or so he thought at the time, and they had kissed. It was the first time they had touched since the night Miguel was shot and he had been afraid that what had happened between them on the steps of the veranda that night was all just a figment of his imagination.

But no, they had kissed and he had held her close, oh, so close, and she had liked it. He could tell. There was none of this business of her pulling away from him in fear. In fact,

329

he wondered if she had actually organized that kiss, as well as the walk.

They had walked afterwards for miles, still holding hands, until it was almost too dark to see the way back, but it didn't matter. It felt right. It had never felt that right between him and Margaret.

'Go to sleep, Davy,' he said, and when he closed his own eyes, a smile played about his mouth.

'Aye, Rob. Goodnight.'

★　★　★

Matt crept around the *estancia* as stealthily as a marauding fox. He had waited a long time for the opportunity to return. For too long he had been holed up in the mountains until he was sure those wild *gauchos* had given up the idea of him ever coming back. He had watched them come and go, and Rob and Davy with them. Once, but only once, did he consider carrying out his plan during the daytime, when the ranch was pretty well deserted. However, the idea paled when he realized how the hillsides and plains would be teaming with men who could see for miles around. Even if he could get away with it at the ranch, overpowering the women, he would never be able to escape unseen.

No, the night was his friend. It hid a lot. And those men were too deep in their slumbers to worry about intruders. He knew by now that only two men rode the perimeters of *El Paraiso* like mounted guards. Trouble was rare in this part of the world, not like it was up north where there were endless robberies and shootings. Now that he was getting used to handling a rifle, Matt thought he might head up there. It could be exciting. But he didn't want to do it alone. Solitude was not something he took kindly to.

The place was dark and silent. No lights shone from any of the windows, nothing moved, not even the trees. And without the vigilant presence of the old guard dogs, he was able to move about undetected.

Matt had made one or two dry runs, so he knew the lie of the land. He even knew where everyone slept. That was the most important thing, for he couldn't afford any more mistakes.

As he tiptoed around the main building, his presence must have disturbed the horses in a nearby corral. There was a shuffle of nervous hoofs and a low whinnying. Matt flattened himself against the white wall and prayed that they were all heavy sleepers inside. He had chosen a moonless night, just to be on the safe side.

Sidling along, hands flat against the rough stone, he counted the windows along the back of the house. He knew exactly which one he had to enter by, and in exactly which room he would find her. Taken by surprise like that, she wouldn't be able to do anything about it. She would be butter in his hands once they were away from this place and she realized where her future lay.

Matt had already gone to the trouble to steal two good horses from the well-stocked corral and had left them hidden at the edge of the tree line where his escape route lay. It wasn't far to go, even carrying a struggling female.

As he eased the thick blade of a skinning knife into the soft wood of the window frame he couldn't help grinning with anticipation. With only a little careful work, he had the window open. It slid up with a minimum of noise. Nevertheless, he waited, holding his breath, feeling his heart thump hollowly in his chest, echoing eerily in his ears.

When he was sure he was still safe, he slipped inside. The room he wanted was on the left. The floorboards creaked as he crept through a small sitting room and gripped the door handle, turning it slowly so as not to disturb the occupant of the room. Like a starving man inhaling the odours of roasting meat, he started salivating at the thought of what he was going to enjoy in so short a time.

The door opened easily. He didn't dare put on a light or strike a match, but there she was, a lumpy silhouette, lying beneath a thick quilt, all snuggled into it. He could hear soft feminine breathing as he approached the bed and reached out. The one thing he couldn't risk was that she woke up and started screaming. He bent down low over the sleeping form, felt for her hair and took a handful of it, but before the sleeping woman could call out, his fist struck. He heard a slight grunt, then silence.

Working blindly, he picked up woman and quilt together, pleased to find that she was lighter than he had expected. He carried her out of the room, stepping carefully over the windowsill with her. Hardly daring to breathe, he ran with his trophy to the waiting horses.

He got there without mishap, blessing his luck. Then he slung the unconscious girl over the back of one of the horses and quickly tied her securely. With one last look about him to make sure he was not being observed, he leapt into the saddle of the other horse and rode off into the night, chuckling to himself. He had pulled it off and nobody was the wiser.

But somebody soon was the wiser. Coming back from the kitchen, a lighted candle in one hand, a cup of warmed milk and honey in the other, Gwyneth entered her room and frowned at the empty, rumpled bed. She put the milk down and went out again, tapping gently on the bathroom door.

'Dora? Are you in there?'

There was no answer. Gwyneth tried the door and it opened, revealing nothing but empty space. Then she felt a waft of cold air and saw the open window. And the wood was splintered where someone had forced it.

A second waft of air blew out the candle she was holding. Gwyneth breathed heavily through her nose as she fought off the feeling of dread that rose within her. With her heart tumbling over itself and threatening to choke her, she fumbled with shaking fingers to light an oil lamp. As soon as the glow from it was sufficient to see by, she carried it with her to the other side of the house and rapped urgently on Therese's bedroom door.

'Therese! Therese, come quick! Something terrible has happened!'

She dared not raise her voice, not wishing to disturb Miguel in a room down the hall. He was still recovering from his gunshot wound. However, Antonio, who was always hovering near his friend with close attention, put his head out and gave her a curious stare. She noticed he was fully dressed and ready for trouble.

'Antonio! Please go to the bunkhouse and alert the men. Dora's been kidnapped!'

As she spoke, Therese appeared, heavy-lidded and yawning, but she came fully awake when Gwyneth's words sank in.

'My little Dora? Kidnapped? But how . . . who . . . ?'

'I saw nothing, Therese,' Gwyneth told her and gave a shudder. 'I was fetching some warm milk from the kitchen. She couldn't sleep because she had had a bad dream. That's why she was in my room instead of . . . Oh, God! It must have been Matt.'

Therese stared at her anxiously, slow to comprehend at first, then the truth dawned and her hands flew to her mouth to stop her cry of despair.

'Oh, poor child!' She cried breathlessly. 'In the hands of that brute. We must do something . . . the men . . .'

'Antonio has gone to rouse them. I must . . . I must speak to Rob and Davy.'

Gwyneth, the lamp still in her hand, fled out of the house in Antonio's footsteps. The keen night air stung her through her flimsy nightdress and the ground was hard and sharp beneath her bare feet.

She was a few yards from the bunkhouse, hearing the rumpus that erupted inside as Antonio told the men what had happened. As she might expect, Rob and Davy, still in their underwear and struggling into their pants, were first to burst through the door. She flung herself at Rob, clinging to him breathlessly.

'Rob, it has to be Matt,' she panted. 'Who else would do a thing like that? Poor Dora. She must be terrified.'

'Didn't you hear anything?' Davy asked, wild-eyed with worry.

She repeated what she had said to Therese. By now her teeth were chattering with the cold, but she ignored it.

'Davy,' Rob gave his brother a push. 'Go get a blanket for Gwyneth before she freezes to death . . . and bring my coat will you.'

Davy disappeared back into the bunk-house, where most of the men were hurriedly dressing, excited at the prospect of a manhunt. He reappeared thirty seconds later with blanket and coat.

'What are we going to do, Rob? This is our business, isn't it? We have to take responsibility for that bastard.'

Rob inclined his head, then slipped the

blanket around Gwyneth's shaking shoulders.

'First, let's be sure of our facts, Davy. I'll take Gwyneth back to the *hacienda*. It'll be dawn soon, then we can go after him. There's not much sense in setting out in the dark. He may know where he's going, but we don't.'

'But what about Dora?' Davy looked ready to explode.

'We'll go at first light. He can't make much headway in the dark. Indian Joe will come with us. I hear he's a pretty good tracker.'

Gwyneth shook her head as he led her away, his arm tightly around her.

'No, Rob. Indian Joe is too old now. He's full of rheumatism and half blind. I'll go with you. I know this territory well. I used to roam about here long before I met Therese and Miguel.'

'I won't let you, Gwyneth. It's too dangerous.'

'So is Patagonia, if you don't know your way around. Believe me, I know what I'm talking about.'

He argued with her all the way back to the *hacienda*, but she was adamant and in the end he grudgingly gave way. After all, he knew her well enough now to realize how stubborn she was. Even if he had continued to refuse, he couldn't stop her from going. She was a good tracker and better than most men on horseback. And she knew how to find her way through the mountains and past glaciers.

Gwyneth drew in a deep breath, thinking of the glaciers, those gigantic ice flows from another age that were so beautiful and yet so deadly to the inexperienced traveller. Many men had lost their lives thinking they could cross them. She didn't care if Matt became one of the statistics, but she hated the idea of him taking Dora with him.

'Rob, you might think this silly, but I don't think Matt came here for Dora.'

He pressed a hand on her shoulder, his fingers massaging the flesh beneath the blanket.

'I've already worked that out, Gwyneth,' he said, pushing her down onto a chair at the dining table, where Juanita, looking old and flustered, was already producing food and hot drinks.

'Aie! Señor Barker!' the housekeeper cried when she saw his half-dressed state and that of Gwyneth. 'Is not good you sit at table like that. You go get your clothes on, and you too Señorita Gwyneth. Have you no shame?'

But Therese was quick to tell the old woman to be quiet and attend to the business of breakfast.

'There are more important things at stake

today, Juanita, than respectability,' she said. 'Go and prepare a hot meal and a basket of food . . . enough for a few days. Rob and Davy will have need of it.'

'Enough for three, Juanita,' Gwyneth said to Juanita's broad back as she disappeared back into the recesses of the kitchen. 'And some extra for Dora when we find her.'

Therese looked shocked. 'Gwyneth, you cannot go. It is not for any woman to go hunting down dangerous men.'

'I'm going anyway,' Gwyneth told her. 'Without me, Rob and Davy could lose themselves in the mountains.'

'You are a fool, Gwyneth. They are not your people, after all.'

Gwyneth did not have time to argue. Dora and Davy, and particularly Rob, had become her family, along with the old Welshwoman who had supported her for as long as she could remember. They were not blood relations, but they were good, warm-hearted people and she loved them. She loved them all. And that was something precious that she never thought she would have in her life.

She kissed Therese on both cheeks. 'You mean well, Therese, so thank you for that.'

'Mean well? *Cara*, I had dreams of your becoming my sister-in-law. Miguel was so close to changing. No other woman has meant so much to him. Do not break my heart, Gwyneth, I beg of you.'

'Miguel is happy with Antonio, Therese. They have been together a long time. As for me, I must follow my own heart, now that I've discovered I have one. I'm sorry that it does not lie with Miguel.'

Seeing Therese's eyes fill with tears, she kissed her again and after a brief hug, she rushed off to prepare for what could turn out to be a long and dangerous journey.

She was already waiting astride the gleaming black Diablo when Rob and Davy appeared, both carrying rifles, which she had taught them to use.

'Here!' she said, tossing them each a pistol. 'Sometimes a rifle is not the best weapon.'

'I don't want to shoot anybody!' Davy complained.

'Perhaps you won't have to,' she told him gently.

Rob was regarding her with narrowed eyes. She gave him a reassuring smile.

'Come on,' she said huskily. Get your horses and let's be off. I think I know where Matt is headed. The tracks are still fresh, but if it snows in the mountains we will lose him quickly.'

'I don't care about losing that bugger,' Davy swore and his jaw was set firmly, showing his hate and determination. 'It's Dora I'm worried about.'

'I don't like any of this,' Rob said as he fixed the rifle in place and swung himself up into his saddle.

'None of us like it, Rob,' Gwyneth said, as she urged Diablo to take the lead and drew behind her a packhorse laden with the necessary provisions. 'But in life there are some times when we have to do what goes against the grain.'

She dug her heels into Diablo's sides and went off at a gallop, leaving Rob and Davy to follow.

★ ★ ★

Dora groaned. The world seemed to be spinning around and there wasn't a part of her that didn't hurt. Deep inside her there was a pain that refused to go away. With her eyes still tightly closed, she tried to remember what had happened, but it was all very hazy.

She recalled going to Gwyneth's room because she was having difficulty sleeping and needed the comfort of female companionship. Gwyneth reminded her of Blodwen. They were both tough on the outside, and yet so soft and warm once you broke through the brittle veneer. Gwyneth, too, was awake and willing to talk. She had gone to warm up some milk and then . . .

Dora figured she must have dozed off, lying warmly beneath Gwyneth's quilt. She heard what she thought was Gwyneth moving around the room. Then something hit her hard and there was nothing. She had come to briefly and realized that something awful was happening to her. The jerky, rocking movements of a galloping horse made themselves felt, digging into her stomach, her chest, her face. She was slung over a hard saddle and she could see, in a blur, the uneven ground racing past.

Then the blackness descended again to shut out the fear and the pain. At least, now, she wasn't strung like a side of bacon over the hard saddle of a horse. She was lying on her back on stony ground, gripped by the extreme cold to such an extent it acted as an anaesthetic to reduce the pain, except the pain in her head, which throbbed mercilessly.

'You awake, then?'

The recognizable sound of Matt's voice jerked her into full consciousness and made her heart pound with fearful, irregular beats.

'Matt?' she said in a croaking voice that seemed to be coming from deep within her head. 'What's happening? Where are we?'

'Never you mind.'

She forced her eyes to open and saw him sitting on his hunkers in the old miner's traditional position, though there was no cosy miner's cottage with the open coal fire and his family all around him. She saw the faint glimmer from a pathetically small fire that he had managed to get started. Between them, the ground was dark brown and frozen. Beyond, all she could see from her prone position was a grey-white blur. Snowflakes fell softly, floating before her eyes, making her feel dizzy and sick.

Dora struggled to sit up. Matt, watching her in brooding silence, didn't offer to help her. She winced and cried out as pain once more seared through her insides. Maybe she was going to die and Davy wasn't even there to comfort her.

Oh, heavens, she thought and offered up a little prayer, the best she knew, taught to her by the sweetshop lady who had taken her in and nurtured her after she left the orphanage.

Lord keep me safe from all that is evil and let me live to prove that I am of some worth.

'What are you muttering about, bitch?'

Matt poked the fire with a stick of brushwood before tossing it onto the flames. It flared up for a few seconds, sending tongues of flame two feet high, then died. The fire would be out before long and it was already cold enough to freeze the toes from his feet.

He glanced at Dora's bare toes peeping from her quilt and gave a shrug. Silly bitch. What had she been doing sleeping in Gwyneth Johnns's bed? As if things weren't bad enough, he had to go and make a fatal error like that. At least with the *Indios* girl he would have had enough fight on his hands to keep them both warm. And she would have succumbed, eventually. This one was no fun, and no pleasure at all with her skinny body and her abject fear of anything touching her. Especially her husband.

Matt roused himself, suddenly reminded of the fact that no matter what he thought of Dora, she was still his wife. He got up and went to her, pulling back the quilt. His fingers were numb as he reached down and ripped the front of her nightdress open to the navel. She shrank back, as she always did, but there was something other than fear in her face. There was the look of real pain. That was when he saw the purple and red bruises spreading over her chest and down to her belly.

'Damn and blast you, girl!'

He sank a kick into her side and retreated, leaving her alone to pull her nightdress back together again, and huddle once more beneath the quilt, ignoring the agony of her injuries in an attempt to roll herself more securely in it against the cold.

★ ★ ★

Pressing onward through a flurry of snow, and then a blizzard, Gwyneth stopped and slumped low and weary in her saddle.

'It's no good. I can't see the tracks any more. We'll have to take shelter for the night. Maybe it will blow over by morning.'

'But we can't stop now!' Davy was just as exhausted, but he refused to admit it, needing to go on heedlessly in his search for Dora.

Rob dismounted and patted the boy's leg. He understood Davy's feelings, but there was a limit to their endurance in these difficult conditions on strange territory. They were even getting out of Gwyneth's range of knowledge by now.

'Davy, be sensible, lad,' he said. 'If we can't go on, then it's reasonable to suppose that Matt can't either. Especially with Dora.'

'But I'm scared for her life, Rob. If she dies . . . '

'Rob's right, Davy,' Gwyneth said, also dismounting and leaning against Diablo's steaming shoulder. 'We have to find shelter, if not for us, for the horses. Out here, we could perish on foot.'

For the first time, Rob looked around him instead of keeping his head down as he followed the tracks made by Gwyneth's stallion. His eyes became dazzled by the flurries of snow that blew this way and that. All around them, the foothills were climbing ever higher, with snow lying everywhere, getting deeper and deeper. The silence that surrounded them was eerie.

'There's a cave not too far from here,' Gwyneth announced, getting her bearings and pointing at a mass of rocks and trees pushing up out of the ground as if propelled by some force too powerful to resist. 'Come on.'

Leading the horses, Rob and Davy followed her, their feet sinking into the deepening snow that was fast drifting into thick mounds, disguising the contours of the land.

It was a steep climb to reach the cave, which was only a small space in the cliff face, though there was enough room for the horses and the mules to shelter in the entrance. Inside, it smelt dank of animal dung and rotting vegetation, but was otherwise much warmer than outside, and there was enough dry tumbleweed to pack under their sleeping bags to soften the impact of the unyielding floor. While the men were making a fire from conifer branches, Gwyneth rubbed down the animals, drying them off so they wouldn't catch a chill.

'Gawd, it's perishing!' Davy said through chattering teeth as they bedded down. 'I hate to think what that bloody Matt's up to right now . . . and how can poor Dora stand this, her with that baby inside her?'

'Let's not be negative,' Gwyneth told him gently. She had placed herself between the two men at Rob's insistence and offered no objection to the close proximity of their bodies.

'I can't do anything else. I feel so helpless.'

'Tomorrow,' she told him, 'we will be able to turn ourselves to more positive action, when we can see what we're doing and think more clearly. As Rob said, Matt is no better off than us in these conditions. If anything, he's worse off.'

'That's what's bloody worrying me,' Davy muttered.

When he turned on his side with a sigh, Gwyneth shuffled along until she was pressed up against him. She draped an arm about him and looked over her shoulder at Rob, who was still staying a respectable distance from her.

'This is no time for being prim and proper,

Rob,' she said with a half smile. 'If we all keep very close it could save our lives. Otherwise, even with the fire, we could die from hypothermia.'

He took no second telling. He eased himself over the space that was between them until he was pressing up against her back. His arm, beneath the heavy blankets, snaked about her slim waist and held her tight. He heard her sigh, then her breathing told him she was already asleep. As for his part, he didn't think that sleep would be one of his bedfellows that night.

However, he did eventually fall into a deep slumber, but dreamed of blinding snow and glaciers and Matt laughing at them as he dragged poor little Dora, her hands tied together as if in supplication, her great blue eyes now white, sightless orbs and her face distorted out of all recognition.

He awoke with a start, thinking that some creature was trying to find its way into the cave, but it was only Gwyneth, moving about stealthily as she rekindled the fire and placed a pot of ice over the flames so she could make *maté* to revive them and get the day started.

'I didn't feel you move,' he said, noticing that the space between him and Davy was already cooled down.

She smiled and concentrated on getting out some food from the hamper Juanita had provided; enough to keep them going for the next few hours. There was some dried beef, stale bread and cheese and some sweet carrot cake.

'That's some breakfast,' he said, struggling to extricate himself from the blankets, shivering as the first blast of cold air hit him from the mouth of the cave. 'Where are the horses?'

'There's a little brook a few yards from here where the grazing is still good. Don't worry. I tethered them well, but at least they can refresh themselves too, until we are ready to go on. You'd better wake Davy. I don't want to spend any more time here than necessary. It was daylight half an hour ago.'

There was a groan from Davy and he emerged, pink-faced, from having had his head beneath the blankets.

'I'm awake,' he told them unnecessarily and stretched with a loud yawn. 'Let's get going.'

'First we eat,' Gwyneth said firmly and Rob backed her up when Davy looked like giving her an argument.

'I'm not hungry,' Davy said, taking a piece of stale bread and looking at it in disgust.

'Eat!' Gwyneth ordered. 'I don't want you

letting us down because you have no energy in your belly.'

Davy glowered at her just for a second, then dunked his bread into the pot of steaming *maté* that she passed to him.

'One day I might even get a liking for this stuff,' he said gloomily, reaching for a chunk of dried beef and a slice of cheese.

Breakfast over, Gwyneth repacked their belongings and hoisted the saddle panniers onto her shoulder.

'I'll get the horses ready,' she said, and stepped out of the cave.

Rob's eyes followed her hungrily as he remembered how he had spent the night pressed into her back and couldn't believe that he had been able to ignore the fact in favour of sleeping. It hadn't been easy, but he had done it. Perhaps, had they been alone, without Davy's intrusive presence, the experience might have been very different.

'That's some woman,' Davy said as he sat, cross-legged, on the floor of the cave, finishing off the last of the food, despite his avowal that he had no appetite.

'Yes, isn't she,' Rob said, heading in the same direction as Gwyneth and calling to his brother over his shoulder, 'Clear up there, Davy. I'm going to help Gwyneth with the horses.'

'Aye, aye, sir!' He heard the echo of Davy's mocking words and was glad that the lad was more light-hearted this morning, for nothing good was ever achieved by black-hearted anger.

Gwyneth had already saddled Diablo and was tightening the cinch straps. Rob started on the other horses and caught a curious glance from Gwyneth above the black stallion's broad back.

'Thank you for last night,' she said.

He raised an enquiring eyebrow at her. 'Last night? What did I do?'

'Nothing,' she said. 'And that's what I'm thanking you for. You could have taken advantage of the situation, but you didn't. I'm grateful for that.'

Her words took him a little by surprise. Without responding verbally, he simply nodded and went on saddling the horses. They were in luck, he thought. The sky was clear and blue and the sun was already beginning to shine. It was a good day for catching a murdering kidnapper.

Everything else could wait. There was plenty of time.

16

They found Dora huddled beneath a makeshift shelter with the smouldering remains of a fire that didn't look as if it had ever been big enough to keep her warm. At first, they thought she was dead, but then, as Gwyneth and the two men started to rub her hands and feet vigorously, she stirred and her eyelids flickered.

'Oh, Dora, love!' Davy fought back his emotions as he wrapped his big riding coat around her and she cried out in pain. 'I'm here, love. You're safe now.'

'What the hell did the bastard do to her?' Rob said through gritted teeth.

'Never mind that, now,' Gwyneth told him, straightening up and scanning the distant, icebound horizon. 'Let's get her back to the *hacienda* before she freezes to death. That is, if it's not too late. She looks pretty bad to me.'

'Aye, come on, let's go.' Davy was hugging the semi-comatose girl to his chest. 'She can ride up with me.'

'Just a minute,' Gwyneth delved into her saddlebags and brought out items of warm clothing and they struggled to pull them onto Dora's limp, rag doll body.

Lifting her, they saw that the blanket she had been lying on was stained with blood. Rob felt his own blood run cold inside his veins. He wasn't too experienced when it came to women and their bodies, but it looked to him as if she had lost the baby she was carrying, and no wonder.

'If you go quickly, Davy,' he said, you'll be able to follow our tracks back to *El Paraiso*.'

He took out some food from their supply bag and stuffed his pockets with it. Davy and Gwyneth were watching him intriguingly.

'What are you doing, Rob?' Gwyneth asked as he took ammunition and a spare rifle and strapped it to his sleeping roll behind his saddle, then jumped up and turned the horse towards the way Matt had gone.

'You go back with Davy and Dora,' he said, his face set in a determined scowl. 'I'm going after Matt.'

'You can't!'

Both Davy and Gwyneth spoke together, their faces stricken with disbelief.

'Go, I said! This business is now between Matt and me.'

'You're not planning to kill him, Rob, are you? You can't! Not you, of all people!' Davy had gone pale at the thought.

'My intention is to find him and bring him back, by whatever means is available to me, but bring him back I will. He has a lot to answer for. I think the onus is on me to see things through to the end, one way or another.'

'How do you figure that, our Rob,' Davy shouted and the pitch of his voice disturbed Dora, making her whimper pitifully.

'You're a fool, Rob!' Gwyneth was holding tightly on to his stirrup as if she had no intention of letting him go. 'You may not be a killer, but he is. He's proved it more than once now. He won't stop at pulling the trigger or sticking a knife in you. Believe me. I know the type. He's just another Brin Johnns and he'll stop at nothing to get what he wants.'

Rob bent down and cupped her chin in his hand. He kissed her lightly on the top of her head and offered her a sad smile.

'He hasn't anything left to have, Gwyneth.'

'But Rob . . . '

'Now, tell me which way you think he would have gone beyond here, just in case I lose his tracks.'

She blinked furiously as the icy wind whipped around her, stinging her eyes and producing tears that oozed out onto her frosted cheeks.

'There's only one way from here,' she

pointed. 'Through the Twin Horn Pass
. . . there!'

He followed her finger. Two massive
columns of black rock rose like crooked
fingers. Between them the ground was thick
with snow and ice. Beyond, there was the
turquoise blue of a tall glacier rising like a
solid wall. It looked an impossible passage,
but if Matt could get through it, then so
could he.

'Go with Davy!' He said, kicking the sides
of his mount, and she was obliged to let go of
the stirrup and move back out of the way. 'I'll
be back for you . . . if you'll have me.'

Gwyneth watched him ride off. *If you'll
have me!* There was no other man in the
world she would rather have. Didn't he know
that by now?

'Do you think, Davy,' she said, turning now
to Rob's brother, 'that you can find your way
back without me?'

'Aye, but what are you going to do,
Gwyneth?'

'I'm going after Rob. The fool will get
himself lost or killed if I'm not there to stop
it.' She flashed her eyes at Davy. 'Well, what
are you waiting for? Go!'

She slapped the rump of Davy's horse and
it bounded forward with an anxious snort.

'You take care, Gwyneth,' he shouted into

the silent, frozen air. 'I don't want to lose either of you.'

She gazed after him, her heart torn to shreds. He and Dora were so young. If he got lost, both of them could perish. Dora could die anyway, the state she was in. But she had to go with Rob to protect him. Nothing was going to stand in their way now. Not Matt, not the glacier, not even the Andes themselves. She wouldn't let them.

Without wasting any more time, she hauled herself up into the saddle and urged Diablo forward, cursing the fact that they could not fly like the wind on this treacherous terrain. She couldn't risk Diablo breaking a leg and the packhorse she was trailing behind her slowed their progress considerably. It was for the best, she told herself sensibly, though her heart was inclined to ignore the dangers. She knew that if the worst came to the worst, she would risk her own life to save Rob. Especially if it involved Matthew Riley.

*   *   *

Matt had never felt so alone. His insides were burning from the raw Bourbon he had been gulping down along the route. The bottle was empty now. He stared hatefully at it for a split second, then threw it at a rock where it smashed, filling the eerie silence with a deafening noise.

The alcohol didn't appear to be having any noticeable effect. It was not dulling his brain, or suppressing his black thoughts. If only he could get roaring drunk, like he used to back home in Gateshead, it would help him forget his inadequacies; forget the killings, and the bullet meant for the only friend he had ever had. It would make him forget Dora, the little bride he had brought with him to this Godforsaken land. He had soon learnt to hate and despise her, but now he was filled with remorse at the mental picture of her tortured little face as he beat her black and blue. It kept haunting even his waking hours. He hadn't been able to stop hitting her and kicking her, as if she was the cause of all his problems. Poor little beggar. All she was guilty of was being stupid enough to marry him.

He had tried to make her comfortable before he deserted her. What was bothering him now was that she might never be found . . . or be found too late to save her. He couldn't afford to spend too much time pondering on that. His first priority was to get over this damned glacier. The old Indian had told him that there was a vast green land beyond, where a man could lose himself and still live like a king. It was as good a place as any to head for. After all, what did he have to lose?

After an hour of trying to cross the ice at the foot of the glacier, Matt's filly missed its footing and fell, and him with it. The damned silly creature had him pinned beneath her. She was screaming and writhing with pain, her front legs broken where they had slipped into a crevice. He took his pistol out from his belt and put a couple of bullets through her head, then eased his own damaged leg out from under her and limped away.

He couldn't seem to walk in a straight line. The ground kept tipping beneath his unsteady feet. All he could see, after a while, was a white blur and some bright blue patches where the ice had been compacted over hundreds of years as the glacier grew and moved like a living thing over the land, inch by inch. Straight ahead, the Indian had said. Don't deviate or you will be lost.

The trouble was, he had lost his sense of direction half an hour ago and floundered about so much it was difficult to tell if he was still going in the same straight line as the one he had started out on. Pulling an old woollen shawl up around his face, he fixed his sights hypnotically on the darkest blue of the glacier and forged on.

Rob's horse gave a startled jerk at the reverberating sound of gunshots. He was halfway through the narrow pass that separated the Twin Horns. Overhead, there was a strange creaking sound, then a deep-throated rumble and he felt the vibration of it. He looked up in time to see a mass of ice and snow come hurtling down towards him from a great height.

With a shout he forced his horse to leap forward out of the path of the avalanche. It was a frantic dash, but he made it with seconds to spare. And, he was glad to note, it hadn't totally blocked off the pass. He would, at least, be able to get back. That was, if he was lucky enough to survive the next few hours.

Beyond the pass, it soon became patently clear that the terrain was impossible for horses. This was confirmed when, having tethered his mount to a lone pine tree, he continued on foot and came across Matt's dead horse. Matt must be in a bad way, he thought, for he hadn't even taken his saddlebags with him and they were full of essential supplies and spare clothing.

Crazy, crazy fool!

Rob could see the direction in which Matt

had gone, though his trail seemed to be a little uncertain, veering to the right instead of going straight ahead, which would have been the more obvious choice. To the right, the glacier rose higher and became a series of jagged crevasses, some of them deep enough to sink a ship in.

Shading his eyes, Rob surveyed the vast panorama, stiffening when he saw a black blob moving a mile or so ahead. It had to be Matt.

Rob took one step forward, then heard the sound behind him of snow and ice being crunched and feet slithering on the hard ground. He spun around, thinking it was his horse, having pulled free of its tethering.

'Gwyneth!' He couldn't believe his eyes when he saw her walking towards him, as sure-footed now as a gazelle.

She was bundled up in just about every piece of clothing she had brought with her. Her rifle was slung across her back and she had a determined expression on her face, all set for the argument she knew he would give her.

'You idiot! You know I have to go after Matt. It . . . it's a matter of principle. Please, Gwyneth. It's not too late. Catch up with Davy. He'll need help with Dora.'

'No! You are the one who needs me,

Geordie English.' She used the term she had attached to him when they first met. 'I'm staying. Where you go, I go.'

Rob heaved a great sigh and held out a hand to her, which she took. He lifted her fingers to his mouth and kissed them through the woollen gloves.

'He's there,' he told her, pointing.

'Yes, I see him, but he is going the wrong way. No man climbs the heart of a glacier and lives to tell the story. If we go after him, we could all be killed.'

'Then let's get to him before he gets too far,' Rob said.

'Look how he walks,' Gwyneth pointed out. 'He must be drunk. It cannot be snow blindness. Not yet. Later, that will come, if he gets far enough.'

They were moving more quickly than Matt, who stumbled a lot. As the distance between them shortened and Matt stopped, perhaps to catch his breath, they saw him look over his shoulder. The way he hesitated, standing like a statue, then jerked into hasty motion, told them that he had spotted them.

Rob raised an arm, calling out Matt's name, but Gwyneth shook her head at the floundering figure less than half a mile ahead of them now.

'He will not stop now, Rob,' she said. 'He

has nothing to gain by being caught, even by you.'

'Especially by me,' Rob told her through tightened jaws as anger boiled inside him where friendship had once warmed him.

Suddenly, Matt disappeared from sight. There was no sign of him as they drew close.

'He has to be in a crevasse,' Gwyneth said, inspecting the wall of ice with its encrustations of moraine deposited in the glacier over thousands of years.

'Look! Over there!' Rob had spotted something lying on the impacted snow, something glinting metallic in the sunlight.

It was the fob watch he had given Matt for his twenty-first birthday. It was lying face down, watch and chain intact, the end of which still had a bit of dark material attached where it had been torn from Matt's coat.

'He must have squeezed through here.'

Gwyneth indicated a narrow aperture in the ice that looked as if it had been recently disturbed by something scraping against the walls. Beyond it, reaching deep within the glacier, the light was grey and unwelcoming, but there was a definite cleft that seemed to climb gradually upwards through the ice.

'Stay here, Gwyneth,' Rob said. 'It would be senseless for us both to get trapped in there.'

Gwyneth said nothing, but he was satisfied that she did not follow when he slipped into the gap, thanking the gods that he was not as bulky as Matt, and a lot surer of step.

He followed the cleft up through the silent body of the glacier, surprised that he went easily enough with the minimum of effort. But then the passage became two, spreading out into a 'V' and there was nothing to point him in the right direction.

'Come on, bastard!' he muttered, hearing his own voice echo back at him in an eerie whisper. 'Make a sound so I can tell which way to go!'

A tiny shower of ice particles answered him on the left. There was no guarantee that the disturbance had been due to Matt, but he headed in that direction.

The walls of the crevasse seemed to close in on him, the higher he went. He started to lose his footing and there was little in the way of handholds. What he wouldn't have given right now, he thought, for a pit pickaxe or hewing tool to help his progress.

Fumbling, with frozen fingers, in his pockets, he came up with a heavy-duty penknife. He opened it cagily and thrust it into the wall of ice above his head. The blade sank in to the hilt and he found he was able to pull himself up sufficiently to reach the next negotiable ledge.

After a couple of similar actions, he could see the sky opening up above him, feel the cold waft of the wind on his head. He could also feel the icy grip of fear and doubt working in his insides. Somehow, he couldn't imagine that Matt had come this way. He was a strong man, but he wasn't a capable one. The climb would surely have beaten him before he got this far, desperate though he must be.

At last, he could get a grip on the sharp edges of the ice wall as they burst into the open. It took all his strength to get himself up there, but he did it. And as he stepped out onto the ragged tooth surface, he heard a rattle and grunt, and when he looked up there was Matt, twenty-five yards from him, having chosen the other passage and got there before him. He was already perched precariously, with his rifle trained on Rob, and although it appeared to be wavering, it would be hard for him to miss at that range.

'Well, well!' Matt shouted across the undulating gap between them. 'I never thought you had this much spunk in you, Rob.'

'Ever heard of principles, Matt?' Rob called back, finding it difficult to speak, his lips were so frozen. 'Put that rifle down, man. I'm taking you back to Puerto Daffyd where you can stand trial and take your chances with the judge and jury.'

'Lynch mob, more like! You'll not take me in, Rob. Not alive. Not at any price.'

Rob tested the ground beneath him. It was solid, but so jagged like a serrated knife, it was difficult to get a good hold without twisting an ankle. He moved forward at a snail's pace, putting one foot cautiously after the other, praying he wouldn't fall and injure himself. An accident now would serve no good purpose.

'Stay where you are, you bloody fool! I'll kill ye if I have to.'

'Then you'll have to kill me, Matt, and have that, too, on your conscience. I'm not leaving here without you, but I'd rather take you back alive. You see, unlike you, my friend, I don't thrive on the blood of others.'

He saw Matt stagger slightly as he raised his rifle again, peering down the sights of it directly at Rob. The click of the safety mechanism being pulled back brought Rob's heart into his throat as he drew closer and closer to his quarry. Any minute now, he thought, Matt was going to pull the trigger and he would have to rely on him being unsteady on his feet, and a bad shot.

As it happened, he didn't have to rely on

anything of the sort. There was another sound, so loud that it made both men stand rigid. It all seemed to happen in some kind of slow motion as Gwyneth stepped into view behind Matt. The leather thong of her whip snaked through the air, wrapping itself around the rifle barrel and sending it flying, skittering across the ice field to disappear from sight down a deep fissure some yards away.

'Gwyneth, for God's sake, be careful!' Rob yelled.

He wanted to swear at her for ignoring his instructions and putting herself in danger on his behalf. She had obviously followed him and taken the other fork in the ice passage, coming out at the exact spot where Matt had emerged.

Matt had recovered himself now and was laughing loudly, though there was no real mirth in the sound. He was approaching Gwyneth, mindless of the whip, for she had gone down on her knees in her bid to rid him of the rifle, her feet sliding out from under her with the force of it.

Rob shouted at the top of his voice and plunged forward, but there was no haste to be made on this lethal terrain and for every step he took forward, he seemed to take another one back or to the side. He felt so helpless that his mind was clogged with frustration, seeing Matt almost on top of Gwyneth as she struggled to rise.

'Rob!' she cried out, desperately. 'My foot's caught!'

That was when Rob saw the knife in Matt's hand. It was no pen-knife, either. It was a long, broad-bladed thing that the *gauchos* used for skinning cows and guanacos. It could cut through the thickest hide like a hot knife through butter. If he turned it on Gwyneth now she wouldn't stand a chance.

'Come on, Matt!' he said, trying to keep his voice steady, though panic was tearing his guts apart. 'Enough! This isn't what we came to Patagonia for, man!'

'Oh, no? It seems like you got what you wanted, mate. Aye, and everything I wanted too. Let's be havin' you, old friend. I might be on me way out, but I'm goin' to take you wi' me!'

A part of Rob felt relief, realizing that Matt was set on killing him rather than Gwyneth. But then, what would become of her if she was left in Matt's crazy hands?

'Rob, stay away from him!' Gwyneth said as she tugged desperately at the trapped foot that was wedged in the ice. 'He's mad!'

'Aye, I suppose I must be.' Matt's voice was low, but Rob heard every syllable. 'But don't worry, pet. Ye'll get to like it after a while, when there's nothing else to have.'

Rob was so close, it took only one mighty leap and his body collided with that of Matt's, sending him flying, the knife still in his grip, but not, happily, embedded in Rob. Together, they grappled and rolled over one another, first this way, then that. It was hard to tell which man was the stronger. In reality, it should have been Rob, but Matt was driven by a wild desperation to survive at all odds. He had the killer instinct strong in him and nothing to lose. When Rob looked, for one crazy instant, into his eyes, he saw what he should have seen long ago, and was afraid.

He somehow got the better of Matt, just as he thought he had lost the battle. He hauled the other man to his feet and raised a tight fist, ready to pound it into Matt's face. Unfortunately, he had forgotten the knife. Matt's arm swung and Rob felt the cold steel slice through his shoulder. It looked as if the fight was all but over, but then a shot rang out, nicking Matt's head.

Gwyneth, having freed her foot, had taken careful aim and pulled the trigger. She wanted to kill him, but her hands were too numb, too gripped by emotion at the thought that she might lose the only man who had ever respected her. However, the bullet had caused Matt to stagger backwards.

'Matt!' Rob started forward after him, his arms reaching out to grab him, but Matt fell into the gaping crevasse with a wild shout and they could hear him slithering down into nothing, his fingers clawing at the ice walls, grappling futilely for something to hold on to.

'Be careful, Rob!' Gwyneth screamed. 'It's deep!'

Rob fell flat and crawled on his belly to the edge of the gaping hole. He saw Mat clinging on to a ledge a few feet down, his eyes wild and starting from his head.

'Matt, if you can stand up, I think I can reach you.'

Rob got as near to the edge as he could safely go and felt Gwyneth behind him, hooking herself around his ankles like an anchor.

'No! Leave me!' Matt's voice echoed up from the crevasse.

'Don't be stupid, man! I can save you.'

'For what? A rope around me neck?'

And then, before Rob's eyes, Matt threw himself off the ledge. There was no scream, no sound, except the dull *zunk* as Matt's body came to rest, speared by a sharp pinnacle of ice. He twitched for a few seconds, then was still. Rob drew in a great gulp of air and felt Gwyneth tugging at him, pulling him back from the abyss.

'He's gone,' he said, his voice a mere croak.

They clung to one another. Then, almost as if the glacier was digesting its meal of human flesh, there was a loud groaning and a creaking as an enormous slice of the ravine wall came adrift, plunging down, effectively burying Matt in a timeless tomb. Perhaps, one day, hundreds of years from now, Rob thought, his body would be carried out with the moraine, into a world curious to know how he got there.

Gwyneth was shuddering in Rob's arms. 'Oh, Rob, your shoulder!'

He held her tightly against him, kissing her hair, her face, rubbing his hands over her to bring back the life they had both nearly lost.

'It's nothing. I'll survive.'

'I thought I'd lost you,' she said with another convulsive shudder.

'Let's go,' he said gruffly. 'And this time, I'll follow you.'

'I won't ever let you out of my sight again,' she told him with a quivering smile.

'That's something I'm very glad to hear.'

He kissed her once more, this time gently on the lips, then she led him safely back out of the glacier. Outside, the sky was blue and the horses, when they finally reached them, whinnied with the pleasure of seeing them again. Behind them, the glacier stood silently in all its terrible beauty.

17

The ladies of Puerto Daffyd had moved Blodwen's bed so she could gaze out on the town and the sea beyond. In the summer, if the Good Lord had not seen fit to take her before, they would carry her onto the veranda every afternoon, so she could breathe some fresh air and smell her roses.

Right now it was spring and she was feeling restless. It was a long time since she had seen her loved ones and sometimes fear niggled at her innards in case she would not see them one more time before she died.

Only days ago, a letter had arrived by messenger from Rob. It was just like the boy to care enough to put her mind at rest. For weeks she had worried about them isolated out there at the *hacienda*. She felt that nothing had gone according to her great plan, for it looked as if Gwyneth, the silly girl, was getting far too attached to that Spaniard, Miguel. And Davy was wasting his time pining over Dora, married to that rogue, Matthew Riley, her own great-nephew, though she refused to acknowledge him as such. And who would be left that was worthy of her lovely Rob? She had seen such a future for him with Gwyneth, but there you have it; those who tried to play Cupid often came adrift.

It was a very short letter that Rob had penned to her, and she had to get one of the Elders to read it to her, her eyes being so bad. No doubt the news would be all over Puerto Daffyd by now, but she didn't care. It would put a few minds at rest, hearing of the death of that boy Matt. He had, according to Rob, fallen down a crevasse while trying to escape over a glacier just north of *El Paraiso*.

Blodwen often thought about it, trying to summon up some pity for the lad, but all her failing Christian heart could feel was suppressed contempt that God could give her such a poisoned present as Matthew Riley for a relation. If she was ever allowed through those pearly gates when her time came, she would have words with the Man in Charge and he would know a little of the tongue-lashing of Blodwen Evans, Griffiths that was.

'Are you all right, Widow Evans? Can I get anything for you now before I go and make tea for my man, and a nice cake for you for tomorrow?'

Winifred Jenkins was looking almost pretty

now that she had married Howard Cummings, the oldest bachelor in Puerto Daffyd. He had looked after his old mother till she almost outlived him, and now it was time for the poor man to have some coddling. He was so shortsighted that he probably never noticed that his bride looked both ways at once and her long nose was like the bill of a condor poised over a mouth that didn't know how to form a proper smile.

But the woman had a good heart after all and Blodwen had become quite fond of her.

'I don't want cake,' she told Winifred with a twist of her shrunken face. 'A nice bit of bread and butter is all I seem to be able to get down these days.'

'In that case, that's what I'll bring you. Now, then, your chamber pot is right here to hand and there's water in the jug. I'll pop back and see that you're all tucked up and shut in for the night in an hour or so.'

'You're a good woman, Winifred,' Blodwen smiled and patted the hand that fussed about her bed covers. 'Will you make me a pot of *maté* before you go?'

'I'll do that, yes. And maybe tomorrow you might be able to swallow a bowl of my chicken soup. It's good for anything that ails you. My Howard, bless his heart, swears by it.'

Blodwen nodded and smiled, fighting off the desire to drift off into a slumber.

'Howard Cummings has fallen on his feet, I would say, Winifred. You take care of him, now, look you.'

'Oh, there's no fear on that score, Widow Evans. Now, have you . . . ?'

She stopped chattering and the sudden silence forced Blodwen's eyes to flicker open. For a moment she wondered if she had gone deaf, because it wasn't normal not to hear Winifred's monotone voice. But she could still hear the birds chirruping outside the window. And there was a rumble of distant muted voices . . . and something else. The clippety-clop of hoofs and wagon wheels.

'What is it? What's happening?' She struggled to sit up more highly, stretching her neck, though she knew she couldn't see up the road where people were staring, shading their eyes from the late afternoon sun.

Winifred stepped out onto the veranda, hovered curiously, then came back and gripped Blodwen's hand, which made the old lady's heart sink, for people didn't do that unless there was bad news.

'They've come back!' Winifred announced, and for once her face cracked wide open into the biggest smile Blodwen had ever seen there.

'Who are you talking about, girl?'

'Your little family, that's who,' Winifred was almost jumping up and down in excitement and when the meaning of her words sank in, Blodwen felt she could almost leap out of bed and join her. 'Look, you, Blodwen Evans! They've come back to see you and to cheer you up. They're all there . . . well, all except that nephew of yours . . . '

She looked immediately apologetic, sensing that her words could be offensive, but Blodwen tutted at her and flapped an emaciated hand in her direction, letting the woman know that she didn't care what she said about Matthew Riley, as long as the rest was true.

'It's Rob, is it?' she asked, feeling a fluttery agitation in her breast. 'And Davy?'

'Yes, yes! And the girl, Dora, looking as pretty as a picture. They're all there, I tell you, and they're heading this way.'

'And where else would they be heading, Winifred Jenkins that was? This is their home, look you!'

But there was a heaviness sinking through the delight the news brought to her old, tired heart. Where was Gwyneth?

'Maybe you'll want me to bake you some cakes after all?' Winifred said, hanging on to the doorframe, her head popping in and out like a child's yo-yo toy.

'Maybe I will,' Blodwen said. 'But before you disappear, bring me my best white bonnet and a clean shawl. I can't receive my lovelies looking like an old ragbag, now, can I?'

As Winifred rushed about the place finding this and straightening that, Blodwen pinched her cheeks to make them pink and healthy-looking. By the time she heard footsteps ringing out on the sidewalk boards she appeared perfectly composed, though her fingers, twitching nervously at her coverlet, revealed how excited she was.

Davy and Dora were first through the door and a happy sight the two of them were. The boy had hardened muscles and a healthy tan, and the girl had blossomed magically. The love that shone out of the pair of them near broke Blodwen's heart, so tangible an emotion it was.

'Well, what a sight for sore eyes, the pair of you are. Now, where's my Rob? Ah!'

It was with great relief she saw him, filling the door space, his fine grey eyes shining and still looking the very embodiment of her precious Huw.

'Hello, Blodwen,' he said, then frowned. 'What's this? Taken to your bed, have you? You're not ill, I hope?'

'Och, it's nothing but my old age making itself felt,' she assured him, but then Winifred pushed through and made herself busy plumping up her pillows and wouldn't be shooed away.

'She was viciously attacked by that friend of yours, her nephew whose name is no longer mentioned in this house, or indeed this town.'

'God rest his soul,' added Blodwen.

'Aye, God rest his soul!' Winifred said quickly. 'Well, I'll leave you to get reacquainted, but I'll be back to see to you, Blodwen, as usual, in the morning.'

She hurried out with a shy glance at the three young people filling the tiny living room.

'Oh, Aunty Blodwen,' Dora flung herself at the frail old lady and hugged her so tight that Blodwen felt she might break, but she loved the girl for it anyway. 'Matt hurt you?'

'Yes, girl, but it's over now. Come, tell me all about your adventures in *El Paraiso*, eh. Rob, if you would, put the kettle on and make some *maté*. That silly Winifred seems to have forgotten.'

'Perhaps I can do that, Blodwen.'

Blodwen blinked and looked beyond Rob's tall frame. Just inside the door, silhouetted by the setting sun, Gwyneth stood, with more beauty on her than Blodwen had ever thought possible. The girl glowed as if the sun itself radiated out of her.

'My darling, lovely Gwyneth,' she cried, opening her arms to embrace the young woman whose future had been her concern for many years. 'But where's that Spaniard of yours? Have you brought him to meet me?'

'No, Blodwen!' Gwyneth's eyes slid shyly away and she looked up into Rob's handsome face and laughed; and he laughed back.

Blodwen's eyes narrowed to slits. She looked around the room, regarding each one of them closely.

'I think perhaps you have some things to tell me, isn't it?' she said and patted the bed for them all to sit down there.

'Well, first of all,' Rob began, but was beaten to it by Davy, in a state of little-boy excitement and Blodwen blessed his youthful enthusiasm and hoped he would never lose it.

'Dora and I want to get married, Aunty Blodwen,' he blurted out and she pretended to look disapproving, just for a moment, but she couldn't keep it up and beamed at the young couple.

'It does me good to hear it, for the pair of you were meant to be together and I think perhaps you knew it the minute you met.'

'Aye,' Davy nodded. 'I think you're right. It

was just a pity that Matt got there first.'

'Well, he's not in the way now, so make the most of your life together.'

'We'd like to get married here, in Puerto Daffyd, Aunty Blodwen, if that's all right with you.' Dora smiled and bit on her lip.

'Of course it is, girl. I wouldn't have it any other way.'

'And then . . . ' Davy hesitated, not wanting to offend, but his mind was, Blodwen knew, firmly made up as to the future. 'And then we're going back to the *hacienda*. I'm going to be assistant foreman and Dora, here, is going to be the new housekeeper when Juanita is too old to boss everybody about.'

Blodwen glanced at Rob for confirmation, needing his approval of Davy's decision.

'It's all right, Blodwen,' Rob said. 'They're good people and Davy has taken to ranching like a duck to water.'

'Aye, and Dora's a fine cook, better even than me mam, eh?' Davy pinched Dora's pink cheek and it grew rosier.

'And you, Rob, my lovely? What are your plans? Back to the *estancia*, you too? It would be a waste of all that talent you have working with wood.'

'Well, I don't know about that, Blodwen, but I'm not going back to *El Paraiso*. Davy and I are going our separate ways, but we won't lose touch.'

'And where are you going, pray?'

'There's a place at the end of the world called Ushuaia . . . a pioneer town on the Beagle Channel. I thought I'd try my luck as a cabinet maker down there . . . and take my wife with me.'

'Your wife, is it? And who . . . ?' Blodwen saw the bloom deepen on Gwyneth's cheeks. 'Tell me I'm not mistaken, please God!'

'No, you're not mistaken, Blodwen,' Rob laughed and, leaning forward, took her hand and squeezed it. 'Gwyneth and I are to be married and we'd like to do it alongside Davy and Dora . . . here in Puerto Daffyd, so you can be guest of honour.'

'The Lord be praised!' Blodwen cried, throwing her hands in the air with the joy of his news. 'If I'm called to my Maker right here and now, I can assure you that I will go happily with no regrets whatsoever. This is what I have been waiting for, my lovelies, but I beg of you, don't make me wait too long, for I haven't much time now.'

★ ★ ★

Rob and Gwyneth, alongside Davy and Dora, were married in the little chapel that Blodwen

381

had helped to build half a century earlier. To see the old lady dressed so prettily, and sitting erect in the first pew, was a thing of beauty in itself. And when the ceremony was over and the wedding hymns were being sung, Blodwen's strident voice could be heard above all the others.

'When I tread the verge of Jordan, bid my anxious fears subside; death of death, and hell's destruction land me safe on Canaan's side. Songs of praises, songs of praises, I will ever give to thee . . . '

The two brides, one as lovely and as happy as the other, presented her with their bouquets. She sat, clutching them all the way back to her little house, where people gathered and ate the delicious cakes and pastries of Winifred Jenkins that was, and the place smelled like the shop of Lewis the Bread, for he had brought enough bread for the whole town, it seemed, and it was still warm.

She saw her lovely Gwyneth dance in the arms of her best boy, Rob. Such a grand sight it was. And that dear girl, Dora, sat holding her hand and humming happily to the music of Branwell the Fiddle and Olwen the Piano. And even Irish McGinty appeared, once the Elders had departed, claiming that the bottles he brought contained nothing more lethal than 'Adam's Wine', though the liquid in them sent her old head in a whirl.

She waited until the elation had simmered down to a quiet pleasure, with only her closest friends around her, then Blodwen smiled and closed her eyes and her grip on Dora's hand slackened so suddenly that the girl knew immediately that her spirit had finally flown.

'Davy,' Dora whispered to her new husband who was putting a flame to the fire, for it was still chilly in the evenings. 'Davy, I think Aunty Blodwen has died.'

He turned and saw Dora's huge blue eyes fill with tears, but she brushed them away, swallowed her grief and squared her shoulders, much in the way the old Welsh woman used to do when she needed that extra bit of courage to get her by.

'What is it?' Rob and Gwyneth came in from a short, hand-holding walk along a road where people had smiled and nodded to them, the respectable, married couple.

'It's Aunty Blodwen,' Davy said, all choked up and cursing himself for showing more weakness than his little wife.

Rob held back. He was not one to show emotion and this wasn't the time to start. Blodwen would not have wanted it.

'She's gone,' Gwyneth said, feeling the old

woman's pulse at her neck and stroking the satiny smooth skin. 'But she already knew her time had come.'

'Aye,' said Irish McGinty, standing over the tiny form and placing a hand tenderly on the snow-white head. 'She did that. She had been ready for a wee while, but she hung on until you four got here. Now, she can go to her place in Heaven with no worries left behind her.'

'How come you know so much about Aunty Blodwen?' Davy wanted to know and Irish gave a sly chuckle.

'It was yer aunty what owned my tavern,' he said to the surprise of all present. 'And it was yer aunty who bailed me out when things got tough . . . ye remember, when the place burned down? And she was a good friend to all my girls, when they needed one. And I'm not the only one in this town that doesn't owe her the clothes he stands up in. She was a feisty little woman, but that heart of hers . . . ' He gave a gulp and shook his head. 'Look in the dresser drawer over there. That's where she keeps a copy of her will. I think you'll find it very pleasing, all four of you, but I'm warning you now that she's left me this little house to live out my retirement.'

With a touch of a finger to his forelock, he took his leave and the other wedding guests with him, not sure whether they should be mourning or celebrating, but already regretting harsh words they had ever said or thought against the Widow Blodwen Evans.

★ ★ ★

They buried Blodwen in the small cemetery, under the lilac tree, just as she had instructed them in her will, and Dora planted roses on her grave. The day after the funeral, the Barker brothers embraced fondly before taking leave of one another.

'Mind you write, Davy, lad,' Rob said with a playful punch to his brother's shoulder. 'I know how you hate writing, but I want to know that you're safe, you and Dora here. And you take care of that lass, do you hear?'

'Aye, I will an' all. I know when I'm well off, our Rob, and so do you, I'd say.'

Davy's eyes swivelled around and came to rest on Gwyneth, all decked out in a dress and looking quite a lady, that would have made his aunty Blodwen proud to see. 'We've both struck lucky, eh?'

Rob's eyes misted over. He couldn't believe the love he had in his heart for the black-haired beauty he once thought would never see him as a man worth having.

He watched as Gwyneth and Dora hugged

and kissed, then he stepped in and draped a protective arm about his wife's shoulders, placing a kiss on her cheek.

'Are you ready, then?' he asked, his voice a trifle unsteady.

'I'm ready, Rob,' she answered, reaching up to touch his cheek.

'In that case, let's go in search of the rest of our lives.'

The two couples set off in different directions. At frequent intervals, until they lost sight of each other completely, they turned and waved.

'I can't see them any more,' Gwyneth said, registering disappointment.

'They'll be all right,' Rob said. 'We'll see them again. I'm sure you'll want to visit Therese and Miguel some day, if only to show off our family.'

'Family?' Gwyneth frowned at him and saw the corners of his mouth twitch.

'Aye.' He touched the flat of his hand to her stomach and she looked at it nonplussed. 'I hear that we're expecting an addition.'

Out of the corner of his eye he saw Gwyneth's mouth drop open.

'A baby?' She was shaking her head, still puzzled.

'Well, according to Blodwen, we are, and she's never wrong, is she?'

A radiant smile was spreading over Gwyneth's face. She stroked the place where Rob's hand had rested. 'No, I suppose not.'

'Don't worry. I'll have a nice house built for you before your time comes.'

'Tell me again where we're going?'

'Ushuaia,' Rob said, flicking the reins at the rumps of the two horses pulling their wagon, making them go faster. 'Or, if you prefer, to the ends of the earth . . . which is where I would go any day if it was to find you again.'

Gwyneth's chin quivered as she looked up at the sky so blue with one fluffy white cloud floating directly overhead. It reminded her of Blodwen's halo of hair, so she said a silent *thank you, Blodwen*.

'Tell her thank you from me too,' Rob said, reading her mind.

She laughed and leaned against him, feeling totally safe for the first time in her life.

We do hope that you have enjoyed reading this large print book.

Did you know that all of our titles are available for purchase?

We publish a wide range of high quality large print books including:
Romances, Mysteries, Classics
General Fiction
Non Fiction and Westerns

Special interest titles available in large print are:
The Little Oxford Dictionary
Music Book
Song Book
Hymn Book
Service Book

Also available from us courtesy of Oxford University Press:
Young Readers' Dictionary
(large print edition)
Young Readers' Thesaurus
(large print edition)

For further information or a free brochure, please contact us at:
Ulverscroft Large Print Books Ltd.,
The Green, Bradgate Road, Anstey,
Leicester, LE7 7FU, England.
Tel: (00 44) **0116 236 4325**
Fax: (00 44) **0116 234 0205**

Other titles published by
The House of Ulverscroft:

THE JEALOUS LAND

June Gadsby

Following the death of her parents, Sophie is sent to live with relatives in London, where she is treated like a servant. Later, her chance to escape an imposed life of hardship comes in the form of Daniel Clayton — a formidable explorer and photographer. Sophie agrees to his proposal of a loveless marriage, but this union plunges her into the midst of a family feud. She faces unforeseen treachery, a terrible secret in her husband's past and her greatest dilemma yet.

WHEN TOMORROW COMES

June Gadsby

Hildie Thompson is an eternal optimist, but even her indomitable sense of humour is shaken when war is declared. Hildie's war, however, is a fight to the last to support her family and friends who are battling wars of their own. An unhappy marriage, an illicit love affair, infidelity, a pit disaster and a murder all within that one little mining family just about knocks Hildie off her perch. But, through it all, she must submerge her own secret dreams and make the best of things. Then, she receives a mysterious letter that could change her life . . .

THE IRON MASTER

June Gadsby

Newcastle, 1908: Turning down a proposal of marriage from her older employer is perhaps the first mistake in Ellie Martin's young life. Running back to a family in trouble is the second. A new beginning awaits them in Durham, but at what cost? Her mother, with a dark secret in her past, mysteriously obtains jobs for her men in an iron foundry — and Ellie finds the magic she dreams of with Adam, son of the iron master of ill-repute. However, the hatred harboured by Ellie's mother for the Rockwells leads Ellie to believe that she is in love with her half-brother. And so she returns to Newcastle and tries to ignore her heart . . .

IF TRUTH BE KNOWN

Patricia Werner

Susan Franks, research director of the Association for Honesty in Government, was involved in one of its biggest cases. Law-enforcement agencies were suspected of circulating false reports on private citizens. Susan was to present her findings to a congressional subcommittee. After meeting Geoffrey Winston, she wasn't sure if they shared a dynamic attraction — or if he would use his position as a congressman to undermine the AHG: he had warned her not to dig too deeply into the matter. Susan did investigate further. When the case proved to have international ramifications, she desperately hoped Geoffrey wasn't involved . . .